TRACK
OF
THE
SCORPION

TRACK
OF
THE
SCORPION

VAL DAVIS

St. Martin's Press ✠ New York

A THOMAS DUNNE BOOK.
An imprint of St. Martin's Press.

TRACK OF THE SCORPION. Copyright © 1996 by Val Davis. All rights reserved. Printed in the United States of America. No part of this book may
be used or reproduced in any manner whatsoever without written permission except in the case of brief quotations embodied in critical articles or re-
views. For information, address St. Martin's Press, 175 Fifth Avenue, New
York, N.Y. 10010

Design by Nancy Resnick

Library of Congress Cataloging-in-Publication Data

Davis, Val.
    Track of the scorpion / Val Davis.—1st ed.
      p. cm.
    "A Thomas Dunne book."
    ISBN 0-312-14437-7
    1. Women archaeologists—New Mexico—Fiction.
2. Conspiracies—Fiction. 3. Bombers—Fiction. I. Title.
PS3554.A937836T73   1996   96-2038
813'.54—dc20   CIP

First Edition: August 1996

10 9 8 7 6 5 4 3 2 1

*To Frank Ashley
for his memories*

TRACK
OF
THE
SCORPION

PROLOGUE

January 1945
An Island in the Pacific

It had been raining for three days, with a low overcast that made everything outside the four-engine B-17 bomber look as gray as a navy paint job. One hundred yards out from the plane, a small army of MPs had set up a security perimeter. All incoming and outgoing air traffic into the island had been either canceled or diverted, and would continue to be banned until well after the takeoff.

Navigator Ross McKinnon left his seat and moved forward to join the bombardier, Howard Kelly, who was peering through the nose cone at the wind-driven rain pelting the Plexiglas.

"Christ," Kelly said, "nothing ever changes. Hurry up and wait. That's the army. We could have stayed in bed another hour and a half."

McKinnon leaned forward to wipe mist from the Plexi. "What kind of visibility do you think we've got?"

Kelly squinted. "A quarter of a mile at least. No sweat. Our intrepid captain could take off in a blizzard."

"It's more like a hundred yards, if you ask me. I can't see the MPs anymore."

Kelly sighed and wiped his own peephole. "There you go. Two o'clock, big as life. No wonder they washed you out of pilot training. Maybe we ought to have your eyes tested before we take off. I wouldn't want to get lost now that we're going home."

"I'll get you there."

The pilot, Captain Dennis Atwood, came on the interphone. "Decker, do you see anything?"

Technical Sergeant Paul Decker, their upper turret gunner, had been issued binoculars for the mission. "Nothing's happening on the beach, sir. They're just standing around like they've been doing since we got here. The colonel's pacing back and forth waving his arms at the MPs and looking mad as hell. Situation normal, all fucked up."

"I told you," Kelly said to McKinnon off-mike. "That beach is four hundred yards if it's a foot. If Decker can see that far, we've got plenty of visibility for a takeoff."

McKinnon returned to his seat and plugged into the interphone system before retrieving his diary from the map case. Keeping it there was strictly against regulations, but it was the safest place in the cramped navigator's compartment. Not only was the map case made of steel, but it sealed out most of the moisture and mildew that made life on the islands in the Pacific so miserable.

He opened the diary, spread it on his navigator's table, and made his first entry of the day. *Sunday, January 7, 1945. Midway Island. Rain for the third day in a row. Temperature, 66.*

He closed his eyes and thought about his wife until Atwood said, "Anyone got to take a leak?"

Slipping the diary inside his flight suit, McKinnon dropped through the forward entry hatch and moved away from the plane to relieve himself. In the open air, he saw that Kelly had been right. Visibility was a quarter of a mile at least, not that it mattered. There was nothing to run into; the only hill on Midway was six feet high.

Above him, copilot John Curtis cracked open the cockpit's side window. "Are we lost yet, Ross?"

McKinnon pointed east, toward Japan. "That's the way home, I think."

"The captain wants to turn over the props."

Technically, McKinnon knew, the propellers didn't have to be turned over unless they'd been standing for two hours or more.

"Are you asking for a volunteer?" McKinnon said.

"You're already wet."

McKinnon zipped up his fly and went to work. Ashton and the other waist gunner, Jim Parish, joined him so that nobody had to get too wet.

When Curtis gave him a thumbs-up signal, McKinnon climbed back inside the B-17, settled into his seat, and turned to a fresh page in his diary.

> My Dearest Lael,
> I'm writing to you from on board my plane, while we're waiting to take off on a special mission. They've promised us leave when we're done. If all goes well, I'll be able to deliver this letter in person, my love. I'll be able to hold you in my arms again. Sometimes I wake up at night and think I smell your perfume, but when I open my eyes all I smell is mildew and old tent canvas.

He paused, thinking about the censors and wondering if he should write anything personal, especially since their mission was so secret. Finally, he shook his head and went back to the letter.

We've renamed our ship. Our sexy pinup has been re-placed by a scorpion. It wasn't our idea. It was orders, but I'm not supposed to write about that. Anyway, we've now got a mean-looking scorpion painted on the nose. It's bright yellow with red eyes. If the Japs ever get close enough to us to see it, it ought to scare the you-know-what out of them.

Atwood came on the interphone. "We're picking up war news from the tower."

The pilot switched the shortwave broadcast to the B-17's internal radio system. "In Europe, U. S. and British forces have advanced three miles along the Germans' northern flank in Belgium. Our casualties have been light, while enemies losses have been described as extremely heavy."

"Sheeit," Kelly cut in. "Get to the important news, will you? Are we clobbering the Japs or not? I don't want to have to come all the way back here after we get home."

The radio announcer continued. "In the Pacific, our carrier-based planes simultaneously attacked in Formosa and Taiwan, sinking twenty-five Japanese ships and destroying one hundred eleven enemy aircraft."

"That's more like it," Kelly whooped.

Sergeant Decker's voice broke in. "Captain, submarine sur-facing now."

"I see it."

Atwood began his start-up procedures, switching off the turbo controls, opening the fuel shutoff valves, and cracking the throttles while his copilot, John Curtis, checked hydraulic pressure, cowl flaps, intercooler, and fire extinguisher controls. Finally, one by one, the twelve-hundred-horsepower Curtiss-Wright engines roared to life.

"They're coming ashore in a rubber boat," Decker said on the interphone.

4

Atwood scanned the gauges again, and looked at his copilot, who nodded that everything was okay.

"They're on the beach, Captain. One of them looks like a goddamn general."

"That's probably our passenger," the pilot said. "Remember security. Nothing specific, not even on the interphone."

"Nobody said anything about generals."

"I have him in sight now," the pilot said. "You can stow your binoculars, Decker, and stand by for takeoff. Ashton, you and Parish see to our passenger when he comes aboard."

"Yes, sir," said the waist gunner.

"Sir," Decker said, "now that he's closer, I think he's an admiral."

"What would you expect from a submarine?"

The moment the fuselage door closed, the B-17 began rolling down the tarmac. It's bright, freshly painted nose art, an attacking scorpion, gleamed in the prop wash.

Thirteen hundred miles later, the *Scorpion* put down at Hickam Field in Honolulu, taxing to the end of an auxiliary runway that had been sealed off in advance by military policemen. A ground crew was waiting with a fuel truck and immediately began topping off the B-17's fuel tanks.

Atwood spoke to the tower. "My passenger would like to stretch his legs."

"Negative, *Scorpion*. No one is to leave the plane."

"What about a ground inspection?"

"Our ground crew will take care of it."

"Bullshit," Curtis said on the interphone. "That's a pilot's prerogative. Are you going to let them get away with it?"

"We volunteered, didn't we?" Atwood tapped his copilot on the shoulder to point out that the MPs surrounding the plane were carrying Thompson submachine guns.

"You are clear to take off," the tower said. "Radio silence is now in effect until you reach your next destination."

"I don't like it," Curtis said.

"Tell me that when we're home."

The flight to Hamilton Field north of San Francisco, the staging area for B-17 traffic across the Pacific, took a little less than fourteen hours. Once again the tower directed the *Scorpion* to taxi to a remote parking area, where a fuel truck, a ground crew, and MPs were already waiting.

Even after the engines were cut, Atwood continued to feel the vibrations. His copilot looked as exhausted as he felt, and they still had another twenty-five hundred miles to go.

Atwood grabbed his mike and spoke to the tower. "We're out of sandwiches, the toilet's full, and we need some rest."

"A mess truck and portable toilet are on the way."

"What about a few hours' sleep?"

"You know your destination. Important people are waiting for you there."

Their orders had been specific. The destination, Washington, D.C., was never to be mentioned on the radio.

While they were eating, a meteorologist came on board to brief them on the weather conditions over the continental United States. A storm front was centered over the Rocky Mountains, running all the way from Canada south into Colorado. To avoid it, they would be routed south, across Arizona, New Mexico, the Texas panhandle, and Oklahoma before gradually veering north. Snow flurries were predicted along the East Coast, but nothing serious enough to warrant aborting the mission. Weather updates would be transmitted to them when available.

As soon as the meteorologist left, an ordnance truck arrived, driven by a technical sergeant who had orders to remove all .50-caliber ammunition now that the *Scorpion* was out of the war zone. The bomb racks had been empty since takeoff.

"I feel naked," Decker said immediately from his top turret.

"I don't think we're going to run into any Zeros," Atwood answered. "Now, check in."

When all crew members were accounted for, including their passenger, Atwood took a deep breath and rubbed his eyes.

"*Scorpion,*" the tower said, "you are cleared for start-up."

Atwood glanced at his copilot. "Let's go by the book, John. I don't want to make any mistakes now that we're home."

When they'd completed the checklist, Atwood called his navigator on the interphone. "How's our passenger, McKinnon?"

"Safe and sound and talking about baseball."

"Okay, fasten his seat belt. We're on our way."

McKinnon tracked their progress closely on his maps, calling out state lines and points of interest along the way. California's Death Valley and Arizona's Grand Canyon were behind them when he said, "As of right now, we're crossing into New Mexico."

"If we're not lost," Curtis said.

"Have I ever got us lost?"

"Only when we're on the ground."

"Keep talking," the pilot said. "Otherwise I'm going to fall asleep."

As the miles passed, the landscape beneath them grew more and more barren, until all signs of vegetation disappeared.

"Remind me to stay out of New Mexico," Atwood said.

"You should see it through my bombsight," Kelly answered. "I'd be doing the state a favor if I bombed the place."

"We've got ourselves an escort," Decker said from his top turret. "Little friends at ten o'clock."

Atwood, who'd been rubbing his eyes, saw nothing but spots in that part of the sky. "Not Zeroes," he joked.

"Ours," Decker reported. "P-38s. They're coming down, now."

"A beautiful sight," Curtis said.

Atwood was still nodding agreement when his mouth dropped open. "What the hell?"

1

August 1996
New Mexico

Nick Scott moved to the lip of the cave and shaded her eyes against the blinding sky. Once again the radio had lied. The promised clouds were nowhere to be seen. The sun beat down on the desert as if intent on incinerating the already scarce vegetation. Badlands, the map called this part of New Mexico. An understatement as far as she was concerned. Carry water at all times, the map legend warned. That was fine and dandy when you had a four-wheel drive, but what about the Indians who'd built a civilization here, the Anasazi, the reason for her suffering presence. What had they done for water on brutal days like this?

Next time stay home, she told herself. Don't volunteer. The Anasazi were her father's passion, not hers.

Fat chance, she thought, laughing at herself. She'd volunteer for a dig anywhere, especially if there was a chance of an important discovery. Hell, any kind of discovery. The thrill of the hunt was what counted. Anasazi Indians, Inca gold, or old airplanes. They were all buried treasure to her, a siren song that couldn't be resisted.

With a sigh, Nick spun her Cub's baseball cap around until the brim was at the back of her head, then pulled a bandanna from her grubby jeans and mopped her face. Sweat was a good sign, she reminded herself; it meant she was keeping up the proper intake of water.

She backed away from the cave entrance, but the sun had reached its zenith, erasing all shade from the cliff dwelling and turning the sandstone cavern into a kiln. Readjusting her cap brim to soften the glare, she checked the thermometer, one of the few items she'd managed to screen from direct sunlight. One hundred and ten degrees. Whoever said only mad dogs and Englishmen went out in the noonday sun had failed to take archaeologists into account.

Three stories above her, in the Anasazi cliff dwelling named Site ES No. 1 in honor of her father, Elliot Scott, a voice shouted, "Send up more lemonade and beer."

She craned her neck and glared at Pete Dees, one of her father's students, who was lowering a basket on the end of a rope. He was one of ten students who were earning class credits by providing slave labor for her father's university-sponsored dig.

"If you don't mind, please, Dr. Scott, we need more water," Dees amended.

She loaded the plastic bottles, a brand she'd never heard of outside of this part of New Mexico, and called, "Make sure my father drinks his full ration."

Dees raised the basket without comment. No student, even one verging on a Ph.D., as he was, would dare offer advice to the grand old man of Southwestern archaeology. Not so old, Nick reminded herself. Now that she was thirty, her father's fifty-six didn't seem that ancient.

Nick heard a rustling overhead and immediately scanned the rock face above the cliff dwelling. Some twenty feet above the top story, there was a fissure in the rock, a natural chimney for venting smoke from the ancient Anasazi fires. It had become home to a small colony of bats. Nick had climbed among them once, looking for stashed artifacts. What she found was bat dropping and a passage large enough to wiggle through, but only if you were desperate enough. At the moment nothing was moving up there, so maybe the fluttering had been her imagination.

She opened a liter bottle, her fourth of the day, and drank deeply. Warm, it tasted even worse than what came out of the tap at their motel in town. The town was called Cibola and their motel, the Seven Cities, had probably been named in an attempt to capture the luster of the fabled seven golden cities of Cibola that had lured the Spanish explorer Coronado to New Mexico. Not only did the motel lack luster, it was short on amenities.

She pulled another bottle from its cardboard carton and checked the seal, wondering if the mayor, who owned the general store, wasn't substituting local water to boost his profit margin. But the seal looked unbroken.

She sighed and retreated to the rear of the cave in a vain hope of finding shade. Sweat stung her eyes as she stacked empty water cartons high enough to create a sun screen. Then she sat on the cave's rocky floor next to the aboveground kiva, wiped her face again, and began bagging and cataloguing the last basketful of artifacts that her father had personally lowered. She wasn't a recognized expert on the Anasazi—her speciality being historical archaeology, the near past—but she saw nothing to prove her father's latest theory, that the Anasazi were cannibals. His theory made some kind of sense, considering the landscape. What else was there to eat in such a godforsaken desert? And even the term *Anasazi* translated as "enemy ancestors," apt enough if they were eating their relatives, no matter how far distant.

Gingerly, she leaned against the kiva wall. Usually kivas were pits sunk into the ground, but in bedrock caves such as this one, they had to be constructed at ground level and then surrounded by rocks to create an underground atmosphere. Kivas were the spiritual centers of Anasazi life and were thought of as the sacred entrances into the earth from which the Anasazi's ancestors had once emerged. Her father had found water jugs in this one, causing him to speculate that in such a desolate location water might have been as much a part of the Anasazi's religious ritual as human sacrifice.

"Coming down!" her father called to her.

Nick left her patch of shade to hold the aluminum extension ladder, which wobbled badly when extended two full stories, especially under the weight of a man as bulky as Elliot Scott. Watching him climb down, moving casually as if the possibility of falling was no concern of his, she marveled. Nothing seemed to faze him. Heat, cold, it didn't matter as long as he was on the track of his beloved Anasazi.

The moment he stepped off the last rung, he towered above her, the size of a linebacker, six two, two hundred and twenty pounds. His hair was combed, his shirt buttoned; he made no concession to the oppressive heat.

"If you weren't so damned tall," she said, "you wouldn't get half the respect. Grand old man, indeed."

"Never argue with a woman, that's my motto. Which is why I've decided to pay for my sins by giving you the rest of the day off."

"I take it you need something from town."

"Not exactly."

"You could send one of your students."

"They're paying for the privilege of working with me on an important dig."

"You may not have noticed it, Dad, but it's a hundred and ten degrees in here. If we took a vote, I think every one of them would opt for an air-conditioned movie."

"Sometimes, Nicolette, you sound just like your mother."

Nick clenched her teeth, which caused Elliot to duck his head, all the apology she was likely to get for such a remark.

She said, "A woman's work is never done, is that it?"

"Come on, Nick, you know someone's got to handle the logistics. If we run out of water or some damned thing, we're in big trouble. Besides, I don't want you climbing up and down that ladder all day doing the grunt work. And I can't trust the cataloguing to someone less experienced, not if I expect my work to stand scrutiny."

"I didn't see any tasty-looking bones today," she said, relenting. "Nothing to gnaw on, anyway."

"I was hoping to have something more concrete by the time Clark arrived. If not some bones, then maybe an ancient well."

"We've been over every inch of this place."

"The old riverbed is out there, Nick, not fifty yards from where we stand."

"And it's been bone dry since the Middle Ages."

"The water's still down there, running underground, I know it. Look at the map of Anasazi sites in this area. They're all located along the course of that old river."

"And they left when it dried up," Nick pointed out. "The great Anasazi migration of 1300."

"If they sank wells, they could have stayed on. Small groups could have survived. A hard life that might have eventually disintegrated into cannibalism." He grinned. "Besides, I bet Guthrie ten dollars I'd find a well by the time he got here."

"You've still got a week."

"God, I forgot to tell you. My memory must be going. He called last night and said he'd be flying into Gallup this afternoon. That's why I climbed down, to see why you hadn't left to pick him up."

Gallup was a hundred miles west, a four-hour drive taking into account that the first twenty miles were dirt road between here and what passed for a state highway.

"We won't be back much before midnight," she said.

"You don't have to go all the way to Gallup. Mayor Tuttle is getting a shipment of groceries today and has arranged for Clark to ride along."

Nick shook her head slowly, finding it hard to imagine Clark Guthrie, chairmen emeritus of the University of New Mexico's Department of Anthropology, mentor to Nick and to her father before her, riding in a grocery truck.

"The trouble is," Elliot continued, "I would have bet big money on that well being here."

"Are you that sure of the underground water?"

"I had the geology department study the survey maps before we left. They say there's a good chance I'm right, but we'd have to drill down a ways to prove it."

"Look at this country. I wouldn't want to bet my life on finding water out here, no matter how far down we dug."

"It can't be too deep. Otherwise, the Anasazi would never have reached it." Elliot handed her a ten-dollar bill. "According to the mayor, and taking into account all the stops along the way, Clark ought to arrive in Cibola about three-thirty or four this afternoon. That gives you plenty of time to get there before he does."

"Sure, with thirty seconds to spare."

Her father shrugged his well-muscled shoulders. "Give him the money and tell him it will be double or nothing the next time. Then settle him into the motel and we'll go out to dinner when I get to town."

"I thought you'd want me to do the cooking," she said sarcastically.

"Your cooking's as bad as your mother's."

"I know," she taunted, "you would have been happier with a son to follow in your footsteps."

"I named you Nick because your mother said I married her in the nick of time, not because I wanted a boy."

"So you like to say." She turned on her heel and headed for the pair of four-wheel-drive Isuzu Troopers they'd rented for the summer.

"Sorry, Nick," he called after her. "You're nothing like your mother."

It was an old argument, more ritual than anything else, with the emotional heat long since dissipated, on the surface anyway.

She raised a hand, acknowledging his apology, but kept on walking. When she reached the Troopers, she selected the one with its rear seats removed to provide space for supplies. From under the driver's seat, she removed the towel she kept there and spread it over the sun-blistered Naugahyde. Only then did she ease onto the seat and start the engine, immediately switching the air conditioner to maximum.

Stinging sweat, abetted by sunblock, flooded her eyes. She backed out of the Trooper and waited for the air conditioner to make driving bearable. Her bandanna, already sodden, did little more than rearrange the moisture on her face. Clenching her fists to keep from rubbing her eyes, she moved around to the shady side of the Isuzu and crouched down, exhaust fumes being preferable to the fierce sunlight.

A catcher's crouch, she thought, very unladylike. Her mother had liked to crouch too, usually behind the sofa, hiding from demons that only she could see. Never in Elliot's presence, though. For all he knew, Elaine had been the perfect wife, elegantly dressed with dinner waiting whenever he came home.

"It's our secret," Elaine would say while Nick helped her pick out a dress and shoes to match.

Nick rubbed her eyes but the memory of her mother wouldn't go away. "You do the cooking for me, Nick. We don't want to disappoint your father."

To hell with the heat, Nick thought, rising to her feet and

climbing into the Isuzu. With fingertips only, she tested the steering wheel. The breeze from the air-conditioning vents had made gripping it tolerable. She checked the temperature gauge, which was already climbing out of the normal range. Three or four miles was as far as she'd get before she'd have to switch off the air-conditioning altogether. Once she reached blacktop, twenty miles away, the Trooper usually tolerated a low fan setting, but she'd have to keep a close eye on the temperature just the same. A boil-over was the last thing she needed in this kind of country.

By rote, she inspected the bottled water supply, five gallons as always, and her rifle, stowed behind the seat along with two days' worth of high-energy food rations. Emergency precautions she'd been taking since her first dig, when she was a precocious nine-year-old, driving her father's students crazy with questions. A crack shot even then with a .30-.30, the terror of tin cans and road signs alike.

"It's not right, the two of you leaving me home alone," Elaine said from the past. "Rough living may be all right for a man, but not a lady. A lady doesn't grub in the dirt. Think of your nails."

Nick switched on the radio, which she kept tuned to KQNM, the fifty-thousand-watt Gallup station, cranked up the volume until Elaine's voice disappeared, and then headed for town, for Cibola.

2

Cibola's city-limit sign claimed a population of one thousand and six. Since there was only one street, Main Street, and that ran for only a quarter of a mile along State Highway 371, Nick figured the town fathers had to be counting everything and everyone for miles around.

She crossed the bridge spanning Conejos Wash and headed for Cibola's one and only motel, the Seven Cities, a row of squat stucco cabins vaguely disguised as a pueblo. On the outside, unmilled pine logs protruded from the stucco a foot below the roof line; inside the logs provided a rough-hewn ceiling, which was a haven to some of the largest spiders Nick had seen since her own archaeological dig in New Guinea.

She parked the Isuzu under the log lean-to that served as her cabin's carport, rolled the windows down to take advantage of the shade, then went inside to relieve herself. The sight of the shower was tempting, but it was now three-thirty, time for Clark Guthrie to be delivered to Tuttle's General Store along with the groceries. Sighing, Nick settled for a quick wash and a change of bra and shirt.

She drove the block and a half to Tuttle's, where Mayor Ralph, as he insisted upon being called, was behind the counter, wearing a white apron over a short-sleeve checkered shirt. His councilmen, Jay Ferrin and Bill Latimer, were with him. Their presence meant that the desk at the Seven Cities Motel was unmanned and that the town's only service station wasn't pumping gas. Tuttle's store had the advantage of true air-conditioning, not just the noisy window models the councilmen had to live with.

"Your truck got held up in Thoreau," the mayor told her, "though why they even stop there I don't know. They claim a population of over a thousand, but they can't hold a candle to Cibola. Mark my words, young lady, one day this town is going to be on the map."

Both councilmen nodded agreement, though Nick found it hard to believe that Cibola had survived as long as it had. The town's only attraction was its proximity to the Anasazi ruins, where some of the cliff dwellings ran to hundreds of rooms. The land around Cibola, with vegetation as sparse as the yearly rainfall, wasn't fit for anything but minimal ranching. What livestock she'd seen wandering around looked scrawny and bedraggled.

"When do you expect the truck?" she asked.

"The driver called not fifteen minutes ago. He blew a radiator hose climbing the pass near Powell Mountain. If he hadn't been able to coast down the other side, he and your friend would still be out there stranded. They do have a gas station in Thoreau, don't they, Bill?"

Latimer made a face. "The last time I heard, they did, but I wouldn't count on them being as well stocked as I am. Could be they may have to send all the way to Gallup for that hose. In that case"—the service station owner spread his hands— "they could be hung up overnight."

"I hope not, for your friend's sake," Ferrin added. "You

won't find a motel as nice as my Seven Cities between here and Gallup. The fact is, I've been thinking about expanding the place. What do you think, Mayor Ralph?"

Nick sighed. As it was, she, Elliot, and his students were occupying seven of the motel's nine cabins. Number eight was reserved for Clark Guthrie. Usually, the Seven Cities closed down altogether in the hot summer months, or so the Navajo woman who cleaned the rooms had told her. Which was why Nick and her father had been able to negotiate cheap off-season rates allowing them to stay within the university's meager budget.

"When will we know about the radiator hose?" Nick said.

The three of them looked at one another and burst out laughing.

"All right," she said, "just tell me when the truck's due?"

"If you turn around you can see it yourself, coming up Main Street," Mayor Ralph said.

Clark Guthrie stepped down from the refrigerated truck, shook the driver's hand, then clasped Nick in the remnants of a cool, air-conditioned hug.

"I see your father's using you as his gofer again," he said into her ear before stepping back from the embrace to look her over.

As far as she could see, he hadn't changed since her student days, a square blunt man, heavy-set and powerful looking despite his seventy years, with an ageless face and unruly snow white hair.

"The Anasazi have him in their clutches," Nick said. "Once that happens, the rest of us are only ghosts, invisible unless he needs our help."

Guthrie smiled. "You're the same way with your airplanes."

"The trouble is, they're few and far between."

"Your fame is spreading. Have you seen the latest *National Geographic*?"

19

"You mean, I made it?"

"I've got a copy in my briefcase."

The comment sent the truck driver back into his cab to retrieve Guthrie's luggage, a canvas bag the color of army surplus, and a dented aluminum briefcase. He handed both to Nick, who stowed the bag in the back of the Trooper while Guthrie carried his case into Tuttle's store to get out of the sun.

By the time Nick joined him inside, Guthrie was spreading the magazine on the counter next to the cash register. The mayor and his councilmen were peering over Guthrie's shoulder with the ardor of *Penthouse* fans.

Mayor Ralph shook his head. "I thought you people only dug up Indians."

"There's more Indian relics and burial grounds than lost airplanes, that's for sure," Guthrie replied. "But sometimes fifty years ago is just as mysterious as a millennium. Take this find, for instance." He tapped the *National Geographic* with his forefinger. "A B-24 bomber was lost in the Pacific during World War Two, and its crew was listed as missing for all those years. Nick found it in the jungle of southeastern New Guinea and made sure those men finally got a proper burial."

"How come *they* get buried and Indians get dug up?"

"That's right," Councilman Latimer put in. "I have a lot of Indian customers who don't like what you people are doing out there."

Nick came to the rescue. "Give the man a break, will you please? He's had a long trip. I'll walk him across the street to the Zuni for a cold drink, if you don't mind, Mayor Ralph, and then come back for my supplies."

The Zuni Café was a narrow, single-story building with two plate-glass windows flanking the central doorway. The structure looked vaguely Victorian, with a bracketed cornice beneath the flat roof and frosted glass transoms above the larger windows. One of the transoms had been replaced with an air conditioner. Each time Nick saw the place, she was reminded of those Western movies the Italians used to make that featured grimy, grittier-than-life sets.

Guthrie led the way inside. They were the only customers, and there was no sign of Mom Bennett, who ran the place. The infusion of outside air caused the transom air conditioner to shift gears, generating vibrations that rattled the front windows without producing any breeze that Nick could feel.

"Sit down," Guthrie said, "and tell me about your father's progress."

"You know Elliot. He'll raise hell if I spoil his surprise." Nick slid into a booth anyway.

"I understand this site's well off the beaten track."

"The middle of nowhere is more like it. No trees, no water, a few stunted tumbleweeds that aren't well enough fed to leave home. I took one look at the place and said, 'Elliot, your beloved Anasazi had to be retarded to settle here.' "

"They could have been outcasts, I suppose. More importantly, has he found any good bones?"

"I just bag them. Interpreting them I leave to my father."

"Come on, Nick. I trained you better than that. You know what you're looking at."

"You also trained me not to step on my colleagues' toes, whether I'm related to them or not."

Guthrie grunted approvingly. "I see you're learning the politics of the business. No wonder they hired you at Berkeley. When do you get tenure?"

Nick shrugged. "Dad did give me this, though." She pulled the limp ten-dollar bill from her jeans and gave it to him. "He's talking about digging his own well now."

"He's probably right about the subterranean water being there."

"When it comes to the Anasazi, I know better than to question anything my father says."

"You're damn right. I never figured to win this bet."

"It's all right for you two," Nick said, "but I'd like to spend one of my summers someplace cool. Maybe writing a book so I could get tenure at least."

"It won't hurt your reputation any if your father makes a real find here."

They both knew that Site ES No. 1, though a major enough discovery to have earned Elliot the honor of having it named after him, was miles from the main Anasazi ruins at Pueblo Bonito and Chetro Ketl and quite small by comparison. Over the years, thousands of sites had been excavated in Utah, Colorado, Arizona, and New Mexico, but only a few had contained broken and charred human bones, leaving archaeologists with a number of theories. Were the bones evidence of ritual slaughter taking place only at the important population centers, were they the spoils of war, or had there been widespread cannibalism? If similar bones were found at a relatively obscure site, like ES No. 1, Elliot would have backing for his theory that the Anasazi destroyed their civilization, or what remained of it after the great drought that began in 1276 and lasted for twenty-three years. That long without rain, without crops, would leave them only one sure source of protein—one another.

"Now's the time to leave Berkeley, Nick, and join your father in Albuquerque. Between the two of us, I think we can guarantee you immediate tenure. Besides, he's not getting any younger. He needs you."

"I'm here, aren't I? Like always, spending my summers hauling supplies and running errands."

"All digs depend on logistics, you know that as well as I do. If Elliot left that up to one of his students, something could go wrong. His work could be compromised."

"I heard that speech already today."

"It's true nevertheless."

"If I hadn't left the University of New Mexico after graduation," she said, "people would be yelling nepotism behind my back. I want to be accepted for my own work, not Elliot's."

Guthrie laid a hand on hers. "The *National Geographic* may not be the *Journal of Archaeological Research*, but it's bound to get you taken seriously."

"I've loved airplanes ever since I was old enough to read about them, but I'm not crazy to think I can make a career out of them. To make it as an historical archaeologist, you have to restore Colonial Williamsburg or Civil War battlefields. Otherwise, the grant money isn't there."

"Maybe we can find you something like that if you come back to us. Towns along the old Santa Fe Trail need restoring if we're not going to lose our heritage to subdivisions. You know the drill. Renovate a frontier town, spruce up boot hill, and the next thing you know you'll have a tourist attraction."

"The Professor Guthrie who taught me Archaeology 101 would have flunked any student who suggested something like that."

"So stick to the Anasazi, that's my advice. Besides, Elliot already told me he's found some promising artifacts. He'll share the credit with you, you know that."

"Or the blame."

Guthrie ducked his head. "Seriously, Nick, I think your father depends on you more than you realize. The Anasazi may not be your speciality, but you know more about them than anyone else in the department, with the exception of your father."

She sighed. "Don't think I haven't agonized over my decision to leave you two, but I'm tired of protecting him. I've been doing it all my life."

Her comment provoked an inquisitive stare, which she escaped by sliding out of the booth and stepping behind the lunch counter.

"Mom," she called, "I'm going to get us some sodas."

"You know where they are, dear," a woman called back. "I'll be out in a minute."

"What kind of protection?" Guthrie asked.

Nick turned her back on him long enough to retrieve cans of Coke from the refrigerator. The cool air soothed her and made her wonder if she wasn't dehydrated, maybe on the verge of heat prostration. Why else would she have blurted out something so personal? That part of her life was off-limits.

"This damn place is getting to me," she said, returning to the booth. "I need a real summer vacation, or at least a real air conditioner."

"It was a hundred and twelve degrees when you found that plane in Texas last year, and you were living in a tent, not a motel."

She shrugged.

"You're a natural in this business. I said so when you were my student. You're like Schliemann. He read about Troy and believed it was real when everybody said it was a city Homer made up. So he went out and found it, just like you did with that bomber. You've already had two major finds. That's more than most archaeologists achieve in a lifetime."

She sipped her soda. Guthrie was right about one thing. Finding that bomber in Texas, a twin-engine B-25, the same kind Jimmy Doolittle flew off an aircraft carrier to bomb Tokyo, had been so exciting she hadn't thought about the heat for one moment, not even while scouring the badlands of Texas, talking to old-timers who had nothing better to do than tell stories about lost mines and lost planes. Painstakingly, she'd sorted out fact and fiction, cross-referencing everything with Army Air Corps records, until finally she was ready to go out into the desert to look for herself.

Mom Bennett appeared, wearing her usual flowered apron, her gray hair done up in a bun like a Norman Rockwell grandmother. One look at Guthrie, a new man in town in her age group, and Mom's face lit up.

"I make my own pies," she told him. "Mom's home cooking. The first slice is on the house."

Since Nick wasn't included in the offer, she headed for the door. "I'll leave you to your pie, Professor."

Guthrie looked trapped.

"I'll be back in ten minutes," she added, "as soon as I load the supplies we need for tomorrow morning."

A sign on the front door of Tuttle's store said BACK IN FIFTEEN MINUTES. Nick's supplies were stacked on the porch next to the door.

"You could have put them in the Trooper for me," she muttered, then realized the mayor would never risk it while her Isuzu was parked in the sun.

Gritting her teeth, she went to work. By the time she'd finished, Nick was soaking wet and thirsty enough to tear open one of the cardboard cartoons containing the new brand of bottled water she'd ordered. She drank half a liter and poured the rest over her head, feeling refreshed until she caught sight of her disheveled reflection in the plate glass. She ran her fingers through her short red hair, but that made matters worse, creating droopy-looking spikes. All she could do was hide the mess under her Cub's cap. On top of everything else, the new brand of water tasted as bad as the old one.

Feeling bedraggled, not to mention outgeneraled by Mayor Ralph, she U-turned the Trooper, parked in front of the café, and went inside to collect Guthrie. Mom Bennett was sitting across from him in the booth, as well as an older man Nick had never seen before. Both were studying the *National Geographic*.

"You look exhausted, dear," Mom said the moment Nick

sat next to Guthrie. "Let me get you another cold drink."

Nick shook her head. "I'm not thirsty. I think my blood sugar's low."

"One piece of pie, coming up. Anybody else?"

"Apple pie à la mode all around," Guthrie said. "On me." When Mom went to fetch the pie, Guthrie added, "This is Gus Beckstead, Nick. He's a fan of yours."

Beckstead, bone thin with a sun-wrinkled face the color of old leather, looked from Nick to her photograph and back again. Finally, squinting skeptically, he tapped a stained fingernail on the magazine. "It says here you dig up airplanes."

"I've been lucky enough to find a couple."

"Is there any money in it?"

"That picture's all the payment I'm likely to get."

"It's like I told you," Guthrie said. "Nick Scott is a famous archaeologist, and one of my best students. Planes are more of a hobby with her than anything else. Mostly, she digs up Indians like the rest of us. You see, her speciality, historical archaeology, deals with only the last few hundred years. In this country, excluding the Indians, that begins with the arrival of Columbus."

"Is there money in any of this?"

"Mostly we do it for love," Guthrie said. "And for the universities who pay us."

Beckstead's gaze settled on Nick's breasts, no doubt accentuated by the water she'd spilled down the front of her shirt. The look on his face was more doubtful than sexual, as if having breasts somehow disqualified her from scientific work. She'd seen it on men his age before. He was, she guessed, somewhere in his seventies.

"Gus is a prospector," Guthrie said. "He digs for gold."

The man raised his sights to stare her in the eye. "There's not much digging to it. Mostly, I use a metal detector. It beats the old days, I can tell you, scratching around out there in the desert, eating dirt and dust. Now I just turn the damned thing on and wander around. You should hear the bastard beep when I find a big nugget."

Mom served the pie. "You'd better dig right in. The ice cream won't last long in this kind of heat."

"Aren't you having one?" Guthrie asked her.

"It's getting close to dinnertime. My first customers will be arriving in the next few minutes. You come back sometime when we can be alone and get to know each other and I'll let you buy me a piece of pie." Mom disappeared into the kitchen.

"Like I was saying," Beckstead said, "Gold nuggets have been washing down from the Chuska Mountains west of here for thousands of years, not that we get much rain. But when it does come, it's a gully washer, by God."

"Do you make a living looking for nuggets?" Nick asked.

"Among other things," he said, winking.

"Ask him what other things," Guthrie said.

Nick stared at her old professor, who looked as sly as when he asked trick questions on his final exams.

"All right," she said, "what's going on?"

While Beckstead grinned, Guthrie said, "Gus tells me he's found an airplane out in the desert."

"I hope you don't expect me to fall for that one."

"It's the truth. Gus wasn't going to do anything about it until we got to talking and I showed him your picture in the magazine."

"I can't say I'm going to do anything about it now," Beckstead added.

Nick toyed with her pie, now swimming in melted ice cream. "What kind of airplane?"

"How the hell would I know? I don't have the time to dig it up."

"You say it's buried?"

"Sandstorms cover up anything that's not moving out in

the desert. I wouldn't have found it without my metal detector."

"If it's covered up, how do you know what it is?"

"I shifted enough sand to see part of a wing. It had an insignia on it."

"Show me."

He pulled a paper napkin from the booth's dispenser, then used Guthrie's pen to make a rough sketch.

"It could be a World War Two emblem," Nick said.

He eyed her closely. "You weren't born in time for that war."

"I've known her since she was a child," Guthrie said. "When other little girls were playing with dolls, she was a tomboy building model planes."

Nick smiled grimly. Building models had nothing to do with being a tomboy. She'd built Spitfires, Mustangs, and B-17s as a means of escape, the same way her father had done when he spent his weekends absorbed in scale models of his beloved Indian cliff dwellings. Studying cockpit layouts was preferable to dealing with her mother.

"Tell me, Gus," she said, "have you heard any stories of a plane being lost around here?"

"Until I heard about you, I didn't know anybody who'd give a damn."

"Are you asking me to take a look at it?"

"If you dig up my plane, I want my picture in a magazine, too."

Beneath the tabletop, Nick nudged Guthrie with her knee, prompting him to say, "Archaeology isn't as easy as it seems. There's a lot of hard work involved, not to mention the cost."

"Does that mean you'll charge me to take a look-see?"

Guthrie chuckled. "If I know my Nick, you couldn't keep her away from an airplane. You might be able to charge *her* admission."

Beckstead scratched a sideburn as if thinking that over. "How about we take a look first thing in the morning?"

"I think my father can get by without me for a couple of hours," Nick said.

Guthrie snorted. "He'll be so busy showing me his site, he won't even miss you, Nick. I'll ride out with him tomorrow and you can play with your airplane."

Beckstead fingered the *National Geographic*. "What about my picture?"

"I'll do my best for you," she said.

"You're at the Seven Cities like everyone else, aren't you?" She nodded.

Beckstead stood up. "I'll meet you there first thing tomorrow morning."

3

Nick sat up in the dark, wondering what had awakened her. The knock on the door repeated itself.

"It's me, Gus Beckstead."

She switched on the bedside light. For Christ's sake, it was five o'clock. To her, first thing in the morning meant sometime after eight o'clock.

She swung out of bed, went to the door, and opened it the length of the security chain. "Did you bring coffee?"

"No, ma'am."

"Give me fifteen minutes," she said.

"That's what I figured. Women are always late starters. I'll be waiting in the truck."

Sighing, Nick closed the door, plugged in the coffeemaker she'd filled the night before, then headed for the shower. Ten minutes later, with a trowel in one hand and a full thermos in the other, she climbed into Beckstead's pickup truck, a battered Chevy that rode high on oversize tires. The tires looked new, the tools in the back well kept. Five-gallon gas cans had been lashed to the truck's side panels, along with fiberglass water jugs.

As they pulled out of the parking lot, the rising sun was in their eyes but had yet to erase the desert chill. The air smelled damp, though there wasn't a trace of surface water for fifty miles in any direction.

"I brought an extra cup," she said, adjusting her position on the tattered truck seat to accommodate the hand trowel in her pocket.

"My father used to say, 'You can judge a woman by the coffee she makes.' " He blew on his cup, took a careful sip, and swished the coffee around in his mouth. When he finally swallowed, he made a face and shook his head.

She tested it for herself. It tasted worse than usual.

"The water in this town is terrible," Beckstead said. "If you ask me you scientists polluted it with your atomic bomb testing. Now fasten your seat belt. It's a rough ride where we're going." He handed back the cup. "Too rough to be drinking coffee."

"It's rough anywhere in this desert."

"If it was paradise, it would be too expensive for the likes of me."

Heading out of town, they crossed the old concrete WPA bridge that spanned Conejos Wash. At that time of the morning the hundred-foot gorge was still in deep shade. Looking down its steep bank with the wind rushing by, Nick had the impression that the Conejos River was running, though she knew its short life was confined to the rainy season.

Halfway to her father's dig site, Beckstead swung off the highway, following tire tracks that Nick had never noticed before. The tracks wound northwest in the general direction of the Navajo Indian reservation, crossing a landscape that was only slightly less barren than the red-rock canyon where the

Anasazi had chosen to live a thousand years ago.

When Beckstead slowed the truck to a crawl, Nick took the opportunity to pour herself a second cup of coffee. It was on the way to her lips when the truck careened into a shallow gully. The jolt splashed hot coffee down the front of her workshirt.

"That's where I find my nuggets," Beckstead said, "in gullies like this. They crisscross this whole area."

Between gullies, Nick stowed the thermos under the seat and cranked down the window to dry out her shirt. In the few minutes since leaving town, the sun had gone to work. The air temperature was up, well into the seventies, she guessed, with no hint of dew. The locals claimed that the desert vegetation was ideal for range cattle, though Nick had yet to see anything worth eating.

"There it is, up ahead," Beckstead said ten minutes later. "I call it my oasis."

A quarter of a mile ahead a yellow ribbon fluttered from the top of a metal rod. When they got closer, she saw that the ribbon was really plastic tape and the rod was a telescoping car antenna.

Beckstead stopped beside the marker. "From here on, this is my land. If you ever drive out here on your own, stick to the road. Otherwise, you'll hit deep sand. I made that mistake my first trip out and got stuck up to the axle. If I hadn't had four-wheel drive, my bones would be here instead of me."

In low gear, Beckstead crept ahead another fifty yards before parking the truck.

From an archaeologist's point of view, a low mound, maybe a hundred feet long, was the only possible burial site in an otherwise barren and deeply eroded landscape. There were no trees, no brush large enough to provide shade. The only shelter was a shack maybe twice the size of an outhouse. As Nick paced along the base of the mound, she began to sweat, a combination of excitement and the quickly rising temperature.

"The locals call this Hospah Flats," he said, "though you won't find it on the maps. All they show is badlands, lucky for me. Otherwise, some big company might have come in here and stolen my gold claim out from under me."

Nick nodded at Beckstead's truck. "Do you mind if I stand on the cab?"

His indifferent shrug sent her scrambling onto the hot metal. From that vantage point, the mound looked more compact than she'd first thought.

"You told me you'd dug up a wing?" she said.

"I covered it back up again, didn't I? I didn't want anybody else poking around what belongs to me." He grabbed a shovel from the truck bed and waited for Nick to climb down before leading the way out into the soft sand. He started digging at a spot marked by a football-size rock. Nick pulled work gloves from her pocket and got down on her knees, waiting for him to strike metal. The moment he did, she waved him off and began clearing away the loose dirt and sand with her fingers.

"Jesus Christ," Beckstead said, "is that the way you have to do it, by hand?"

"If you want to preserve your find, you have to be careful."

The moment she touched the edge of the wing her fingers tingled with an electric shock of excitement. It took her breath away, as did all such discoveries. She sat back on her haunches to savor the moment.

"Well?" Beckstead said.

She wanted to shout for joy. Instead, she nodded at the prospector and began to dig, using her hand trowel. Within minutes, she'd exposed a perfectly preserved wingtip. Painted on it was a white five-pointed star centered in a faded blue circle, with white bars on either side. Despite the heat, goose bumps climbed her spine.

"Well?" Beckstead demanded.

"It looks like a World War Two insignia all right."

"What kind of plane?"

"Guessing isn't good for an archaeologist's reputation."

"Shit. What difference does it make? It's a plane, isn't it, just like I said?"

"Judging by the shape of it, it could be a B-17 bomber," Nick admitted.

"What the hell's it doing out here in the middle of nowhere?"

"Were there any air bases around here during the war?"

"How would I know? I was stuck in the infantry."

Nick rose to her feet and circled the mound with Beckstead at her heels. The dimensions confirmed the possibility that she'd discovered a plane the size of a bomber.

"May I use your metal detector?" she asked.

He impressed her by producing a state-of-the-art Garrett, complete with expensive earphones. Considering the invest-ment, not to mention the prospector's well-equipped truck, nugget hunting must have been more profitable that she'd first imagined.

Explaining her methods as she went, she began ten yards out from the mound, moving in an ever-tightening circle as she probed for metal fragments. But the Garrett didn't make so much as a peep until she reached the mound's perimeter. Then she climbed the mound, crisscrossing it while getting a con-stant reading from the metal detector. The entire airplane had to be here, she felt certain, not just a wing fragment.

To confirm that, she appropriated Beckstead's makeshift flag pole and made a dozen probe holes. Each time the antenna encountered resistance, conforming to the pattern of a large World War II aircraft. Seventy feet long, she made it, about right for a B-17, or possibly a B-24.

Her initial excitement had passed, leaving her with a spent, weak-kneed feeling.

"Let's get out of the sun." She headed for his shack without waiting for an answer. Inside, the stale air smelled vaguely of manure and felt hot enough to explode. But at least she was out of the glare.

She collapsed to the ground, sitting cross-legged. Her head ached from the hammering sun and the excitement.

"My bones are too old to sit like that," Beckstead said, easing himself onto an empty wooden crate that had once contained dynamite.

"Have you ever seen a B-17?" Nick asked. "They were beautiful planes, deadly, too. Think of what it must have been like during the war. It would be early morning in England when ten young men climbed aboard and flew all the way to Germany and back in broad daylight, six hours flying time with German fighters and flak trying to kill you every mile of the way. By today's standards B-17s aren't that big, but they were our heavy bombers then." She sighed. "I'd give anything to bring one back to life."

"That's why we're here, isn't it, to dig her up and show her off so I can get my picture in one of them fancy magazines?"

"It's too big a job for the two of us."

"What about those students you have digging up Indians out there at the mesa?"

"They belong to my father. Besides, the university is very particular when it comes to funding. When it puts up money for Indian artifacts, that's exactly what it expects."

"I'm seventy-three years old but I can still hold my own when it comes to a day's shoveling."

"Even if the two of us worked like dogs, we'd need to drink gallons to survive every day in this kind of heat. That's a lot of bottled water, and as you know your mayor doesn't give it away free."

"I've got some money. How much would we need?"

"It's a matter of people, too, if we don't want to spend the whole summer here. We'd need three or four diggers at the least. Without that kind of help, it would take more time than I have to spare. Two or three days, that's the most I can be away from my father's dig. I'm sorry."

"If I can get us some diggers, will you help?"

Nick took a deep breath, expelling it slowly while she massaged the back of her neck. Working out on that mound, fully exposed to the sun, made her father's cave dwelling seem like a garden spot. There, at least, shade prevailed during some of the morning. Even so, she'd risk a lot of sunburn and dehydration for the chance at a well-preserved bomber. Besides, like Clark Guthrie said, publicity was one way to get tenure quickly.

"One thing's in our favor," she said. "It wouldn't be like digging up an ancient civilization, where site preservation is absolutely critical. We wouldn't have to be so careful digging. That would save some time."

Beckstead had the bewildered look of someone hearing their first used-car pitch.

"Normally, we'd have to lay the entire site out in grids," she explained, "then sink shafts to determine geological strata inch by inch so that every artifact could be properly dated in context. Here, we know we've got a World War Two airplane, so all we have to do is be reasonably careful and not cause any further damage to the craft. Site stripping, we call it. It's a technique used when time or approaching bad weather is a factor. Like I said, time is my critical factor. Of course, I'm not certain how long my father can spare me, or if he even will."

By so stating, Nick was giving herself a way out should the need arise. Elliot would never stand in the way of one of her beloved planes. Even so, she wouldn't abandon him for too long, bomber or no bomber. Still, Clark Guthrie could take over most of her chores, at least on a temporary basis.

Beckstead rose from the crate and put his hands to the small of his back. "I don't want to be paying diggers, if you aren't willing to do your part. I want a commitment from you. And I want to know for sure if this plane will get us publicity like you and your friend, Guthrie, said."

Nick got to her feet, adjusted her cap to shade her eyes, and stepped outside to take another look at the burial mound. Chances were that Beckstead was all talk, especially when it came to laying out his own money. Certainly, he'd never get volunteers, not to work in a blast furnace like this. But if he did come up with a crew, she might be able to get some kind of reimbursement from one of the museums that were always on the lookout for heritage aircraft.

"If you get a crew," she said, "I'll donate my time. The publicity I can't guarantee, but finding a bomber ought to attract somebody's attention."

Beckstead grabbed her hand and shook it formally. "By the way, missy, I've filed for this land legally, so don't try any claim jumping. Now come with me and I'll show you the safe places to turn around in without hitting deep sand. I don't want to have to baby-sit you all the time."

4

Gus Beckstead wore his poker face during the drive back into town. Even after exchanging dirt ruts for the state highway's blacktop, he forced himself to clench the steering wheel rather than have his fingers betray him by tapping out the beat of excitement throbbing inside his head. By his reckoning, he was halfway to making a name for himself. God, he could see it now, the looks on people's faces when they had to eat crow for all the things they'd said about him over the years. They'd have to take it all back, that he was nothing but a crazy old desert rat, a scrounger, that the only gold he ever found was in his Social Security check.

He pressed his lips together to keep from laughing. Maybe he could get someone else to pay for the diggers. Now, wouldn't that be the perfect payback for all those insults. Someone else financing his fame, his picture, and his plane on the cover of one of those big magazines. Someone like his high and mighty holiness, the mayor. And why settle for *National Geographic*? He'd go for *Time* or *Newsweek*, or maybe even

People. For once, he'd be somebody important. And who knows? With luck, he might also pocket a little money if he played his cards just right.

He stole a quick glance at his passenger to see if she was aware of his excitement. Her eyes were closed; her baseball cap was in her lap and her arms were crossed, hiding those fine breasts of hers. He let out a breath. A good-looking woman, even in jeans and an old shirt. Not what he'd expected at all when he first heard there was a lady scientist in town. The photo in the *National Geographic* hadn't done her justice. Of course, she'd been out in the sun, wearing that damned cap of hers. It was a crime to hide pretty red hair like that.

He slowed, driving more carefully than usual as he turned into the motel's graveled parking lot. In one motion he switched off the engine and opened his door, then trotted around to the passenger side. With just the hint of a bow, he opened the door and offered Nick a helping hand. She accepted it, but the puzzled look on her face told him to cool it.

"I'll get back to you, partner," he said.

She smiled and disappeared into her room at the Seven Cities.

On the way out of the parking lot, Beckstead fought off the urge to pop the clutch and send gravel flying. Instead, he coasted down the street to park in front of the general store. Nodding to himself, he unlocked the glove compartment and took out the copy of the *National Geographic* he'd scrounged the night before. He'd already dog-eared the article about Nicolette Scott, whom the magazine called "a recognized expert in the field of twentieth-century archaeology."

Beckstead smacked his lips. "All that and great boobs, too."

He rolled up the magazine and stuck it in the back pocket of his jeans before going inside. Mayor Ralph was alone, sitting in front of the air-conditioning vent reading the *Albu-*

querque Journal, which arrived by mail a day late.

"How's business?" Beckstead asked as he always did, surprised that his voice sounded so calm.

"It would be better if you bought something once in a while," the mayor said without looking up.

"Everything I wear I bought here."

The mayor snorted. "Another change of clothes would be appreciated by more folks than me."

Beckstead sniffed in the direction of an armpit. "The only thing I smell is fame for this town of ours."

Deliberately, the mayor folded his paper, slid it under his chair, and tucked his reading glasses into his shirt pocket. Only then did he fix Beckstead with a questioning stare.

"Cibola's population is shrinking worse than your cotton goods," Beckstead said. "Those who haven't moved away drive into Gallup to do most of their shopping."

"I survive."

"Only thirty people turned out to vote for you last time."

"I was unopposed."

Beckstead nodded. "The fact is, Cibola's dying and the mayor, no matter who he is, can't do anything about it."

"What's your point, Gus?"

"The interstate has passed us by and all we've got going for us is some old Indian ruins, too far off the beaten track to attract tourists. The next thing you know, they'll be deleting Cibola from the maps altogether. We'll be nothing but an intersection branching off the state highway."

"Jesus Christ," the mayor said. "I don't need to hear this again. I already get it from my wife and every loudmouth who shows up at the council meetings."

"Step over to the counter," Beckstead said, leading the way.

When the mayor joined him, Beckstead drew the magazine from his back pocket and slapped it down on the counter.

"Take a look, Mayor Ralph. Opportunity is knocking right in front of you."

The mayor squinted at the magazine. "So? I've seen it before."

"Put on your glasses, for Christ's sake."

"You're a pain in the ass, Gus, do you know that?" the mayor said, but did as he was asked. "All I see is our lady archaeologist."

"Look closer."

"She's got a hell of a shape, is that what you want me to say?"

"She's a professor and she's famous, a celebrity. With her help and my airplane we can get a little publicity and put Cibola back on the map. She's agreed to help us dig it up."

"What airplane?"

"The one I found out there on my land."

"What the hell would a plane be doing out there?"

"It's a bomber, she said. It must have crashed." Beckstead fingered the *National Geographic*. "If my plane gets famous, so does Cibola."

"She actually saw the plane?"

"Part of it, anyway. We uncovered a wingtip."

"What did she say about it?"

"Not much, but you should have seen the look on her face. For her, it was like striking gold."

Lips pursed, Mayor Ralph paced back and forth in front of the cash register. "We can't expect tourists to drive across all that desert just to look at an old airplane."

"You're missing the point."

"Which is?"

"Reporters will be showing up. They'll want to interview me, along with other important people in town like the mayor. You'll get your picture taken, too. You'll see your name in print. You could throw in a plug for the town."

The mayor licked his lips.

"You could talk about the desert climate," Beckstead continued. "You could call Cibola a retirement community, and maybe sell off some of that acreage of yours."

"Do you think so?"

"Absolutely," Beckstead lied. He faked a cough to keep from smiling. He had the mayor on the hook; all he had to do was reel him in.

"What kind of plane did you say it was?" the mayor said.

"The *professor*," Beckstead said, lingering over the title to give a ring of authority to his plan, "thinks it's probably a B-17, the kind they used to bomb Germany with."

"A B-29 might have been better, what with Los Alamos being so close by. On the other hand, why alienate Japanese tourists unnecessarily?"

Beckstead thought the mayor was being a little overoptimistic if he figured anyone but New Mexicans would come to a place like Cibola, and then only those with nothing better to do.

"All we've got to do is come to an understanding," Beckstead said. "I've got the plane. All we need now is the workers to dig it up."

"I thought that was your professor's job?"

"You haven't seen the plane yet. It's a big bastard we're talking about, a four-engine bomber. Remember that old movie, *Twelve O'clock High*, with Gregory Peck? Those were B-17s. I looked it up."

"How much money are we talking about?" the mayor said.

"The professor said we'd need three or four diggers if we want it uncovered in less than a week."

The mayor leaned against his cash register. "I ought to bring my council in on this."

"That's up to you," Beckstead said, giving the mayor a little more line. "Share the cost, that's my motto. Still, how much could it be if we kicked in four ways, you, me, Bill Latimer, and Jay Ferrin?"

"I know a few ranch hands who'll work for fifty dollars a day. So maybe a couple of hundred dollars will do it."

"Even if it's twice that, split four ways it only comes to a hundred apiece. That's cheap enough, I say, to get our pictures in an important magazine."

"Don't forget the newspapers," the mayor said. "I know a guy at the *Journal* in Albuquerque. What do you think?"

"Absolutely. That's the place to start."

"All right, then. Let's see what the others have to say." The mayor reached for the phone.

Half an hour later, Beckstead added his name to an agreement already signed by the mayor and his councilmen, acting strictly as private citizens. Once copies were handed out, the mayor tossed Beckstead the key to the soda machine. "We ought to have a toast. Drinks are on the house."

"Let's hope that free drinks are only the first miracle," Beckstead said before fetching the icy cans.

After a long swallow, Mayor Ralph said, "Now's as good a time as any to start our publicity campaign."

He opened the cash register, removed a stack of business cards from one of the coin bins, and began sorting through them. "Yes, here it is. Will Smith, editor of the *Albuquerque Journal*. He came through Cibola a couple of years ago, on one of those tours of the Indian ruins. I seem to remember the Navajos were raising some kind of a fuss at the time. They wanted the bones of their ancestors back, or some damned thing."

Ferrin nodded. "He stayed at my motel."

"I pumped gas for him," Latimer added.

43

"He said to call him if the Indians ever went on the war path," the mayor said. "I guess he figured that's the only kind of news Cibola would be good for."

They all gathered around as the mayor phoned, angling the receiver away from his ear so they could listen in. A secretary answered. After closely questioning the mayor, she put him through to Smith, who asked the same questions she had.

Finally, Smith said, "Cibola's a long way to send a reporter on spec."

Beckstead waved the magazine.

"Have you seen the latest *National Geographic*?" the mayor relayed. "They have a story about the same archaeologist who's going to dig up our plane."

"Give me her name and I'll run it through the computer."

"Nicolette Scott."

They could hear the editor hitting keys. "I get two Scotts, Elliot and Nicolette."

"They're both here in Cibola," the mayor said. "Elliot Scott is head of the Department of Anthropology at the University of New Mexico."

"He's working on the plane, too?"

Mayor Tuttle winked at his partners and crossed his fingers. "He and his daughter are staying here in town and working together. They have been all summer. But the plane I'm talking about is going to be uncovered in the next day or two."

"The *Journal*'s on a tight budget. You don't have your own newspaper there, do you, someone who could act as our stringer?"

Ferrin gestured for the mayor's attention. "Hold on a moment, will you please, Mr. Smith."

As soon as the mayor covered the mouthpiece, Ferrin said, "I've got one room left at the motel. I'll donate it to the cause."

The mayor looked at Latimer, who nodded. "I'll kick in the gas."

"We can provide gas," Tuttle said, "plus a motel room and meals, if that will help."

"You've got a deal," Smith said. "I'll have a man there tomorrow."

5

Will Smith disconnected his headset, swung his feet up on the city-room desk, and gave a war whoop. "Goddamn, I'm good, which is why they pay me the big bucks."

"Which leaves spit for the rest of us," reporter Mark Douglas fired back.

"Show a little respect. I'm about to hand you a scoop on a platter. What would you say to an all-expenses-paid vacation to a desert wonderland?"

"Look out the window," Douglas said. "Albuquerque *is* the desert."

Smith beckoned to his reporter. "You've lived too long in California. This is the real world. Now, step into my parlor, my boy, and I'll make you famous."

Groaning for effect, Douglas grabbed his cane, levered himself to his feet, and maneuvered past the two intervening desks to reach the *Journal*'s city editor. The editor's desk, like its siblings throughout the vast, carpeted newsroom, was a mixture of metal and plastic masquerading as wood.

"How long has it been since your accident?" Smith asked.

"Damn near three months."

"Take it from me, what you need is exercise, fresh air, and sunshine. You don't want to start making a career out of being a gimp."

Douglas rolled his eyes. The *Journal*'s fresh-air policy had gotten his leg broken in the first place, the first day the newspaper's no-smoking policy had gone into effect. After two hours of on-the-job abstinence, Douglas gave up on his gum and ran for the fire exit to light up. Only he hadn't counted on one of Albuquerque's infrequent rainstorms turning the metal stairway into a ski jump.

Douglas hadn't smoked a cigarette since, though the craving still haunted him, particularly after meals. After sex was supposed to be a big deal, too, but you had to have a girlfriend to appreciate that.

"What do you know about Cibola?" Smith asked.

"Please, not another of your treasure hunts."

"Humor me."

Douglas limped back and forth, trying to work the stiffness out of his leg. "If I remember my history, Spanish explorers roamed New Mexico sometime in the sixteenth century seeking Cibola's fabled seven cities of gold. Why the hell they bothered, I don't know. One look at this godforsaken state should have told them that the Indians were lucky to survive, let along amass riches."

"The explorer we're talking about is Francisco Coronado," Smith said. "Practically our patron saint."

"If you say so."

"What I say is that our beloved Coronado wasn't looking hard enough, because I've found the gold, right in Cibola where it should be." Smith swiveled around in his chair before charging the twenty-foot wall map, where he stabbed a finger into the state's northwestern badlands. "For the benefit of foreigners like yourself, let me explain that the state of New Mexico has a town named Cibola."

Douglas moved close enough to the map to see a minuscule dot.

"That was their mayor on the phone just now," Smith went on. "The silly bastard's sitting on one hell of a story and doesn't know it. I strung the gazooney along until he agreed to pay your expenses. Hell, one call to a TV station would have got him a chopper in there, with live coverage if the satellites are in working order." The editor thumped the map with the palm of his hand. "But as of now, this exclusive is all yours."

Douglas eyed the map. Cibola's part of New Mexico was color coded white, like a salt flat. "Hold it." He snatched up the day's edition of the *Journal* and turned to the weather section. Cibola wasn't listed, but the nearest town of any size, Thoreau, showed a temperature of one hundred and ten degrees. "No, you don't. I'm on restricted duty. Doctor's orders."

"Like I said, don't start coddling yourself at your young age. Besides, it can't be more than a hundred miles to Cibola. And a hundred ten is a spring day. Hell, we used to play doubleheaders in worse than that when I was on the university baseball team."

Exaggerating his limp, Douglas collapsed onto the metal folding chair next to Smith's desk, the one everybody in the newsroom called the "hot seat."

Smith returned to his own cushioned chair and phoned the research department. "Bring me the latest edition of the *National Geographic.* Now!"

To Douglas, he added, "Cibola's found itself an old World War Two airplane buried out in the boondocks. Maybe it's a B-17, though it's too early to be sure. Whatever it is, I want you there when they dig her up."

"Who's 'they' and who's doing the digging?"

"That's the kicker. They've got themselves a couple of experts. Very famous archaeologists. Elliot Scott, for one."

"I thought he was supposed to be an authority on the Anasazi Indians."

"He is, he is, but he's got a daughter. She's our hook. Ah, here comes our magazine now. I'll show you what I mean."

Smith nodded a thank-you at the editorial assistant, then handed the *National Geographic* to Douglas. "Turn to the article on New Guinea."

Once Douglas had the proper page, Smith took back the magazine, glanced around the newsroom to make certain they weren't being overheard, then did a Groucho Marx imitation complete with raised eyebrow and imaginary cigar. "Tits and nostalgia, that's what sells newspapers. The daughter in question is Nicolette Scott, called Nick for short." He held up her picture for Douglas to admire.

"What kind of plane is that behind her?" Douglas asked.

"Jesus Christ, I think maybe you broke more than your leg on those stairs."

Douglas knew better than to fight back.

"I want close-ups of this lady archaeologist," Smith went on, "cleavage if you can manage it."

Douglas sighed. Smith was all talk. Catch him away from the *Journal*, where he wasn't living up to some long-gone image of the hard-bitten newsman, and he was a pussy cat. If Douglas actually substituted sex for an honest-to-God story, he'd find himself back on obituaries, praying for mass murder to fight off the boredom.

"Any chance of taking a photographer with me?" Douglas asked, hoping that someone else might do the driving.

Smith shook his head. "Aim and shoot, that's all you have to do with these new cameras."

Nodding his acceptance of the inevitable, Douglas said, "What's my deadline?"

"God knows how long it will take them to actually dig up

49

the thing, but I want you in at the start just the same. As long as we don't tip our hand to TV, you can sit on it until you're ready. You'd better drive down tonight, though, in the dark when it's cool. Take a cellular phone with you just in case you run into trouble on the highway. I wouldn't want a tenderfoot like you on my conscience."

Douglas smiled.

"Don't get cocky, and don't think you can take the rest of the afternoon off, just because I'm letting you drive at night. I want you on the phone to the air force. Find out if the bastards have lost any planes."

Sure, Douglas thought, he'd look it up in the phone book. The air force would be there certainly, listed under the U.S. government, but he doubted there'd be a subheading for missing fifty-year-old bombers.

Smith must have read his mind. "Start with Kirtland Air Force Base, fer Chrissake. It's just south of town, the last time I looked."

Clenching his teeth, Douglas hobbled back to his desk.

"You might try Captain Ken Roberts," Smith called after him. "He's the press liaison officer out there. You can mention my name to the asshole. You never know, it might be worth something. And knock off the limp. I'm not feeling sorry for you."

Smith was still laughing when Douglas made the call, feeling as if he wasn't fit for much more than obits at the moment. Captain Roberts didn't help bolster his confidence when he immediately put Douglas on hold. He was still holding when Roberts called back on another line.

"Sorry about that," the captain said, "but when someone tells me he's a reporter I always make sure who I'm talking to. Now, what can I do for you?"

Briefly, Douglas outlined the situation, that he was on his

way to Cibola to check on reports that a World War II bomber had been found in the desert.

"I'm looking at our maps now," Roberts answered. "There were a lot of bases in New Mexico during the war, but I don't see any that were designated for bomber training. Mostly fighter squadrons, I think, but I'd have to do some research to be sure."

"We've been told some archaeologists are already on the scene."

"Let me put you on hold again and check a couple of my history books."

Douglas was starting to crave a cigarette by the time Roberts came back on the line.

"I hope you're not on a wild-goose chase," the captain said, "but I can't find any documentation that there were bomber bases in the area. Of course, that doesn't mean a plane couldn't have gone down in the desert. If it had, though, you'd think we'd know about it. We'd also have picked up the pieces. Most likely, that's all you're going to find, a piece of a plane or something. Still, I wish you luck."

"I'd appreciate it if you kept quiet about this for the moment," Douglas said.

"You can count on me. I've been press liaison long enough to know the importance of an exclusive."

The smile left Captain Roberts's face the moment he hung up the phone. Journalists were a pain in the ass. Even if you made them happy, they wouldn't take the time to thank you. But rile them and they'd be on you like a pack of wolves. Either way, you lost.

He left his desk to check the map one more time, aligning the benchmarks to make absolutely certain that the plastic overlay was positioned correctly. There was no mistake. Cibola and environs were well outside the security zone that encircled Los Alamos and its testing grounds. Of course, the no-fly zone must have been larger during the war. No doubt there'd been fighter bases to enforce it.

Roberts shook his head. That was ancient history, just like he was. Too old and too long in grade. If he didn't make major on the forthcoming promotion list, he'd never survive the next cutback. If that happened, ten years would be shot to hell.

Ancient history or not, he decided to follow the first rule of military survival: cover your ass. A memorandum for the record was the usual method, to be filed for future bailouts. Only this time, he decided, he'd buck a copy up to the CO, Colonel Fortunato.

Colonel Joseph Fortunato waited until Captain Roberts left his office before slumping in his chair. All he wanted to do was coast through the next five months until retirement. No bumps, no waves, that was the way to a short-timer's heart.

He groaned. The captain's memo was more than a bump. It was a goddamn roadblock. And he couldn't ignore it, not if he wanted to survive. Of course, if blame needed to be assessed, he would dump everything on Roberts, who was going to be passed over for promotion anyway.

With that decided, the colonel opened his safe and went to work. The classified files on the Los Alamos security zone made no mention of lost airplanes. But there was a red flag, dating from 1945, that said all unusual inquiries concerning the security zone, or vicinity, should be forwarded to the Pentagon, Washington, D.C. No name was given, only a unit designation: S-OPS17.

Fortunato did the arithmetic in his head. The likelihood of anyone from S-OPS17 still being alive was remote enough, let alone being on duty after so many years. But he didn't like the term *vicinity*, not one damn bit. It was too vague, too unmilitary. Every order, red flags included, should have specific map coordinates; that was his idea of how things ought to be done.

Christ, vicinity could mean a neighborhood or a theater of war. In Fortunato's case, the vicinity to worry about was five months. A quiet, hundred-fifty-day neighborhood was all he wanted, not some goddamned war zone with a red-flagged career killer.

On top of everything else, he'd never known a red flag designation to remain in effect so long. No doubt it was the usual clerical screwup, but technically—as long as the red flag was there—security measures were still in effect.

"Shit," he muttered. "Here we go."

Once he responded to the red flag and set things in motion, it would be like an insect landing in a spider's web. Even if the spider was long gone, the vibrations would continue and sooner or later someone was bound to get stuck.

Sighing deeply, Colonel Fortunato addressed a classified cover sheet referring to S-OPS17—as prescribed by red flag procedure—and fed it into the scrambled fax machine, then repeated the process with Captain Roberts's memo explaining the press inquiry.

The moment SAC Headquarters at Offutt Air Force Base, Nebraska, acknowledged receipt, Fortunato shredded everything.

6

Nick examined her plate like a true archaeologist, probing the Zuni Café's dinner special, pot roast à la mode, as if in search of buried artifacts. What she unearthed was a chestnut dressing garnished with apple slices.

"You might as well eat it," her father said. "You know Mom Bennett, she only serves one entree a night. If you don't finish it, you won't get dessert."

Clark Guthrie, who was sitting across the booth from Nick, peeled back the sliced pot roast that was hiding the dressing and tested it for himself. "Am I missing something?" he said. The Zuni Café was full, as it always was on Wednesday, pot roast night. Last Wednesday Nick had thought ahead, stocking up on bread and cheese from the general store.

"Nick has nightmares about dressing," her father said. "Underdone turkey stuffing damn near killed us all when she was a child. When it came to cooking, my wife, God bless her, had her mind on other things."

"Like waiting for you to come back from one of your digs," Nick put in.

"When it came to food Elaine was totally dyslexic. Isn't that right, Nick?"

She ignored the question, variations of which she'd been hearing for years, and speared an apple slice with her fork. When she brought it to her mouth, it smelled of sage and sausage. In a heartbeat, the aroma erased Cibola and replaced it with Thanksgiving at home. Nick was eleven again, setting the table with white linen and sterling, following the pictured instructions in one of her mother's etiquette books, and hoping her father wouldn't get home too soon and spoil the surprise.

"You ought to try this dressing," Guthrie said. "It doesn't taste a bit like turkey stuffing."

With a sigh, Nick gingerly nibbled one of the apple slices. Her stomach knotted instantly. She knew it was a conditioned reflex, that memory was overriding reality, but she couldn't help herself. She got up, excusing herself to go to the bathroom, where she flushed away the mouthful she hadn't wanted to spit out in public.

By the time she got back to the table, her father had eaten her portion of pot roast and dressing, leaving her to cope only with the potatoes and string beans. She thanked him with a flickering smile, wondering if she'd ever be able to tell him the truth about that disastrous Thanksgiving dinner. He'd been out of town the entire week before, she remembered, called away to an unexpected dig made necessary because an Anasazi site was being threatened by an unusually heavy storm.

His first words coming through the front door had been, "Thank God I got back in time for one of your Thanksgiving dinners." He'd swept both Nick and her mother off their feet with a two-armed hug.

Prompted by the memory, Nick looked up from her plate and said, "You know how Mother hated your field trips."

With exaggerated deliberation, Elliot put down his knife

and fork, then wiped his mouth with a paper napkin. "Your mother never complained. She knew it was my job. I don't remember you complaining, either."

"Would it have done any good?"

"I hate coming in on the middle of a soap opera," Guthrie said. "Maybe I should go back to the motel and watch television."

Elliot shook his head. "Pay no attention, it's a family ritual. True archaeologists digging up the past and paying no attention to the present or the future. Your mother always said my homecomings were like having a honeymoon all over again."

But she didn't tell you about sitting in the dark, Nick thought. Day after day spent in her pajamas and robe, with the drapes and blinds drawn, unable to summon the energy or will to dress herself. Talking only when asked a direct question, leaving the housework and cooking to Nick. Her mother's moods of black depression, which she had once described as being trapped at the bottom of a well with glass walls that defied climbing, had haunted Nick's childhood.

"Mother told me once that she never worried about losing you to another woman," Nick said, "only to a major archaeological find. She said you were obsessive."

Elliot was about to respond when Gus Beckstead arrived, along with Mom Bennett's hot apple Betty topped with a mountainous scoop of vanilla ice cream.

"I know your tricks, Gus," Mom said. "Don't expect dessert without paying for dinner first."

"He can have mine." Nick moved over in the booth so Beckstead could squeeze in beside her.

Mom shook her head. "Don't think I didn't see how you treated my pot roast, young lady. Nobody leaves my place hungry. Now you eat your apple Betty and I'll bring another plate for Gus, not that he deserves it."

Beckstead waited until he was served and Mom Bennett

was out of earshot before speaking. "Good news, Professor. I've got your men. Four cowboy diggers ready and waiting to start first thing tomorrow morning. I told them to be there at six A.M. so we could get a jump on the heat."

"What the hell's going on?" Elliot said.

"I told you about it," Guthrie said. "Gus here's the prospector who found a plane buried out in the desert."

"Where?"

Beckstead provided directions.

"I thought it was all talk." Elliot condemned his daughter with a hard-eyed stare.

"Don't blame me," she said. "I didn't know he'd be able to come up with the money."

Beckstead grinned. "The mayor and his council kicked in. They figure it will be good for the town, having their own B-17 on display. Do you want me to pick you up in the morning?"

"I'll manage to get there by myself."

"Don't forget what I told you about the deep sand out there at my oasis. Stick to the road and my tire tracks." Beckstead lowered his head and went to work on his apple Betty.

"What about *my* dig?" Elliot said.

"Relax," Guthrie told him. "I'll fill in. Besides, how often do buried B-17s come along?"

"Talk about obsessive," Elliot said, unable to suppress a grin. "My daughter doesn't have lovers, she has airplanes."

7

Nick arrived at Beckstead's oasis at exactly six the next morning. Even so, half a dozen pickup trucks were there ahead of her, parked in a line adjacent to the burial mound. Being careful to stay in the well-worn tire tracks, she pulled her Trooper in behind the last truck and killed the engine. The moment she stepped outside, the rising sun hammered her; its glare started her eyes watering. When she blinked, waves of tears amplified the shimmering mirage lake that ran the length of the horizon. The temperature was way beyond yesterday's though that didn't seem possible.

What was it Beckstead had said? Start early and get a jump on the heat. Some jump this was. They'd all fry their brains by noon.

At the moment, Beckstead was standing with the mayor, who was flanked by his two councilmen and a stranger taking photographs. Four straw-hatted cowboys carrying rifles, her work crew no doubt, stood apart from the others.

She cupped her hands around her mouth and shouted, "This is a dig, not a hunting party."

Mayor Ralph trotted forward to greet her, gesturing for calm. "This is Mark Douglas," he said, indicating the man carrying a camera in one hand and a cane in the other. "He's a reporter from the *Albuquerque Journal*."

Douglas jabbed his cane into the sand, freeing both hands to take Nick's picture.

She glared at Gus Beckstead. "I thought you wanted your picture in a *national* magazine."

"We've gone partners with Gus," the mayor answered. "We'll all be sharing the fame and fortune."

"They promised me a B-17," Douglas said without taking his eye from the viewfinder.

"I don't know what we've got yet," Nick told him. "Now, will somebody tell me why all the guns?"

"Somone spotted a rattlesnake up on the mound where your plane's buried," the reporter said.

The mayor nodded. "We were about to shoot it when you arrived."

Nick shook her head. "For Christ's sake, it's probably more scared than you are. All we have to do is chase it off."

The mayor lowered his voice. "If we don't shoot it, the boys won't like it. They'll be looking around for it all day instead of doing their work."

Beckstead spoke up. "A little target practice will get our juices flowing, ain't that right, boys?"

"Nobody shoots at that mound," Nick said. "Understood?"

"We ain't working here, lady," one of the cowboys said, "not while that snake's around."

She sighed. That's what she got for dealing with amateurs. If she had any sense, she'd climb back into the Trooper and drive back the way she'd come. Except, of course, she'd have to creep in reverse if she didn't want to get stuck in the sand.

"You see a snake, you shoot it," the cowboy added. "That

way you won't be stepping on it some other day. Just give us the word, lady, and bang, it's all over."

A clear case of testosterone overload, she told herself. Experience had taught her there were two ways to counter such macho bullshit. One was to play the helpless female, the other was to attack right back, a prospect she found far more appealing.

She retrieved the .30-.30 from the Isuzu. Expertly, she levered a shell into the rifle's chamber. "Show me the goddamned snake."

The talkative cowboy obliged. The rattler, a five-footer, was coiled in striking position but making no sound.

She assessed her firing angle, found it acceptable in terms of site preservation, and snapped off a shot that cut the snake's head off.

The cowboy whistled his approval, then he and his cohorts quickly stowed their rifles in the window racks of their pickups.

"Where the hell did you learn to shoot like that?" the mayor asked.

"On my first dig. Now, let's get to work. From now on, we do things my way or I walk away from here."

"If she goes," the reporter said, "so does my story."

The mayor held up his hands in surrender. "Whatever you say. We need your help if we're going to turn our B-17 into the mother lode."

"Confidentially," Mayor Ralph went on, making certain the reporter could hear every word, "I've been talking to some of my Navajo contacts. We're thinking of putting our plane on Indian land and turning it into a casino."

Deliberately, Nick turned her back on the mayor and returned her .30-.30 to its hiding place. When she faced him again, she said, "As of now, I want everyone out of here who's not going to be using a shovel. Otherwise, you'll just get in the way."

"Does that include me?" Douglas said.

"She's means us," the mayor said, gesturing at his council-men. "Like I said, Dr. Scott, you win. This is your dig. All we ask is that you keep us informed."

"I think you can count on Gus to do that."

As soon as the politicians were on their way, Nick waved over the cowboys and shook hands all around before escort-ing them to the exposed wingtip. "I want you to start here. We'll work slowly until I think you've got the feel of things. Remember, once you hit metal, back off and use your hands. We want to preserve everything we can, especially serial num-bers and any identification marks. If you spot anything un-usual, give a holler."

"How long do you think this is going to take?" Douglas asked.

Nick wiped the sweat band of her Cub's cap. "Long enough for you to get heatstroke if you don't cover your head."

"I've got an old hat in my truck," Beckstead said, and went to fetch it.

While the men went to work on the wing, Nick positioned wooden stakes on the mound, estimating the location of the nose, the cockpit, and the tail, which, judging by the height of the mound, was no longer attached to the airplane. When enough of the wing was exposed for her to be absolutely cer-tain that it was a B-17, she'd redirect her crew to the staked areas.

By noon, with no shade at all, Nick had consumed more than a gallon of water, the diggers twice that. The temperature had been holding at one hundred and five degrees for the past two hours. The pace of work, at first enthusiastic, had slowed as the temperature rose. Now, seen through the shimmer of heat waves, the men looked as if they were moving underwater.

"Take a break," she shouted. While the men were seeking what shade there was beneath the tailgates of their trucks, she joined Beckstead and Mark Douglas, who was lying on the floor of the prospector's stifling shack, fanning himself with a straw hat. "Tomorrow I want a tent out here," she told Beckstead. "Without real shade, we're all going to die of heat prostration."

The reporter's face looked ashen. His limp, Nick had noticed, had grown worse as the day and the heat progressed. Her own head throbbed. The back of her sunburned neck had been rubbed raw by her collar. Her lips were cracked, and her tongue felt twice normal size. Only the prospect of finding a previously undiscovered relic kept her from saying to hell with the dig.

"Why don't you stay in town until we've unearthed the plane?" she told Douglas.

He smiled grimly. "If it weren't for this damned heat, I'd be enjoying myself. Besides, you never know when your story's going to break."

She shrugged. "Suit yourself. Tomorrow, we'll have some kind of cover, won't we, Mr. Beckstead?"

"I seem to remember that the mayor has an old army tent he uses when he goes hunting."

"We'll need something better than that, something with open sides to provide ventilation and shade at the same time."

She moved to the open doorway, shading her burning eyes to study the site. Already the shape of the airplane was distinct, with the top of the aluminum fuselage exposed at the point where the dorsal aerial mast attached to the base of the tail. The remains of the upper turret, probably sheared away when the plane crashed, had also been exposed, as had the top of the cockpit. The windshield had yet to be cleared.

From now on, as they exposed more and more of the plane, there'd be more dirt to shift. All that debris would also have to be hauled out of the immediate area so it wouldn't clutter their work area.

"In case you haven't noticed," she said, "we did more work in the first two hours today than in the next four. Tomorrow, when we have proper shade, we'll take fifteen-minute breaks every hour."

"If you don't want the mayor's tent, what about attaching some kind of awning to the sides of our trucks?" Beckstead said.

"Whatever works is fine with me. For now, I think we'd best knock off and get a fresh start in the morning."

"The men owe a couple of more hours."

"My day just ended," Nick said.

Shrugging, Beckstead left the shack to talk to his men.

Douglas said, "This plane means a lot to you, doesn't it?"

"We live in a country that has little respect for history. Every day we tear down old buildings in the name of progress and profit." Nick found herself getting angry. "We concrete over the land, losing archaeological sites forever. That's where my job comes in, to save pieces of history every chance I get."

"You're like me. Your job's a bitch sometimes, but you love it anyway."

Love was part of it, most of it, at least Nick hoped so. But sometimes her motives weren't clear, even to herself. Her mother had seen Nick's fascination with airplanes and archaeology as a personal rebuke. In those moments when Elaine had escaped the silent pit of her black depression, she often said, "I know why you're following in your father's footsteps. It's to get away from me. The same way you used to run away from home when you were a little girl."

"I always came back."

"You stayed away until your father went looking for you."

"I was never far away."

"I need you close to me," her mother had said, "not out on some godforsaken dig."

Douglas touched her on the shoulder, interrupting her reverie. "If I do my job right," he said, "my story is going to attract the publicity the mayor is counting on. I don't think that's what you had in mind for this particular piece of history."

"What are you going to write?"

"I see it as strictly a nostalgia piece. Of course, everything depends on what kind of background information we come up with. How did the plane get here? What happened to the crew? That kind of thing."

"Formal identification ought to be easy enough, but tracking down the crew might be impossible after so many years."

Douglas adjusted his bad leg and began massaging it.

She nodded at the leg and said, "Did you get that in the line of duty?"

"Actually, the Surgeon General's to blame, or maybe Philip Morris. You see, I grew up thinking newspapers were full of typewriters and cigarette smoke. Now it's computers, spell checkers, and smoke-free zones. Try to light up in the newsroom and they throw you out in the rain. In my case, onto a slick metal fire escape. To make matters worse, I didn't even have time to inhale before I bounced all the way to the bottom."

Nick couldn't help laughing.

"Breaking that leg was the best thing that ever happened to me. It stopped me smoking. Hell, I wouldn't take another cigarette if the tobacco companies were giving them away."

Before Nick could respond, a car horn sounded in the distance. By the time she stepped out of the shack with Douglas right behind her, her father's Trooper was pulling up behind her own vehicle. As always, Elliot seemed unaffected by the heat. Next to him, Clark Guthrie looked totally disheveled, with a layer of grime clinging to his sweat-soaked work shirt. The handkerchief that he was using to mop his face had turned as red as the sandy soil, leaving behind streaks that reminded Nick of fresh wounds.

"Christ," Guthrie said. "Look at this place. It makes hell seem like a garden spot. You'd think people would be more considerate and misplace their airplanes someplace nice, preferably with a Hilton nearby."

Guthrie pivoted slowly, studying the excavation. "What kind of plane is it?"

"It's definitely not Anasazi." Nick raised an eyebrow at her father, who accepted her unspoken challenge and began pacing the long axis of the mound. When that was done, he climbed the slope to peer at the exposed portions of fuselage.

"I'd say the plane was more than sixty feet long," he called out finally. "Have you found the tail?"

"Not yet, but the top of the cockpit area should have told you what it was."

Elliot rejoined them at the base of the mound. "You're the expert, daughter."

"I think I can confirm that it's definitely a B-17."

"For Christ's sake," Beckstead said. "Why didn't you say so before? Me and Douglas here have been holding our breath all day. Isn't that right?"

The reporter nodded but kept writing in his notebook.

Elliot returned to his Trooper, climbed onto the hood, and then onto the top of the vehicle. When Nick joined him, the metal roof sagged precariously beneath their weight.

After a moment he said, "Haven't you noticed something unusual?"

Nick stared at the site for a long time but didn't spot anything new.

"If your B-17 had crashed," Elliot said, "the wreckage

should have been scattered over a larger area, not confined to a single mound."

She grimaced, knowing that a successful forced landing would have become common knowledge in the area. An unsuccessful one, with the possibility of an explosion, would have scattered debris to some extent at least. But as far as she'd been able to determine with Beckstead's metal detector, everything was concentrated within the immediate area.

Elliot scanned the horizon. "This would be a bad place to land if you had to walk out."

"Their navigator should have known where they were. They'd have water on board, enough to get them to Cibola on foot at least."

"Maybe the plane wasn't worth salvaging, so the authorities just left it here. Have you found any identification numbers yet?"

"The tail's our best bet, but it's not where it should be, as you can see."

"Let's hope it's not miles away."

"I was going to wait until tomorrow to uncover the nose, but as long as you're here we could take a look now. Maybe that will give us a clue."

She climbed down off the Trooper and then offered her father a hand.

"I can still work you into the ground," he said, but accepted the help anyway.

Nick waved over Beckstead. "I'd like to uncover the nose while my father's here," she told him.

"It's a good thing I didn't send my men home like you wanted."

Nick directed the men to the port side of the nose, where she had them dig a shaft the size of a foxhole, being careful not to scrape the aluminum skin with their shovels. They'd gone down about three feet, when she spotted the edge of a painted emblem, faded but still showing color. "Hold it," she said. "I'll take over from here."

As soon as the men were out of the hole, she jumped in and began using her handkerchief to wipe away the dirt that was clinging to the aluminum.

"We're in luck. The nose art's still intact."

Her father joined her in the hole. Together, they used their hands to clear away more of the dirt.

"It's a scorpion," Nick said. "That has to be what the crew named their plane, the *Scorpion.*"

She sat back on the lip of the hole to admire the artwork. Next to it, there was a jagged tear in the plane's aluminum skin. "I'll shoot some pictures of this, then we'll cover it up again for the time being to protect the paint."

"Let me do the honors," Douglas said. "I'll print you as many copies as you want."

Nick nodded.

"What do you think caused that rip in the metal?" Douglas asked.

"Who knows? That skin's not much tougher than a tin can. Any caliber bullet would go right through these planes. The pilots used to scrounge themselves a piece of armor plating to sit on when they flew missions."

Douglas grimaced. "Will the scorpion help you identify the plane?"

"Eventually perhaps, but a tail number would make it easier. That's where we'll concentrate tomorrow. With any luck, I'll be calling the air force for an ID by the end of the day."

8

Air Force General Thomas Moreland, commanding officer of Offutt Air Force Base, Nebraska, SAC Headquarters, clenched his teeth as he reread the fax and accompanying memo. For Christ's sake, didn't his people know better than to talk to the news media? True, it was a newspaper reporter, not one of those damned hyenas from television, but newsmen could be dangerous at any level.

Snatching up a felt-tipped red marking pen, the general circled the offender's name: Roberts, Kenneth, Captain. Soon to be a civilian. As for Colonel Joseph Fortunato, he could spend his last few months of active duty freezing his ass off among the Eskimos.

Moreland switched pens, exchanging red for blue. Polar blue, he decided. Or maybe ice blue.

But at the last moment, he made no mark against Fortunato's name. The poor bastard was only following orders, bucking the memo up the chain of command. But wouldn't it be comforting to shoot the messenger for once?

The general shook his head, a vicious snap back and forth.

No, that kind of thinking could get him eaten by polar bears if he had to pass the information up the chain to the Pentagon. He hoped his superiors would be as forgiving as he was.

He sucked a quick breath, forcing himself to relax, and opened his personal safe. He knew without looking that S-OPS17 would have a coded designation, but he checked the file just the same.

"Shit." There it was, big as life. Top fucking Secret.

He reexamined the procedures set down on the file's cover sheet. He had no leeway, not when it came to coded red flag designations.

With a grunt, the general got up from his desk and locked the office door. The sound of the lock engaging would be enough to signal his aide that there were to be no interruptions.

He paced for a moment, choosing his words in advance, before picking up the scrambled phone that connected him with General Walters at the Pentagon. Only Walters himself was authorized to pick up at the other end. If the call went unanswered for more than four rings, Moreland's number would be recorded in code that would automatically be deleted from the computer files after sixty minutes. At the end of that time, Moreland would have to call again.

This time, however, Walters picked up immediately.

"This is a red-letter day," Moreland said.

"Wait," Walters said.

Moreland smiled grimly, knowing that his superior officer would be going through the same procedure he'd gone through himself only moments before. Red letter and red flag were one and the same.

"Go ahead," Walters said, meaning he had the coded list in his hand.

Quickly and precisely, Moreland summarized the information at hand.

"Are we sure there's an airplane in that area?"

"That's not confirmed as yet since we don't have anybody on the ground, but it's certainly a possibility, considering the fact that there are archaeologists on the site even as we speak. Do you want me to investigate further?"

"Absolutely not," Walters said. "Red flags are worse than booby traps. Fax me everything you have, then destroy your copies."

General Walters resisted the temptation to slam down the phone. Instead, he cradled it gently, and muttered, "Why me, for Christ's sake? And why now?"

He closed his eyes and imagined waves of shit, rising on a tide of red flags, until they swamped everything. With a sigh, he rose from his desk and stepped into the private john adjoining his office. Carefully, so as not to wet his uniform, he splashed cold water on his face. When he looked at himself in the mirror, his eyes fixed on the three stars attached to the epaulettes of his air force uniform. Three down and one to go, he thought, but knew he'd never achieve the highest rank his country had to offer. That was one dream he'd abandoned for another, that of being a millionaire. And that was no longer a dream, but a reality. The first payment of that reality, his consultancy fee, had already been deposited to his off-shore account. More money would follow the moment his retirement papers went through.

It was like stealing candy from a baby, or so he'd thought when he made the deal. Only now he might have to earn his money. The red flag had seen to that.

Christ, he'd hoped to keep a low profile. Take the money, sit back, and enjoy the good life; that was his motto. He'd been looking forward to playing lobbyist and strong-arming his academy buddies whenever a particularly juicy defense contract came up. But that wasn't what they were paying him for;

that was routine, just good business. If he didn't do it, someone else would. But this file? Judging by the looks of it, someone was about to land in deep shit. All specific information had been removed from the military records, that much was immediately obvious. No one in the Pentagon, himself included, knew what S-OPS17 stood for. Only its classified designation remained on file, which by itself was enough to get all references and queries bucked up the chain of command. In theory, though, the buck stopped here, with him. The military buck, that is. From now on, passing the buck was a violation of his oath as an officer. For a million dollars, though, he didn't really give a damn. He would do as he was told, and pass S-OPS17 along to his new employer, CMI. To do that, he'd have to use a more secure line of communication than the Pentagon offered. Of course, CMI had more money than the Pentagon to spend on such niceties.

General Walters returned to his desk and pushed a button, signaling his driver to bring the car up from the basement parking garage. Thirty minutes later, he reached his newly purchased house in Georgetown.

"Is this legal?" his wife had asked when the CMI rep first showed them around the place.

"It's just one of the perks of being a top beltway bandit," the rep had replied. "Keep in mind that escrow doesn't close officially until the general retires."

At the moment, his wife was visiting antique shops with one of the decorators supplied by CMI, so he had the house to himself. Even so, Walters took the precaution of locking the study door behind him.

He switched on the CMI computer—state of the art yet user friendly—that sat on a nineteenth-century English partners desk that cost more than a humvee, or so his wife had said. CMI didn't care. Why should they? They were one of the biggest military contractors in the country. The biggest when it came to contract overruns. They produced everything from jet fighters to small arms. It was said that war couldn't be conducted anywhere in the world without CMI making money. An incredible feat, the general knew, especially since CMI had been nothing but a small metallurgy outfit when it joined the Manhattan Project during World War II. Consolidated Metallurgy, it had been called then. Now it was simply CMI, a logo that appeared on products throughout the world, and not just military hardware, but pharmaceuticals, refrigerators, and even soft drinks.

On the face of it, CMI's achievement seemed impossible. Bigger companies had worked on the Manhattan Project— Allis-Chalmers, General Electric, Westinghouse, Union Carbide, even Du Pont. But CMI had left all those giants in its wake. While they moved like dinosaurs, answering to boards of directors, layers of vice presidents, and stockholders, CMI followed the vision of one man, Leland Hatch. With a Ph.D. in physics by the age of twenty, Hatch had been one of the wunderkinder attached to the Manhattan Project.

Following CMI procedure, the general used his mouse to open a dedicated window on the computer screen. After that, he switched to the keyboard to type in the first of his codes. The entire sequence required two minutes to enter and had been committed totally to memory. On this level, nothing was ever to be written down, that was a prime CMI directive.

When he reached the final entry level, the general hesitated. He'd never been told who had access at the New York end of his computer hookup, but he suspected it had to be someone very high up indeed. At the Pentagon, he had only the Joint Chiefs to contend with, but at CMI there were half a dozen people with more power than any four-star general. Carefully, using one finger to make absolutely certain he hit only correct keys, the general typed in his final access code and hit enter.

After what seemed like an eternity of waiting, TYPE IN RED-FLAG DESIGNATION appeared on the screen.

S-OPS17, he answered, and once again hit the enter key.

WAIT flashed on the screen.

Five minutes went by before his computer beeped. SUMMARIZE THE SITUATION.

Nervously, hitting the wrong keys constantly, the general relayed what information he'd gleaned from the classified faxes he'd received from SAC Headquarters.

ASSESSMENT?

MILITARY LEAKS NOW PLUGGED, BUT NEWS MEDIA UNPREDICTABLE, Walters answered.

AGREED. TAKE NO FURTHER ACTION AT YOUR LEVEL. DESTROY ALL RED-FLAG MATERIAL. WIPE S-OPS17 FROM ALL MEMORIES, YOURS INCLUDED.

The general sighed with relief, then followed procedure, asking for a code confirmation of the destruct order.

He twitched as H-ONE appeared on his screen. Christ. Leland Hatch himself had been at the other end of the line.

9

By nine the next morning, Nick was rocking on her heels and staring openmouthed at the bullet holes in her B-17. The pilot's windshield showed a line of them, gaping .50-calibers, that would have killed him instantly. The copilot's Plexiglas had been blown away completely. Through the opening where it should have been, she saw the desiccated fingers of a detached human hand protruding from the debris that filled the cockpit.

"Look at *these* fuckers over here!" one of her workmen called.

She left her perch directly in front of the cockpit and slid off the fuselage and into the narrow pit that had been cleared along the port side of the aircraft.

"Motherfuckers," the man clarified when he put a fist through one of half a dozen holes that had been punched through the bomber's aluminum skin immediately behind the pilot's seat.

"Cannon fire," she said.

Mark Douglas, who'd been dogging her every move, stopped

taking photographs long enough to say, "What the hell happened here?"

She ignored him to measure the punctures. Until now, she'd only seen photographs of battle damage like this. "Twenty-millimeter cannons, I'd guess, but I'm no expert in ballistics."

"Keep talking," Douglas said.

Nick's only answer was to shake her head. The kind of damage the *Scorpion* had sustained could have come only from heavily armed fighter planes. Yet none of her maps indicated that this part of New Mexico had ever been used as a firing range.

She retreated to the awning's artificial shade, along with Douglas who was still following her. The thermometer read ninety-two, three degrees hotter than yesterday at this time. Even so, she hugged herself against a sudden inner chill.

"I know how you feel," Douglas said. "That mummified hand gave me the creeps, too."

"I hadn't expected it, that's all." Nick pulled off her cap and fanned herself. "The *Scorpion* looks like it was used for target practice, only I don't think they had remote-controlled target planes during World War Two."

"And the hand?"

"It could be a local, I suppose. Maybe an old prospector like Gus Beckstead who got trapped inside somehow."

"Sure. He decides to get out of the sun and then conveniently up and dies knowing an archaeologist like yourself would come along some day and put things right."

"You tell me, then."

"No, you don't. You do the talking and I write it down. That's the way journalism works."

Sighing, Nick took a bottle of water from one of the cartons stacked under the awning, tossed it to Douglas, then grabbed another for herself and drank deeply.

"Hey, Doc," one the men called to her. "There's a whole body in here."

Nick took over immediately, worming her way through the copilot's side window and then digging carefully with her fingers to preserve the find. It took her half an hour to uncover the skull completely. Some mummified flesh clung to it, but no smell remained, thank God.

Another thirty minutes of cautious digging uncovered pieces of a uniform and a badly corroded brass bar, still recognizable as the insignia of a second lieutenant.

Nick switched sides of the aircraft, digging into the cockpit through the port window. Within minutes she found a second skeleton in the pilot's seat. The skull was missing, which came as no surprise considering the number of .50-calibers that had come through his windshield.

She left the skeletons in place and carefully backed out of the cockpit.

"I want pictures before we do any more work," she told Douglas. "My camera's conked out."

"You sound like my editor," he said, moving in for close-ups.

As soon as he finished, he sat on his haunches and rubbed his bad leg. "I don't mind doing your dirty work, but I expect information in return."

Her mind raced, sorting through possible scenarios, none of which seemed logical. In New Guinea, she'd expected to find bodies. In fact, that had been one of her goals, to locate lost airmen, still technically listed as missing in action, and put them to rest once and for all. Here, there shouldn't have been bodies, unless the plane had never been discovered, which seemed unlikely.

"Out loud, if you don't mind," Douglas said.

"Give me a minute."

Before he could protest, Nick led her digging crew to the

point on the starboard side of the bomber where they'd find the main door. "Clear this area next. When you reach the door, don't open it, just give me a shout."

"It doesn't seem right," one of them said. "The air force should have buried these boys long before now."

"We'll have to see to it, then, won't we?"

"You're damned right."

The others nodded and went to work eagerly despite the soaring temperature. While they dug, she stood to one side, marveling at the amount of damage the airplane had sustained. With the removal of each shovelful of sand, more holes were revealed. A couple of them were almost big enough to use as doors themselves.

"You're not talking to me," Douglas said.

"I don't know what to say."

"Look, I know you don't have all the answers yet. Maybe you never will. But it doesn't really matter. Whatever happened out here, this is one hell of a story and you know it. I'm not about to sit on it, either. So I'm telling you in advance, I'm calling it in to the paper as soon as I get back to town. This is a once-in-a-lifetime story, a mystery plane shot down in the desert. Hell, it's *Enquirer* stuff. Only this time it's real and it's mine."

"Give me another day to investigate the site more thoroughly."

Before Douglas could answer, Gus Beckstead drove up, honking his horn continuously the last fifty yards. As soon as his truck stopped, he was out and loping toward them, waving his arms.

"We're rich," he called out as soon as he was in range. "We've got an offer for my plane. Some collector wants to buy the whole shebang."

Douglas clicked his ballpoint pen. "How much?"

"The mayor's still dickering."

"Who's making the offer?"

"Some lawyer called. He says his *client* wishes to remain anonymous."

"Don't make any quick decisions," Douglas said. "I've got a sneaking suspicion that this plane might be worth more than you think."

Beckstead squinted at him suspiciously.

"Show him, Nick," Douglas said. "I'll shoot photos of the two of you studying the bullet holes, and the bodies."

Looking bewildered, Beckstead inspected the B-17. When he'd finished, his chin sank onto his chest. "It can't be worth much shot up like this. It's junk."

"You're not thinking straight," Douglas said. "I can see the headlines now. 'Mystery Bomber Found in Desert. Dead Crew Still on Board.' Once my story hits the paper, you know what happens next, don't you?"

Beckstead shook his head.

"You and your plane will be instant celebrities. Television will be here."

"Do you really think so?"

"If I do my job right, they'll be thicker than flies," Douglas said.

Nick groaned. She'd have to push hard to get her work done before the site was overrun. After that, there'd be chaos, and anything she published would be suspect.

"While you're writing in that notebook of yours," Beckstead said, pointing a finger at the reporter, "take this down. This plane is on my land. It belongs to me. I haven't signed *all* my rights over to the mayor or that council of his."

"I thought you were partners," Nick said.

"This changes things."

"How much was the lawyer's offer?" Douglas asked again.

"It's not worth talking about, son, thanks to you. Now, why

don't I drive you into town so you can send in that story of yours."

Douglas glanced at Nick. "I want to be here when you go inside the plane."

Beckstead spoke up. "These are my men, son. I can shut work down for the rest of the day, if that's what you want."

"Give that order," Nick said, "and you'd better find yourself another archaeologist."

"What about it, son? Do we still need her?"

"If you want to be on the talk shows, we do."

Beckstead's eyes widened. He was offering to shake hands with Nick when one of the workmen came over to say, "We've found the tail."

The tail stabilizer, minus its rudder, was wedged against the B-17's main door. Torn and mangled the way the tail was, it shouldn't have been there. It should have been debris somewhere farther out in the desert. But Nick didn't care, because the tail number was still legible, 44-4013.

She raised a fist in triumph. Identification was now a certainty. All she had to do was make a phone call and that would be the end of Douglas's mystery. Then maybe she'd have some peace and quiet to finish her work.

"I want the men on overtime," she said. "We'll work till dark if the heat doesn't kill us."

10

The dead should stay buried, Leland Hatch thought as he carefully deleted all evidence of the *Scorpion* from his computer files. By the time he was finished, not even the God of hackers himself would be able to reconstruct so much as a byte of information. Even the Cal Techies on his payroll hadn't been able to break in to his system. The thought of all their deflated egos started him chuckling. When he'd issued the challenge, the look on their Techie faces had told him they thought their boss was over the hill, senile even, but he could still run rings around them. He could still—

Only the dead weren't buried, were they? Not in proper graves.

Damn. There it was again, his conscience, creeping up on him along with old age. Sprouting and sending out feelers in hope of finding what? God?

Well, if you're there, God, thanks for keeping my damn conscience at bay for so long.

Night, like now, was the worst. That's when his conscience—if that's what it was—acted up. The light of day chased it away with all the other goblins.

At the moment, the only light in Hatch's library came from the computer screen. Using the remote control, he triggered the main lights. The walls sprang to life with the rich hues of Renoirs and Monets discreetly lit by strategically placed spots.

When it came to consciences, he decided, Catholics had the best idea; they could confess away their sins. But what about physicists? Could they blow up the world, or pieces thereof, and say they're sorry?

Bullshit. He would do it again if he had to, pick up the phone, say a few words, and order men dead. No big deal, not considering the stakes. Besides, there'd been a war on.

He sighed deeply. It was so easy when you were young.

Leaving his desk, Hatch plucked a volume of Freud from one of the shelves of his vast library and ran his fingers over the leather binding. Men crave wealth, Freud wrote somewhere. Wealth, power, fame, and the love of beautiful women.

He held the book at arm's length, talking to it as if addressing Freud personally. "Well, by God, I've had them, you old bastard. To get them, I did what had to be done. Conscience be damned. You said it yourself. Conscience, morality, whatever you call it, was something dreamed up by priests to keep their flock in line. Scare them with God and conscience and they toe the line, you said. There is no God, no right or wrong. No hell, no punishment. But what about the dreams, Sigmund? They got your attention, didn't they?"

Hatch crossed the room to the two-hundred-year-old gold-leafed Florentine mirror that was a memento of his second wife's Italian period. He winked at himself. Blemishes in the glass muted his age spots and wrinkles, and made it easier for him to recognize the man he'd once been.

He held Freud up to the mirror. *You and your dreams. Give*

me the light of day, by God. Keep me from those old sins that cast long shadows in the night.

With a snort, he tossed the book onto a Louis XIV sofa that had come from his wife's French period. *You didn't get it completely right, Sigmund. Men crave more than you thought. We crave immortality.*

God, to be young again. No thought of dying. No thought of God except maybe a little lip service on Sundays. That was the cost of doing business. Belief, subservience, that was for fools. But wouldn't it be nice if there was an afterlife, if you could take your fame, power, wealth, and women with you?

The knock of the door was his wife's. He could tell by the time, 11:45 P.M.

He used the remote control to disengage the lock. With the light behind her, Adela could have been mistaken for a young Elizabeth Taylor. Her black nightgown, one of his gifts, left nothing to the imagination. Which was just the way he liked it. The same went for her street clothes. He loved taking her out, seeing other men drool over her, yet afraid to make a move because of who he was. Not a man to be messed with.

She kissed him, mouth open the way he liked it. "Time to come to bed, Leland."

For an instant he hesitated. The *Scorpion* weighed on his mind. Yet it was late, not the best time to mobilize men into action. And maybe, with luck, it wouldn't come to that.

Seeing the look in his wife's eyes, he allowed himself to be led. Money was one hell of an aphrodisiac. Add power, real power, and women lined up to get a piece of it the best way they could. Adela, of course, wanted a child, someone to inherit. But Hatch had one son already, Leland Jr. The crown prince, people called him.

One prince was quite enough. Add a second and God only knew what might happen, probably civil war when the time came to divide the kingdom.

Tonight, however, no matter what Adela's desires, she'd have to be content with a pat on the ass. He needed sleep; he needed a clear head, because tomorrow decisions would have to be made.

But once under the covers, even with the electric blanket providing a cocoon of warmth, sleep was a long time coming. Memories kept intruding. The past, though growing ever more distant, cast longer and longer shadows. To escape them, he forced his mind to business, the contracts coming up with the Israelis, CMI's nuclear power subsidiary that was under attack from environmentalists, the nasty job he had in mind for General Walters. He lingered over the problem of selling a cost overrun to the air force. The profits would be funneled into the president's reelection campaign. CMI would own more than ex-generals.

The shadows caught up with him at the moment of sleep. Their touch carried grainy black-and-white images, gun-camera film, flickering and shaking as the tracers reached out, missing the B-17 at first, but gradually adjusting until they were on target, striking the wing, then the fuselage.

The angle changed, another gun camera. At each tracer's touch, aluminum debris erupted from the bomber. Smoke streamed from one of the engines; its prop slowed, then stopped.

Hatch felt himself diving at the bomber head-on. His finger pressed the cannon button on the control yoke. The Plexiglas nose shattered.

He changed planes, attacking from above. His bullet streams moved along the fuselage until they reached the upper turret, exploding it. A starboard engine flamed. The B-17 nosed down, shuddering with each new cannon strike. A figure dropped away, body and parachute smoking.

Hatch jerked up in bed, sweat soaked, heart pounding,

gasping for air. That dream would kill him one day. Christ, maybe he was having a heart attack right now.

Adela sat up, too, switched on her bedside lamp, and touched him gently. "What's wrong?"

"A dream, one I thought I'd gotten over. It's not important."

"My analyst says dreams don't keep coming back if they're not important."

Hatch slowed his breathing and forced himself to sound lighthearted. "For the money I pay him, I hope he has more to say than that."

She snuggled against him. "He says a wife has to understand her husband's needs and keep him satisfied."

She went to work, doing her best to arouse him, but without success.

"I think I'll get up for a while," he said finally.

He rose and slipped on his robe. "You go back to sleep, Della. I'll be fine."

Just before she turned out her light, an odd look crossed Adela's face. Disappointment, no doubt. Well, that was the trouble with marrying a younger women. They wanted more from a man than he could supply.

At times like this, he longed to call his first wife. With her, at least, he could talk over shared memories, old radio shows and the like, things Adela had never heard of. Only he couldn't make the call; he couldn't bring himself to expose such weakness.

But what about his son, Lee? An executive vice president of CMI ought to expect an occasional midnight call. But what would Hatch say? *Hi, son. Sorry to wake you, but I just wanted to get a few murders off my chest.*

Hatch snorted. Lee would have to know the truth one day, but this wasn't the time.

In the library, Hatch switched on his movie-size television set and scanned the shelf containing videotaped movies too new to have been released to the general public. Surely he could find something to distract him. When nothing new caught his eye, he selected one of his old favorites, *The Maltese Falcon*. Adela hated it. She said Humphrey Bogart didn't have sex appeal, not like Tom Selleck or Bruce Willis. Maybe he'd talk it over with Lee the next time he got the chance.

Nodding, Hatch fed the tape into the VCR, punched a button, and there was Sam Spade telling Effie to send in Brigid O'Shaughnessy. Hatch settled onto the sofa and marveled at the ease of today's technology, much of it thanks to his own company. Not like the old days. Back then it had been sheer hell threading a film projector, especially if your hands were shaking.

There it was again, the past creeping in. To avoid unnecessary witnesses, Hatch had threaded the gun-camera results personally. Seeing the film that first time had been as exciting as sex. A confirmed kill. His kill. And all he'd had to do was pick up a phone, say a few words, and men died. It had been necessary, essential, not just to him, but to so many others. To this country, even.

Then why the dreams?

Because you've grown an old man's conscience, you fool.

But he wasn't fool enough to think there was more than one plane buried in that godforsaken desert.

Despite the hour, he picked up the phone. Conscience or no conscience, additional precautions would have to be taken in New Mexico. If things went badly, the lawyers would have to step aside. People would have to die again.

11

In her room at the Seven Cities, Nick cranked the already overworked air conditioner to maximum, then kicked off her desert boots and lay on the floor rather than spread sand and grit on the bedspread. The air conditioner shifted gears, rattling the window frame, and finally managed to produce a stale breeze that reminded her of New York City subway air.

With a sigh, Nick closed her eyes and considered her options. It was now Friday evening, too late to start calling government agencies in Washington, D.C. That meant she'd have no access until Monday, though her diggers were prepared to work right on through the weekend.

Option number two involved imposing on an old friend and colleague, Ken Drysdale. Only the last time they'd worked together in New Guinea, he'd ended up asking her to marry him. The look on his face when he realized she only wanted him as a friend still haunted her, so did his attempt to diffuse the tension by then passing his proposal off as a joke. She'd done her best to go along with the pretense, but their parting had been strained.

Sighing, Nick dragged the phone off the nightstand and used her credit card code to call Honolulu, which was three hours behind her time.

Despite being retired from the army, Ken still barked out, "Drysdale speaking," as if he were coming to attention.

"It's time to re-up," she said.

"Damn, Nick, it's good to hear your voice."

"I'm not kidding, Ken. I've found another airplane."

He snorted. "Now I realize my problem. If I'd had wings and a propeller, you would have married me. So tell me about this new love in your life."

Quickly, she summarized her work so far, describing the site, the weather conditions, and the B-17's state of preservation. She concluded by saying, "It's full of bullet holes and the dead crew is still on board."

"You need your old Fifty-seven Foxtrot, don't you?"

"I need more than that. I need your years of experience in the military to cut through the red tape."

Strictly speaking, Fifty-seven Foxtrot (57-F) was the designation of Drysdale's military speciality, graves registration. In Ken's particular case, he'd worked at the Central Identification Laboratory in Hawaii, which handled the bodies coming out of Vietnam. He'd been a master sergeant when Nick first met him and was assigned to her search team when they went looking for the B-24 bomber in the jungles of New Guinea.

"I've got the B-17's tail number," Nick went on, "but it's too late to call Washington."

"I'm your man, then. I'll drive over to the CIL and use one of their computers."

"It's after hours," she reminded him.

"The net's always awake, you know that. Besides, us top sergeants run the military, even when we're retired. I taught my replacement everything he knows."

"I've got nose art, too," she said, and described the scorpion in detail.

"That makes it a piece of cake. I'll be into the National Archives and back to you before you know it."

"How soon will I hear from you?"

"Why the hurry, Nick?"

"I've got a reporter breathing down my neck and the locals are out for publicity. One look at the bullet holes and the bodies and we're talking front-page headlines, probably by tomorrow morning."

"Give me your phone number and I'll get back to you tonight. Hell, I'll hop a plane and join you there if you want."

"There's no funding for this one," she said.

"Give me some credit. Have you ever known a top sergeant to pay when the military has perfectly good airplanes?"

When Nick hesitated, Drysdale added, "Hey, we're friends, right? That's good enough for me."

She closed her eyes and pictured him as she'd seen him last. A big man, as big as her father, with close-cropped sandy hair, he was ten years her senior, a career military man who, but for lack of formal education, could have been a top forensic archaeologist. A good man, too, she thought, but maybe too much like her father to consider as a lover.

"Let's see what you find out first," she said, "before we start making plane reservations."

Drysdale chuckled. "That's lady archaeologists for you. I'll call by midnight, your time. Count on it."

Something must be wrong with me, Drysdale thought as he approached the CIL building. Just the sight of the place, designed with all the military charm of a concrete bunker, eased the sense of loneliness he'd felt ever since talking to Nick. Entering an army base was like coming home.

The MP, known to him by sight, passed Drysdale through

the security barrier with only a glance at the sergeant's ID. Drysdale grimaced. According to regulations, his particular ID required him to have an escort at all times. Had he still been on active duty the MP would have had a combat boot up his ass by now.

Smiling at the image, Drysdale headed for the computer center. His footsteps echoed as he marched along the empty linoleumed hall. Not like the old days, he thought, when a steady stream of casualties was coming out of Vietnam, all to be processed and identified by the lab. Back then, there'd been full shifts twenty-four hours a day. The army had made him an expert in death and its aftermath, and the worst part of it was he missed the excitement.

As soon as he entered the computer room, the duty sergeant waved him over to a workstation that was connected to the Cray mainframe computer. The center was practically deserted. Only two among a long line of workstations were occupied.

"Ain't technology great?" the sergeant said, nodding at the full-color, graphically enhanced hand of solitaire on his computer screen. "What brings an MIA like you among the living?"

"I need some time on the net and I'm too cheap to pay the phone charges on my home computer," Drysdale said, stretching the truth.

"Take your pick. I'll buy you a cup of coffee when you're finished."

Nodding, Drysdale selected a workstation as far away from kibitzers as possible. Once he'd logged on, he queried the computer files at the National Archives in Washington, D.C., punching in Nick's B-17 ID number, 44-4013.

The answer came back quickly: NOT FOUND.

Drysdale tried again, with the same result.

Goddammit, that was the trouble with computers. They

didn't give you a reason, they just dumped on you.

He rechecked his procedures and code entries. He was in the National Archives, sure enough. So what was the problem?

He hated to ask advice from the duty sergeant, since what Drysdale was doing was against regulations. As a civilian using the military net, he was breaking a federal law, although a minor one since security clearances didn't come into it when your were searching for a fifty-year-old aircraft.

So think. Maybe there was a hang-up with the particular file that contained B-17 identification numbers.

He tried another ID number, the next one up: 44-4014. This time the computer coughed up the information: 44-4014 was built at the Boeing plant in Seattle and lost in combat early in 1945. Crew references and combat statistic were available elsewhere.

Once again he typed in 44-4013.

NOT FOUND

He tried 44-4012.

That, too, was another Seattle-built bomber, mothballed in the Arizona desert after the war. For all Drysdale knew it was still there.

So what happened to 44-4013?

He snapped his fingers. Maybe the builders hadn't used the number 13, figuring someone along the line, like a crew member, might be superstitious. If that was the case, Nick had made a mistake, which seemed unlikely knowing her. No doubt he'd written down the number incorrectly.

Taking a deep breath, Drysdale dropped a hundred numbers and typed in 44-3913. Again, the computer obliged by providing the airplane's history.

Resisting the temptation to kick the machine, he logged off the military network and onto the hacker's delight, the Internet, and sent a message to one of his former CIL buddies, Cliff Sawicki, now assigned to the Pentagon. Via computer, they exchanged chitchat until Drysdale got down to business and asked for Sawicki's help tracing a B-17, old 44-4013.

Sawicki promised quick action. The phone rang five minutes after Drysdale returned home.

"I got flagged when I tried searching for your serial number," Sawicki said without preamble. "A goddamned security notice."

"You've got to be kidding. We're talking about ancient history here."

"I'm telling you, the information is classified. By Monday morning the counterintelligence boys are going to be picking my bones. You'd better tell me why you want the information."

"We've found a B-17 in the desert in New Mexico."

"Don't give me that *we* shit. You're in Honolulu, which means you're still doing grunt work and pining away for that lady archaeologist of yours."

"She likes fifty-year-old airplanes, so why not a wreck like me?"

"You'd better hope I don't get my ass in a sling."

"Why would something that old be classified?" Drysdale asked.

"Maybe it's a coincidence. Maybe there's some kind of security flap on, like the time those German cyberpunks tapped into the Star Wars files. Remember how the shit hit the fan? We were ass deep in CIC and FBI agents, crawling over everything and everyone for months."

"Is there any other way to check that ID number for me?"

"Not without going through the records by hand."

Drysdale thought that over for a moment. Today was Friday, so Sawicki wouldn't be able to get at the files until Monday morning at the earliest, and by then he'd be on duty with his own job to worry about.

"You'd better drop the whole thing," Drysdale said.

"I'm sorry to ruin your sex life," Sawicki said, trying to

make a joke out of it, but he sounded more relieved than anything else.

"Don't I wish." Drysdale hung up and was about to dial Nick's number when someone knocked on the door.

Even seen through the peephole and the distortion of its wide-angle lens, the two young men in suits were unmistakable: only Mormon missionaries and counterintelligence agents looked like that.

Since Drysdale didn't want the aggravation no matter who they were, he escaped his apartment through the back door.

12

Gus Beckstead had worn out his welcome at the San Juan Saloon years ago, but the rules had been waived for the victory party, at Mayor Ralph's insistence. Even so, Beckstead hesitated in the street out front; he'd become accustomed to drinking by himself. Besides, he had no intention of letting the mayor get him drunk so he and his councilman could trick him out of his God-given rights to that B-17. He'd promised Grace, his lady, a love-boat cruise if things worked out, maybe even a honeymoon, if she'd have him.

"I don't think we ought to be celebrating just yet," Beckstead told the mayor.

"Relax," Mayor Ralph said. "Cibola's already a winner no matter what. I talked to the *Journal*'s editor not ten minutes ago. Mark Douglas filed his story and our B-17 will be front-page news tomorrow, Monday morning at the latest." He clapped Beckstead on the shoulder. "We're on the map now, no matter what we do with *your* B-17."

Beckstead looked up at the San Juan, which, like almost everything else in Cibola, had a Spanish flavor, complete with a trowel-marked stucco facade and a red tile fascia at the roof line to hide the tar paper beyond.

"Come on," the mayor said, applying enough pressure to start Beckstead moving toward the door. "Everyone's inside waiting to buy you a drink."

"I'm not selling out until I know what it's worth," Beckstead said.

"You're the boss."

"You're damn right."

Beckstead allowed himself to be herded inside. Boilermakers were already set up on the bar, where the mayor's tame councilmen, Ferrin and Latimer, were waiting with expectant smiles. Beckstead smiled right back. They didn't fool him. Besides, he could drink them all under the table if it came to that.

Mayor Ralph leaned his belly against the bar and quickly distributed the brimming shot glasses. "To Cibola," he toasted. "And the *Scorpion.*"

Beckstead made sure the others swallowed their whiskey before he did. He took the same precautions with each of the next half dozen rounds. By then, Ferrin and Latimer had taken up residence in the toilet, being sick.

"Now that we're alone," the mayor said, taking care to enunciate each word, "it's time we got down to business, Gus. Let's face it, to make money out of that plane, it'll need restoring. That costs money, big money. Wouldn't it be better to sell out now and take what profit we can get?"

"You saw the bullet holes," Beckstead said. "That's going to get me on all the talk shows, maybe even Oprah. That reporter said so."

"What happens then?"

Beckstead was still thinking that over when the mayor slid down the front of the bar, unconscious.

Smiling, Beckstead staggered to the toilet and opened the

door. Ferrin and Latimer were still on their knees, their heads half hidden by the porcelain bowl.

"Like I said," Beckstead told them, "I can drink you all under the table."

Outside, the prospector took a deep breath of night air and nearly threw up. That settled it. He was too drunk to drive. What the hell; he'd slept in the truck before. Gracie wouldn't worry; he'd told her he was going on a toot with the boys.

His truck was parked down the block in front of the Feed and Seed, which was dark like every place else in town except the saloon. He was inside the truck, with the door closing behind him and wondering why the overhead light wasn't working before he realized someone was there ahead of him.

"Who the hell are you?" he demanded.

"Your fairy godfather," a man said.

"Bullshit."

"Try me. Make a wish."

Beckstead rubbed his face, hoping to sober himself enough to think straight. "You're here about the B-17, aren't you?"

"Ellsworth Kemp, investment councilor," the man said, reaching up and switching on the truck's interior light. "Here's my card."

Beckstead couldn't focus on the raised lettering. He shook his head sharply. That was boilermakers for you. He tucked the card in his pocket. "I always heard you got three wishes."

"That's genies, not fairy godfathers, but I'll talk to my client and see what we can do."

"Oprah" started to come out of Beckstead's mouth, but he clenched his teeth just in time. No use sounding like a fool, or wasting wishes either, for that matter. This guy looked like money, even under the truck's ceiling light. His fancy suit was like something you see on TV, not in a place like Cibola. He looked fit, too, probably from working out with one of those expensive exercise machines you see advertised on TV. Beckstead revised his estimate. Kemp didn't look like money; he looked like big money. Beckstead's picture in the *National Geographic* or *People*, or even an appearance on Oprah, didn't count for much against that kind of wealth.

"I want to be rich," Beckstead said.

"And famous," Kemp added.

"How'd you know that?"

"Because you're famous already. Why else would I be here? You know where I was this morning? New York City. Just about to get myself laid when I get this phone call from my client. 'Kemp,' he says, 'have you heard about this man Gus Beckstead? He's found just what I want, all the way out in New Mexico.' So the next thing I know, I'm on an airplane with a briefcase full of cash."

Kemp retrieved an aluminum case from the floor of the truck and laid it on his lap. "We want to buy your land and the B-17 both."

"I've been working that claim for years."

"Rich men don't have to work." Kemp inserted a key into the case's lock and opened the lid, exposing stacks of hundred-dollar bills.

Beckstead's mouth dropped open. That case had to be three inches deep and it was full to the brim. "Jesus Christ, how much is in there?"

"More than you can spend in your lifetime."

When Beckstead reached for the case, Kemp snapped the lid closed and said, "First I want to see what I'm buying."

"In the dark?"

"Why wait to be rich?"

Why indeed, Beckstead thought. Besides, if anyone was crazy enough to pay that kind of money for a shot-up airplane and a claim that paid only a bare-bones living, Gus wasn't going to give him time to have second thoughts.

"I've been drinking too much to drive," Beckstead said, "but if you'll drive, I'll be happy to show you the way."

Nodding, Kemp locked the briefcase and handed it to Beckstead for safekeeping. Beckstead clutched it against his chest as they drove out of town.

A mile beyond the Conejos Bridge, Kemp suddenly turned off into the desert.

Beckstead jerked upright, realizing he'd nodded off for a moment, dreaming of all the things his money could buy.

"This isn't the turn. We've got a long ways to go yet."

The truck dipped into a dry wash and came to a stop.

"This will do fine." Kemp left the parking lights on and got out of the truck.

Beckstead followed, bewildered, but still clinging to the briefcase. "I thought you wanted to see my claim?"

"I think you mean *my* claim." Kemp switched on a flashlight and laid it on the truck's hood, then took a paper from his coat and spread it on the metal next to the light. "This is a bill of sale, made out in advance. All you have to do is sign it."

Beckstead held up the case. "You haven't told me how much is in here."

"I'm sorry. I thought you understood. That money's not yours to keep. You're going to give me the land and the B-17, out of the goodness of your heart."

"What the fuck are you talking about?"

"This." Kemp drew a pistol from inside his coat and held it against Beckstead's head.

"Fuck you. You pull the trigger and that claim is still mine."

"As of now, you're quite right."

"You damn betchya."

Kemp put away the gun and took out a pen, which he laid on top of the bill of sale. "Please, as a favor, Gus, sign the paper."

"Fuck you."

"Is that final?"

Beckstead threw the case at Kemp and made a run for it, scrambling up the wash. But he lost his footing and collapsed in pain after only a few steps.

"Goddamned boilermakers," he muttered, clutching his ankle. Only then did he feel the blood and realize he'd been hit from behind.

"I found this tire iron in the back of your truck," Kemp explained as he brought it down on Beckstead's knee.

Beckstead screamed; his leg muscles spasmed.

"I'm not going to carry you back to the truck so you can sign that paper. You'll have to crawl on your own."

Panting, Beckstead breathed, "Please."

"They all beg me before it's over, you know."

"Before they sign?"

"Before they die," Kemp said.

13

Kemp checked his watch. Two in the morning. He was well ahead of schedule. But then Gus Beckstead had been no challenge at all. Of course, he'd keep that information to himself. Let the boss think you're overworked, that was his motto. Overworked and indispensable.

He surveyed the site one more time, then inventoried his own belongings. Everything was in order. Gus Beckstead was now a statistic, one of those drunk driving fatalities that don't rate more than a couple of paragraphs in the obituary column. Broken up the way he was from the crash, the tire iron marks wouldn't show at all.

Satisfied, Kemp crossed Conejos Bridge and headed for his rental car, which was parked at the motel. He didn't meet a soul or see a single car moving on the lonely desert highway.

Before entering the motel's parking lot, he stopped to listen carefully, but there was no sound and no sign of life. He smiled. That lady archaeologist was in for the shock of her life tomorrow morning, if indeed she lived that long. That would depend on the phone call he had to make in—he checked his watch again—twenty minutes.

Inside his room, Kemp unwrapped a Milky Way and began to chew eagerly. What would psychologists make of his need for sweets after a successful assignment? Blame the whole thing on his mother, no doubt, though the plain truth was he had a sweet tooth. But he never indulged during the job itself, because a misplaced candy wrapper was just one more thing to worry about, one more mistake waiting to happen.

As soon as he finished the Milky Way, Kemp began doing push-ups, working up a sweat and counting off repetitions silently to himself, burning off the calories.

At two hundred, he wiped himself dry with a towel and then used his cellular phone to link with the CMI satellite. The scrambling system wasn't absolutely secure, or so said the computer nerds, but they'd yet to break it. Even so, Kemp would be careful what he said. Besides, Leland Hatch preferred it that way, innuendo instead of frontal assault.

Hatch's voice was always a surprise, sounding as if he was in the same room instead of a continent away.

"I have the bill of sale," Kemp said. "The land is now in my name. I'll present my claim Monday morning and take possession."

"I'll have one of our lawyers there tomorrow morning. Now, tell me about your client. What exactly did he know about that airplane?"

The direct question surprised Kemp. "Only what he saw. That it was shot up and had crashed, and that there were bodies still inside."

"Are you certain?"

"There was nothing more to get. He was dry, wrung out by the time I finished with him."

"And the archaeologist? What does she know?"

"She has an identification number from the tail. Is that important?"

"That's been dealt with already."

"She's practically next door. Say the word and I'll wring her dry, too."

"I've taken steps to keep her otherwise occupied. If that fails, we'll make other plans. Now, what about the trucks?"

"They'll be here Monday morning."

"I want them there in time to coordinate with our lawyer tomorrow afternoon."

"They've got a long way to come."

"Do your best, then. Is the woman working tomorrow?"

"Beckstead didn't know. Do you want me to stop her if she tries?"

"Don't bother. I can't see that any more damage can be done in such a short time."

14

Nick indulged herself Sunday morning, ordering hotcakes and bacon, while her father and Clark Guthrie stuck to oatmeal. Mom Bennett had opened the Zuni Café an hour early, because of the full house at the Seven Cities Motel. The café was filled, with Elliot's students lining the counter. Yesterday's new arrival in town, a man named Kemp, had to share a booth with three locals wearing their Sunday best. With that much body heat radiating into such a tight space, the Zuni's air conditioner shimmied constantly as it fought a losing battle.

The outside temperature, Nick figured, was already well over eighty. Tomorrow's forecast called for a slight cooling trend. If that held up, she and her crew ought to be able to clear the fuselage entirely. So today, she could relax with a clear conscience, put her feet up, and maybe read one of the paperback novels she'd brought along on the dig.

"We found some bones yesterday," Elliot said as he added brown sugar and raisins to his cereal.

Nick raised an eyebrow.

"Split open so the marrow could be sucked out."

"Homo sapiens soup," Guthrie added with a wink.

"No, you don't," Nick said. "I'm taking the day off. No cataloguing, no digging, no nothing."

Elliot was opening his mouth to protest when Mayor Ralph stormed through the door, slamming it behind him, and made a beeline for their booth. He grabbed the lone available chair and bellied up against the end of their table. Then he leaned forward and spoke breathlessly, "We just found Gus Beckstead at the bottom of Conejos Wash. The old bastard drove that wreck of a truck of his right through the bridge railing and broke his fool neck. Jesus, you don't want to see what's left of him."

The mayor's breath reeked of stale whiskey. His hands shook and his bloodshot eyes started Nick blinking in sympathy while her mind raced. With Beckstead dead, who had title to his land and to the *Scorpion*? The last time she'd heard from the mayor, he and his council were in favor of selling off her plane. If that happened, all her work would have been for nothing.

Hold it, she told herself. What the hell was she thinking about? That plane was an inanimate object, a thing. Gus Beckstead had been alive and working right beside her only a few hours ago.

"Considering the way we were drinking last night," Mayor Ralph went on, "Gus was crazy to be driving. I couldn't even walk."

Mom Bennett arrived with coffee for the mayor, took one look at his eyes, and condemned him with a shake of her head before moving on to other customers.

Nick let out the breath she'd been holding. She still had time to complete her examination of the *Scorpion*. No buyer, even the most avid collector, would want the plane until the bodies had been exhumed.

The mayor sipped his coffee and shuddered. "Considering

the way my stomach feels, I hope this stays down."

"This may sound callous," Nick said, "but what happens to Gus's land now?"

Elliot snorted. "That's my daughter. When it comes to airplanes, she's got a one-track mind."

"That's why I'm here," the mayor said. "You see that stranger over there?" He indicated yesterday's new arrival at the Seven Cities Motel. "He calls himself Ellsworth Kemp and says he's Gus Beckstead's sole heir, a distant cousin or some damned thing. He was up with the chickens this morning and knocking on my door loud enough to wake the dead. Says his lawyer is arriving later today and they intend to take possession of Gus's claim immediately."

"Did you explain the situation?" Nick said. "Did you tell him who I am and what I'm doing out there?"

"Hell, yes. I told him that me and my council were partners with Gus. I showed him the paper we signed. You know what he said to that? That he'd see me in court."

"I'd better talk to him."

"Tell him we don't want the land, just the plane. Tell him we're willing to share if that's what it takes. Anything to cut our losses."

Nick slid out of the booth and walked across the café to where Kemp was sitting.

"Could I speak to you for a moment?" she said.

"I was just leaving." Kemp stood up and put money on the table. "I know who you are, Ms. Scott. I know your reputation. But I'm not about to surrender any of my rights until I know what I have." He walked out.

Nick was so stunned by his attitude she let him go without saying another word. When she reported the conversation to the mayor, he swallowed so hard his Adam's apple bobbed.

"That's it, then," he said. "We'll have to eat our expenses."

"Has anything been filed in court?" Elliot asked.

"Gus hasn't been dead more than a few hours. Besides, it's Sunday."

"So technically nothing has changed."

The mayor raised his shoulders in a careful shrug. "Goddamn, I wish Gus had told me he had money-grubbing relatives."

"Ownership isn't important to an archaeologist," Elliot said. "Would you have any objections if the three of us went out there today and did some work, at least until the lawyers arrive?"

"Go to it, as far as I'm concerned. Take that reporter with you. The more publicity the better, I say." The mayor pushed back his chair and eased to his feet, grimacing. "If you'll excuse me, I've got to see Mom about some bicarb." Walking stiffly, he disappeared in the kitchen.

"Let's go," Elliot said. "Before it gets too damned hot."

"What about your Anasazi soup bones?" Nick asked.

"No rush," Guthrie said. "They've already been waiting a thousand years."

When they reached the *Scorpion*, Mark Douglas agreed to pitch in, too, despite his bad leg. With the four of them working, they quickly shifted the tail enough to pry open the main fuselage door. One look inside and Nick breathed a sigh of relief. Sand and dirt had seeped in over the years, but no more than a few inches of it. Otherwise, the fuselage was accessible, though the aluminum skin had partially buckled in a few places.

She was the first inside the stifling plane. Light filtering through the cannon and machine-gun holes illuminated the interior, revealing bodies lying side by side. They'd been partially eaten by burrowing rodents but were in good shape by archaeological standards, their remains mummified by the desert climate. Their uniforms were disintegrating but still recognizable.

"Be careful where you step," she said over her shoulder.

Elliot and Guthrie came next, followed by Douglas, who quickly ran off a roll of film using his flash. "I'll take some less candid shots later on. This stuff is a bit grim for a family paper like the *Journal*."

"Look at this one," Elliot said. "He's badly burned but there's no sign of fire in here."

Nick knelt beside the body that lay near the bomb bay. "He's wearing a parachute harness but there's no chute."

Elliot went down on his knees beside her. "If he jumped clear of the plane, why is he here?"

"Maybe the others carried him back after the crash," Douglas said.

"I don't think anybody was alive by then," Nick said. "Let's do a body count."

They found nine in the main fuselage. Only the one body showed burn marks.

Out loud, Nick ticked off the members of a B-17 crew. "Pilot, copilot, bombardier, navigator, radio operator, top gunner, belly gunner, two waist gunners, and tail gunner. Ten in all."

"But we've got eleven," Elliot said, "counting the two in the cockpit."

"Let's check for dog tags."

Nick, Elliot, and Guthrie began examining the bodies in the fuselage again.

"Nothing," Guthrie said finally.

"Something's wrong," Nick said. "The tags should be here. In combat, soldiers only remove a dead buddy's tag if the body has to be abandoned and might not be recoverable later. Otherwise, dog tags are collected by graves registration at the time of burial."

"Maybe they weren't wearing any tags to start with."

Nick was still mulling that over when her father held up a piece of rotting uniform and said, "If I had to guess, this is not U.S. Army Air Corps."

Nick shook her head, not knowing what to think. "Let's see what else we can come up with. Dad, you and Clark start at the tail and work forward. I'll take the nose and work back."

"Where do you want me?" Douglas asked.

For the moment the reporter was in the way, though Nick did want him to provide a complete photographic record. But first, she needed time to sort out exactly what was to be photographed. When she explained that to him, he looked relieved to leave the bodies and go outside.

Nick tied a bandanna around her forehead to keep the sweat out of her eyes and then began working her way forward, squirming sideways to inch past razor-sharp strips of aluminum that had ripped from the skin. Finally, she slipped through the bomb bay's bulkhead and into the navigator's compartment. Everything ahead of that, in the nose where the bombardier would have sat, had been crushed.

There was a gaping hole where the navigator's window should had been; his oxygen regulator hung in shreds; his suit heater outlet came off in her hands. His map case, though punctured, was still intact. Using her flashlight, she looked inside, expecting to find decaying paper. But there was nothing. She stood on tiptoe to check the .50-caliber cartridge box. It, too, was empty.

As she turned to leave the compartment, she brushed against a junction box, partially dislodging it and exposing a small leather-bound book that had been wedged behind it. Carefully, she took hold of its spine and eased it free. It looked like a diary, though she couldn't be sure until she opened it. Time and exposure had turned its flimsy lock into a lump of rust, but that could be remedied when she had the time.

Nick jumped when Douglas spoke through the hole in the fuselage. "We've got company. Four of them. One of them looks like that guy who showed up in town yesterday."

Through the hole, Nick saw four men climb out of a Ford Explorer.

"Stall them," she told Douglas. "I don't want them tramping around in here until we've secured the site."

"I'll do my best."

Quickly, Nick slipped the diary into a self-sealing plastic bag. Since it wasn't much larger than a paperback book, she tucked it into her back pocket and went out to greet the new arrivals. Elliot, Guthrie, and Douglas were there ahead of her.

Standing next to Kemp was an immaculately dressed man in a lightweight summer suit, his lawyer no doubt. The two others reminded Nick of the huge football players who posed as students in her undergraduate classes at the university.

Kemp ignored her outstretched hand. "I thought I made it clear when we spoke in town this morning, Ms. Scott. I have no intention of giving away any of my rights to this land."

"I'm only interested in the plane," she said.

The man in the suit stepped forward and handed Nick his card. He was a lawyer, all right, Joseph Palmer of Palmer and Moyle, Los Angeles.

"You made good time from the coast," she said.

"I've already been before a judge in Albuquerque." He removed a document from his pocket. "You are hereby notified that you are trespassing on private land."

"The government might have something to say about that when they realize that we've found one of their missing planes," Elliot said.

"With dead crewmen still inside," Guthrie added.

"You are to take nothing with you," Palmer said.

"I hope you're not talking about my film," Douglas said.

"We're not that foolish," the attorney said. "We're not

going to give you cause to charge us with anything."

Trust a lawyer to do the right thing, Nick thought as she and the others were escorted to their car. A diary wasn't much of a memento for all that hard work, but it was better than nothing.

Once they were back in the Trooper, she locked the diary in the glove compartment without comment, while her father headed for the highway. No one said a word until they reached the blacktop. Then Douglas snorted, and said, "I'd like to see their faces when they get a look at tomorrow morning's edition of the *Journal*. Your B-17 will be in full color."

"I owe you one," she said.

"Never give that kind of opening to a journalist."

She laughed but took him at his word. She'd keep the diary to herself for the moment. As fragile as it was, it would have to be examined carefully. The safest place for that would be at the Anasazi site, where there'd be no chance of interruption.

15

By the time Nick got back to the motel there was a note pinned to her door. *Ken Drysdale called.* There was no phone number or explanation, which wasn't like Ken, who'd been a stickler for detail when they'd worked together in New Guinea. Once in her room, Nick washed the red desert soil from her hands before using the phone to call him back, but there was no answer in Honolulu. She checked the clock. Dinnertime in New Mexico translated to midafternoon in Hawaii. On the off chance she'd dialed the wrong number the first time, she tried again. Still no answer.

Sighing, she switched her air conditioner to high, then turned on the shower. She was about to step under the spray when the phone rang. She rushed to pick it up.

"I've been calling you every hour," Drysdale said belligerently.

"I just tried your number and got no answer."

"I'm using a pay phone, for Christ's sake."

"You sound upset."

"The air force says no B-17 was ever built with your number."

"It's 44-4013," Nick said from memory.

"That's the one."

"I saw it myself. I have witnesses."

"If you've got a B-17 with that number, then someone's lying to us."

Nick shivered in the lukewarm air coming from the air conditioner. "I haven't got a B-17 anymore," she said and then summarized the situation, starting with Beckstead's accident and progressing to the dramatic change of ownership. As she spoke, her frustration and anger returned with force enough to start her hands trembling.

"About the old guy in truck," Drysdale said, "are they doing an autopsy?"

"I don't know. They said it was drunk driving."

"I don't like it. It smells like the military to me, and I ought to know. I've spent half my life playing their games. They cover up everything, no matter how old and out of date it is. Look at me. I'm old and out of date and I've attracted a couple of sniffers. The bastards are parked outside my place right now, in one of those dead-giveaway government-issue sedans. Either CIC or CIA or FBI, who can tell. They all look alike."

"Are you serious?"

"Why do you think I'm calling you from a pay phone?"

"Maybe it's a coincidence."

"Come on, Nick, this is your old Fifty-seven-Foxtrot you're talking to, so don't shit me. One minute I'm using the computer trying to trace your B-17's tail number and the next an old buddy calls to tell me to log off because there's a security flap on."

"Who could possibly care about a fifty-year-old airplane, even one filled with bodies?"

"How many bodies?"

"Eleven."

"Refresh my memory. What kind of crew does a B-17 carry?"

"Ten, if that's what you're getting at."

"Like I said, something stinks."

"So what do we do now?"

Drysdale expelled a noisy breath. "If I stay here, I'm going to have to talk to those sniffers sooner or later, that's for sure. If I stone-wall them, they might be able to raise hell with my pension."

"Then stay out of it," Nick said.

"On the other hand, they don't know I've spotted them. Which means they can't claim I'm giving them the runaround until they confront me. So maybe I'd be safer there with you than hanging around here. And with me in such close proximity, maybe you'll finally take pity on a poor pensioned-off bachelor."

"If I said yes to one of your proposals, you'd run like hell," Nick said.

"Try me."

Nick smiled, wondering how he would react if she actually said yes. With someone else she might have crossed her fingers and teased him with just such an answer.

"It's a hundred and ten degrees here," she said, "and I'm stuck with it for the duration of my father's dig. I don't see the point of you suffering, too."

"Don't kid me, Nick. You need someone to do your dirty work. I'll fly out of here today."

It was a tempting offer to have an old pro like Drysdale running interference for her. But if he was right about the military being involved, she didn't want to risk his retirement. Or him either, for that matter.

"I don't want you spending your money," she said.

"I'll tell you what, Nicolette. I'll talk to some NCO buddies of mine and see what I come up with. Then we'll see what's next."

Before she could respond, he added, "Cover your back, Nick," and hung up.

16

Nick was dressed and toweling her freshly shampooed hair when Elliot knocked on the door fifteen minutes later.

"We're starving," he called to her.

She ran a hand through her damp hair, then tossed the towel aside. What the hell. She'd go as is. The desert air would dry her hair quickly enough, and she wasn't about to use the blow-dryer again, not after shorting all the fuses the last time around.

"You look like a chipmunk with cowlicks," Elliot said the moment she opened the door.

Douglas and Guthrie were standing right behind him, grinning.

Their smiles faded when she told them what Ken Drysdale had said. "As far as the air force is concerned, our B-17 doesn't exist. They say there's no such ID number."

"They're going to get a hell of a shock when they see my story tomorrow morning," Douglas said. "Complete with a front-page photograph of their nonexistent plane."

"Are you sure?" Nick asked.

114

"I just got off the phone to the Sunday editor. Copies are on his desk right now."

"Why the fuss?" Guthrie said. "You've got expert witnesses, us. We all saw the plane."

"Ken says his computer check backfired and now security people are after him."

"That doesn't make any sense," Elliot said.

"Ken's not a man to imagine things."

"Hold it," Guthrie said. "Let's worry about all this after dinner. Mom Bennett closes up in less than an hour."

There wasn't a soul in the Zuni Café. The tables and counter were already set for tomorrow's breakfast, and Mom looked surprised to see them.

"I'm closing early," she said. "The town's holding a wake for old Gus up at the San Juan and I was just about to leave. You're invited to join us, if you'd like."

"Will there be anything to eat at the wake?" Guthrie asked.

"You poor man, you must be starved."

"We told him you were famous for your Sunday chicken dinners," Elliot said.

"I've already boned those birds for tomorrow's pot pies, but I could fix some sandwiches."

"You're a lifesaver," Guthrie told her.

Mom beamed. "Maybe afterwards you can walk me over to the San Juan. After all, a lady doesn't feel right going into a saloon unaccompanied."

"We'll all go," Nick said, anxious to question the mayor about Ellsworth Kemp's behavior.

Nick helped Mom with the sandwiches, which everyone ate standing around the kitchen. As they were leaving the café twenty minutes later, the windows began to rattle. Even the floorboards trembled.

Mom pointed toward Latimer's service station at the edge of town, where a line of big rigs was hurtling toward them.

115

"They must be doing seventy," she said.

Four of them rumbled by without so much as slowing at the town limits where the state highway turned into Main Street.

"You don't usually see trucks that big around here," she added when they'd disappeared beyond Conejos Bridge. "I hope they get arrested for driving that fast."

"There was a time," Guthrie said, talking Mom's arm and guiding her toward the San Juan, "when truckers were the best drivers on the road."

The passing trucks hadn't been felt or heard in the San Juan Saloon, where a portable stereo had been set up behind the bar, blasting out mariachi music. The noise set Nick's teeth on edge, as did the cigarette smoke thick enough to chew. A hand-written sign, Drinks Half Price Tonight Only, had men lined up two deep along the bar. The women present, half a dozen that Nick could see, were seated at tables.

The mayor broke ranks at the bar to shout, "This was Gus's favorite radio station. It comes all the way from Santa Fe on a clear night."

"That's *your* favorite," Mom shouted back. "Now get us something we can dance to."

Mayor Ralph made a face, but signaled the bartender just the same. A moment later the more sedate notes of big band music filled the saloon.

Nick collared the mayor and said, "We need to talk about this man Kemp."

He jerked a thumb toward the door, pulled Councilman Latimer from the bar crowd, and led the way outside. Mark Douglas started to follow, but the mayor shook his head at him. For a moment, defiance flared in the reporter's eyes, then he shrugged and rejoined Guthrie and Elliot, who were taking turns dancing with Mom Bennett.

The moment the door closed behind them the mayor said, "There's nothing to say. Kemp isn't my problem."

"You were Gus's partner."

"Kemp is Gus's heir."

"Let me get this straight," Nick said. "You and your council paid money out of your own pockets and now you're willing to walk away?"

"We've been compensated," Latimer said.

"I'll do the talking," Mayor Ralph said.

Nick looked from one man to the other. Both avoided her gaze. "You've sold out, haven't you?"

"We've cut our loses," the mayor said. "There's nothing wrong with that."

"And what about all the work I did?"

"Let's face it. We have no way of knowing whether that airplane of yours was real or not."

"Come on. You saw it yourself."

"Hear me out. It could have been a publicity stunt, for all we know. Old Gus could get up to all sorts of things when he put his mind to it."

Nick forced herself to remain calm. "And the bodies?"

"My suggestion to you, Miz Scott, is to go back to your Anasazi Indians and forget all about Gus and his fantasies."

"His fantasy will be on the front page of tomorrow's *Albuquerque Journal.*"

"Jesus Christ," Latimer blurted. "There goes our deal."

Mayor Ralph raised a warning hand. "That's nothing to do with us. It's out of our control."

Nick stormed back inside, fought her way to the bar, and ordered a beer. She was still seething when Mark Douglas worked his way close enough to ask her to dance.

"With your leg?"

"Haven't you noticed. No more cane. All this exercise has cured me."

When she slipped into his arms, he added, "What did the mayor have to say?"

"Who asked me to dance, you or the reporter?"

"We're one and the same."

"If you must know, he and his council are stonewalling me. Probably Kemp and that lawyer of his paid them off for some reason."

Douglas sighed. "As much as I like holding a beautiful woman in my arms, being in here is killing me. It's like smoking a pack a day. If you ever see me reaching for another cigarette, kick me in the shins. My bad shin at that."

Nick nodded. "I'm ready to leave."

The others joined the exodus. Mom Bennett came too, taking Guthrie up on his offer to escort her home.

"It's a shame Grace Miller didn't come," Mom said as they strolled up Main Street toward the residential end of town. "She wasn't really Gus's widow, you know, not officially, but she was as close to family as he had. Gus lived at her place, you know. Of course, they both swore it was strictly a rental arrangement, but most people didn't believe it."

"What do you know," Guthrie said. "There may be life in this town after all."

Mom giggled. "As for me, I say people shouldn't live alone." She nudged Guthrie. "I always thought old Gus would leave everything he owned to Grace, not some distant cousin."

"Maybe she's the one I should talk to," Nick said.

"I'd like to come with you," Douglas said, "but I've been ordered back to the paper for a meeting first thing tomorrow morning. That means driving in the dark."

He shook Nick's hand first. "Call me if you find out what happened to the *Scorpion.*"

17

Grace Miller's two-story clapboard Victorian stood out harshly in the glare from a pair of security floodlights attached to the eaves. Insects swarming around the bulbs cast eerie, flickering shadows over the entire facade. Looking at it, Nick was reminded of some of the student boardinghouses in Berkeley. But there, the Victorian would have fit in; here, flanked on both sides by squat flat-roofed adobes, the house looked enormous and out of scale.

The door opened before Nick could knock. The woman standing on the threshold said, "You must be Nick Scott. Mom Bennett just called and told me you'd be standing on my porch. Come on in."

Grace Miller appeared to be in her sixties and was still trim enough to fit nicely into jeans. The tails of a white loose-fitting man's shirt had been tied in a knot at her waist. Her thick brown hair hung in a ponytail. She was barefoot with brightly painted nails.

"You look like you were expecting me to wear black," she

said as Nick crossed the threshold. "I'm not exactly a two-time widow, despite what people are saying."

Grace escorted Nick into the parlor, which was filled with furniture that looked Victorian enough to have come with the house. Nick settled onto a horsehair sofa; Grace faced her in a matching armchair, tucking her feet underneath her.

"Gus told me about you," Grace said. "He said meeting you was his lucky day. Of course, Gus was always saying things like that. He'd never had much luck, you see, so he figured his turn was just about due. 'Good times are just around the corner,' he liked to say."

"He told me he had good luck finding gold nuggets."

Grace shook her head. "Gus couldn't get away with saying something like that to anyone but an outsider. The only thing he ever found bigger than a pea was that plane. And it wasn't any use until you came along."

"How could he afford that fancy metal detector of his?"

Grace glanced at the wooden mantelpiece filled with framed photographs. Gus Beckstead was nowhere to be seen, at least as far as Nick could tell.

"That metal detector was my gift to him. 'It's all I need,' he said, 'to change my luck.' Well, his luck never did change, getting himself killed like that."

She paused to breathe deeply. "I took pity on Gus when no one else would. He was a drifter, a ne'er-do-well. I knew that the first time I met him. I had no illusions. I also knew he was the exact opposite of my husband, may he rest in peace. You see, my Matt owned the tractor agency in Gallup. His whole life was tractors and farming. I came third. Anyway, he died before the farmers started going bust, otherwise I would never have been able to sell out and buy this house."

"Why here in Cibola?"

"Why else? I was born here."

"And Gus?"

"His folks lived in one of those mobile homes. They never stayed put long enough for him to be from anywhere. But that's not what you're really asking, is it? You want to know about Gus's cousin, Ellsworth Kemp."

This was one sharp lady, Nick decided, which made her relationship with Gus Beckstead all the more difficult to understand. "You're a mind reader."

"Gus used to say the same thing, only I guess I'm not very good at it, because as far as I knew, Gus had no relatives. The fact is, he always said he was leaving everything to me. He wrote out a will to that effect once."

"Do you still have it?"

"Somewhere, probably. But it wouldn't be any good. That cousin of his was already here to show me his will. It was dated this year. That makes mine null and void, though I don't really care. Gus's claim is worthless as far as I know, and what would I do with an old airplane?"

"You could give it to me."

"If it were in my power, I'd do just that."

"Let me ask you a favor, then. Find that will of yours so I can wave it in Mr. Ellsworth Kemp's face."

"Why not?"

Together, they rummaged through the drawers of a narrow Victorian desk until the document was found.

"All I ask," Grace said, "is that you make a copy so I can keep the original."

"I have a portable copier in my room. I'll bring the original back first thing in the morning before I go after Kemp."

18

Armed with a crisp copy of Gus Beckstead's holographic will, Nick went looking for Ellsworth Kemp right after breakfast the next morning. But he'd already checked out of the motel.

"The fact is," Jay Ferrin confided when Nick confronted him in the office, "the bastard woke me up at five this morning to give me his cash and his key. It was still dark, for Christ's sake."

"Did he say where he was going?"

Ferrin shrugged halfheartedly. "Maybe he's out at Gus's claim. That's the way he was heading, anyway, when he drove out of here. I'm surprised he didn't wake you up, the way he took off like a bat out of hell."

Since Guthrie, her father, and his students were already at ES No. 1 looking for more tasty evidence of cannibalism, Nick decided to see her B-17 one last time. But the moment she reached the turnoff leading to Gus's Oasis, she knew something was wrong. The highway was littered with pieces of flattened tumbleweed and dirt clods. Black tire marks streaked the asphalt. The shallow ruts leading off into the desert, barely visible yesterday, now looked deeply grooved and well traveled.

As Nick followed the tracks, she remembered Gus's warning about getting stuck in soft sand and resisted the temptation to hurry. But even driving slowly she almost passed the site without recognizing it. The mound was all but gone, along with any sign of the B-17. Gus Beckstead's shack was missing too, and judging by the tire tracks the old boy's warning about soft sand had been nothing but a tall tale.

Feeling stunned, she killed the Trooper's engine and got out. There were tire tracks everywhere, double sets, probably from the big rigs that had driven through town last night. But why would someone go to all that trouble, not to mention expense, to steal a fifty-year-old war relic? There were rich collectors, of course, but that didn't seem likely. Even the most avid of them would want to see the dead properly buried.

Maybe the answer was in that diary she'd found. Fingers crossed, she climbed back into the Trooper, U-turned without getting stuck, and headed deeper into the badlands, toward ES No. 1. The predicted cooling trend had failed to materialize. The thermometer at the mouth of the cliff dwelling read a hundred and five, though the sun had yet to reach its zenith.

Inside the ovenlike cave, Elliot and Guthrie looked totally oblivious to the furnace heat as they knelt on a ground sheet examining their latest find, a large piece of humerus bone. The half dozen students grouped in a semicircle around them looked as dirty and bedraggled as soldiers coming out of battle.

"Nick!" Elliot shouted when he saw her. "Come over here and tell us what we've got."

Her father and Guthrie exchanged conspiratorial winks as she knelt beside them. Guthrie pointed to a crack along the axis of the arm bone and said, "Show me you were listening during class."

"My B-17 is missing," she replied.

Guthrie squinted at her the same way he'd done when she

missed one of his test questions. "Here, see for yourself where the knife slipped. This bone was deliberately split open so the marrow could be sucked out."

"The whole goddamned plane. Those trucks we saw last night must have hauled it away."

"Nick," her father said, "stop and take a deep breath. Stay calm."

She clenched her teeth, remembering him saying the same thing to her as a child. Then, her mother had been the cause of Nick's agitation. Now it was her father's obsession with the Anasazi.

"Your airplane wasn't a sanctioned dig," he went on. "It was a diversion for you, that's all. Its disappearance is of no historical significance." Dreamy eyed, Elliot gazed up at the three-story cliff dwellings above them. "Here is where we'll find history."

That was pure Elliot, she thought, oblivious to everything else when in proximity to his beloved Indians.

Guthrie said, "Stealing airplanes that won't fly takes a lot of money and manpower."

"Speaking of which," Elliot broke in, glaring at his students until they wearily went back to work, climbing the extension ladder to their most recent dig site two stories above.

When they were out of sight, he shook the humerus at her. "This is a thousand years old. When your airplane's that age, maybe I'll worry about it."

"I think Ken Drysdale may be right," Nick persisted. "There could be some kind of military cover-up going on. Who else would care after so many years?"

Elliot shook his head. "Even the military isn't that goofy."

"You're forgetting something," Guthrie said. "They test bacteria and radiation on civilians all the time without telling them, in the name of national security, naturally. Then they cover their tracks by classifying everything top secret. Come to think of it, Los Alamos isn't that far off. Maybe the poor bastards on that bomber were ordered to fly through a mushroom cloud, or some damned thing."

"What about the bullet holes?" Nick said. "And the diary?" She held it out, still in its plastic baggie.

Guthrie nodded. "You win. The Anasazi can wait awhile longer."

Elliot snorted derisively.

Nick would have preferred to open the diary in a more controlled environment, one without dirt and grit. But both her father and Guthrie were experts in restoration.

With an apologetic nod to her father, she handed the diary to Guthrie, who accepted the offering carefully. "Thank God for our mummifying New Mexican climate," he said, sitting cross-legged on the ground sheet, "otherwise the paper might have disintegrated by now."

Working slowly, he applied oil to the crusted lock and clasp, careful not to wet the leather. After a few minutes, he began scraping away the rust. Several applications of oil were necessary before the mechanism gave way. Next, he worked lanolin into the tips of his fingers and then gently rubbed the oil into the diary's spine to keep it from cracking when opened.

Through it all, Nick wiped Guthrie's brow to keep sweat from dripping onto the book.

Finally, Guthrie took a deep breath and slowly opened the diary. A shiny, perfectly preserved dog tag, complete with chain, fell out onto the ground sheet.

Without touching the disc, Nick bent down to examine it through a magnifying glass. "It looks Japanese."

Elliot confirmed her opinion.

"It must be a war souvenir like the uniform pieces we found," Guthrie said.

"Maybe," Nick said. "But there should have been tags on all the bodies."

Nodding, Guthrie laid the diary on the sheet and slowly spread open the covers. Despite the lanolin, the leather still cracked a bit along the spine, but the diary held together. The writing on the first page was still legible.

The *Scorpion*, January 1945
Ross McKinnon, navigator

"I found it in the navigator's compartment," Nick reminded them.

The second page contained a list of the other nine crew members.

Dennis Atwood, pilot
John Curtis, copilot
Howard Kelly, bombardier
Paul Decker, top gunner
Jack Ashton, waist gunner
Bill Lee, waist gunner
John Emerson, tail gunner
Dave Watson, radio operator
Andy Evans, ball turret

On the next page, a note was addressed to someone named Lael and signed by Ross, the navigator. Using the glass, Guthrie read the letter out loud. " 'My Dearest Lael, I'm writing to you from on board my plane, while we're waiting to take off on a special mission. They've promised us leave when we're done. If all goes well, I'll be able to deliver this letter in person, my love. I'll be able to hold you in my arms again. At night sometimes I wake up and think I smell your perfume, but when I open my eyes all I smell is mildew and tent canvas.' "

Guthrie paused to clear his throat and drink some bottled

water. Nick looked away, knowing it was more than thirst that was choking him.

" 'We renamed our ship,' " Guthrie continued hoarsely. " 'Our sexy pinup has been replaced by a scorpion. It wasn't our idea. It was orders but I'm not supposed to write about that. Anyway, we've now got a scorpion painted on our nose. It's bright yellow with red eyes. If the Japs ever get close enough to see it, it ought to scare the you-know-what out of them.' "

Nick swallowed the lump in her throat. "I wish we knew what that special mission was."

"I don't see how it would help us," Elliot said.

"None of it helps," Guthrie added.

"You're wrong," Nick said. "Names mean service records. We can run them down eventually."

Guthrie went through several more pages. All were blank. He put down the book, stretched, and let out a long sigh before getting to his feet. "You always hope you've hit the jackpot, a revelation that will change your life. But in the end archaeology comes down to hard work."

"And persistence," Nick said, and went over the diary again, transcribing the crew list and letter into her own notebook. After that, she leafed through the blank pages, one after the other. Halfway through the book, as if the diary had been opened at random, she found a message scrawled across both the left- and right-hand pages. Both were stained.

"Jesus." A chill climbed her spine. "Listen to this. 'Our own planes are shooting us down. P-38s. Me and Howard survived the crash. They're still strafing. Hiding this—' "

Both men went down on their knees to read it for themselves.

"Son of a bitch," Elliot said. "No wonder the military's covering up."

"Your father's right, Nicolette. My advice to you is to forget the whole thing. You're half a century too late to help anybody, so why stir up trouble now?"

"Don't waste your breath," Elliot said. "She's as one-tracked as I am."

Nick busied herself copying the navigator's last message into her book. Then she went through the rest of the pages until she was satisfied that there was nothing else to find. Finally, she backtracked and reread the navigator's last letter to his wife. "If she's still alive, someone ought to deliver that letter to her."

"You might not be doing her a favor after so much time," Elliot said.

"Maybe not, but there are other things I can do. So you're going to have to get along here without me."

Guthrie groaned. "That sounds like a plea for volunteers."

Usually when Nick tracked down military artifacts she had full cooperation from the authorities. This time, she didn't know what kind of roadblocks were ahead of her. If it weren't for Mark Douglas's story and pictures in the *Journal*, she'd have no proof the B-17 ever existed. Except, of course, for her witnesses, though skeptics might dismiss both Elliot and Guthrie as being prejudiced.

"I'll take any help I can get," she said.

"Do you know what a professor emeritus does?" Guthrie responded. "He runs around giving speeches and raising funds for the university. I've sucked up to more politicians than you can count. Our governor's one of the good guys, though, the Honorable Michael Elwood Mills. He owes me a couple of favors, so first thing tomorrow morning I'll call him and collect. He's head of the National Guard, for God's sake. If anybody's going to get through to the military, he's our man. Better yet, I'll drive to Santa Fe and camp on his doorstep until he agrees to help."

Nick picked up the Japanese dog tag, tested its tensile strength, and then hung it around her own neck, not as a memento but as evidence she might need one day.

19

The sun was setting by the time Nick returned to the Seven Cities. She stripped off her sweaty clothes, doused herself under the shower, and then, with her own king-size towel wrapped around her, dialed the office and asked if the *Journal* had arrived yet.

"The Sunday edition we don't get till Monday," Jay Ferrin told her. "Unless somebody we know happens to be driving through from Albuquerque."

"And have they?"

"In that case, they'd be at Mayor Ralph's."

"Did I get any calls?" Nick asked.

"He said he'd call back," Ferrin said, and hung up.

Ten minutes later her phone rang and Ken Drysdale said, "Nick, have you been watching your back, like I said?"

"It's too late, I think."

"Are you all right?"

"It's my B-17. Someone arrived during the night and spirited it away. They took everything, even the prospector's shack that was nearby. The only thing they left behind is tire tracks, and those will be gone the first time the wind blows."

Drysdale whistled. "That sounds like the military all right. First come the sniffers, then the sweepers cleaning up behind them. We've had it. Your plane is history."

"Not quite. They missed something, the navigator's diary. The names of the crew were in it."

"Attagirl, Nick. Not only are there personnel files somewhere, but wartime insurance had to be paid out and next of kin notified. Before we do anything else, though, you'd better decide how far you want to go with this. Some of my friends aren't talking to me."

"Technically speaking, without an artifact, an archaeologist is out of work. Which means if I had any sense, I'd cut my loses and go back to schlepping for my father. Only there's something else in that diary. Hold on a minute while I get my notes."

Nick had left the original diary with her father, stored among his Anasazi artifacts, an unlikely place for anyone, sniffers included, to go looking for it. As she retrieved her notebook from the nightstand, she shivered. Her towel suddenly felt cold and clammy. Quickly, she exchanged it for a dry one before going back to the phone.

"What I'm going to read looks hastily written, probably by the navigator, Ross McKinnon. There was a stain on the paper that could have been blood. If I'm any judge, these are the last words he wrote before he was killed. Quote. 'Our own planes are shooting us down. P-38s. Me and Howard survived the crash. They're still strafing. Hiding this—' "

"Jesus Christ. It sounds like we shot down one of our own planes by mistake."

"Do you really think something like that could happen?"

"In a combat area, maybe. But over New Mexico? It hardly seems likely."

"It makes me mad," she said. "Those men deserve a decent

burial, and I intend to see they get one." And maybe deliver his love letter, too, she added to herself. "All eleven of them."

"If someone was hitching a ride, they got more than they bargained for."

"Maybe."

"Okay," Drysdale said. "I'll do some more leg work. Maybe I can dig up something on this man McKinnon. But if I pick up more sniffers, we're in trouble. You watch for them, too, Nick."

"The military has no jurisdiction over me."

"Just keep looking over your shoulder, that's all."

Nick dressed and headed for the Zuni Café to join her father and Clark Guthrie for dinner. Even outside, in the eighty-degree dregs of the day, she continued to feel cold. The chill followed her into the café.

She ordered coffee, something she seldom did after dark because caffeine kept her awake, and wrapped her hands around the cup as soon as Mom Bennett put it on the table. When the Monday night special arrived, Nick dug into the food, hoping calories would dispel her chill.

"Has anyone seen a copy of the *Journal*?" She asked when she came up for air.

"I checked the general store before you got here," Elliot said. "Someone bought up all the copies as soon as they arrived, or so the mayor said."

"Who?"

"He wouldn't say."

Nick shivered and noticed that the food hadn't helped.

20

Leland Hatch ground his teeth as the front page of the *Albuquerque Journal* rolled off his fax machine. The data, originating from cellular equipment inside Ellsworth Kemp's van in the New Mexican desert, was being routed through the CMI satellite and directly into Hatch's RISC System/6000 computer.

As he read the article, Hatch absently ran a hand over the computer's processing unit. As a home computer, the RISC was strictly overkill, providing him with more power than NASA had had available for its Apollo moon shots.

He studied the photograph of the B-17, still partially buried in the sand at the time the picture was taken. Grounded the way it was, the plane looked nothing like the bomber in his dreams.

The lady archaeologist, seen squeezing herself through the pilot's side windshield, showed too much breast outlined against her tightly stretched shirt to be credible. Or so he hoped.

When he picked up the phone, his hand trembled. He

wanted to shout but an act of willpower kept his voice calm. "Kemp, why the hell didn't you tell me there was a reporter on the scene? I was acting under the assumption that you'd wrung that prospector dry. I took you at your word."

"I had no reason to question the old guy on that subject."

"Surely you talked with people around town enough to know the cast of characters."

"Initially, you requested that I keep a low profile," Kemp said.

Hatch paused for breath. Power had its drawbacks. People, especially employees, tended to take his every word as gospel and were afraid to use their own initiative. More than once an offhand remark, spoken inside the CMI building, had been acted upon as if it were carved in stone. Even his son, Lee, had been guilty of such overreaction on occasion. Maybe now was the time to brief him on the situation? Hatch shook his head. There'd be time enough later to end Lee's innocence.

Hatch said, "Are you certain that the site is absolutely clear?"

"I guarantee it."

"I'll hold you to that."

"There is one thing," Kemp said.

"Let's hear it."

"A man named Clark Guthrie, a retired professor, borrowed one of Elliot Scott's cars and is driving to Santa Fe."

"Who's covering him?"

"Wynar."

"That's as far as it goes. If action becomes necessary, I want you to take care of it personally. I don't want anyone else knowledgeable. Do you understand?"

"Absolutely."

"Now, what do you think this man Guthrie's up to?"

"We're monitoring his cellular phone. He put in a call to

the governor's office and made an appointment for tomorrow morning. No subject was discussed."

Jesus Christ. There it was again, lack of initiative. Hatch took a deep breath and spoke precisely. "I don't think we can risk that. You'd better replace Wynar immediately."

"What about the Scott woman?"

Hatch had given her a lot of thought during the past twenty-four hours. His first impulse had been to remove her immediately and be done with it. But her reputation had to be considered. At the moment, it was still intact. She was a recognized expert in her field. Killing her would make headlines, and might necessitate a move against her even more famous father. So, for the time being, he'd take other countermeasures.

He said, "She'll be leaving Cibola soon enough. Once you've finished in Santa Fe, you can pick her up again in Berkeley."

"And the newspaper?" Kemp said.

Hatch sighed. Sometimes he wondered if anyone besides himself had the brains to think ahead. "That's already in the works. And when you get to Berkeley, don't lose her. I want to know her every move."

21

When Nick drove into the desert the next morning, thunderheads hovered along the eastern horizon. The air smelled vaguely of rain, though she felt it was a false promise this time of year.

She'd already marked the ranches nearest the B-17 crash site on her plat map of the area. There were four in all. She wasted nearly three hours checking out the first two ranches, both of which had been abandoned years ago. The third ranch was occupied, but by a couple who'd recently moved to New Mexico for their health and had never heard so much as a rumor about airplanes in the desert.

Number four could only be reached on a rutted trail that was fighting a losing battle against encroaching tumbleweeds. Soon after leaving Highway 371, Nick braked gently to a stop to avoid raising any more dust than necessary, then checked her map against the surrounding landscape. If anything, this particular area looked even more bleak than Gus Beckstead's claim. The track ahead of her, like the road to Gus's, rollercoastered through flash-flood channels that had been eroded deeply into the red soil.

Despite having topped off the fuel tank before leaving town, Nick tapped the gauge with her fingernail. The needle didn't budge from the three-quarters mark. The temperature gauge was well below the red. She shook the water can to make certain it was full, then felt under the seat for her rifle.

Finally, after zeroing the trip counter, she drove slowly north, staying in first gear. The map said the ranch site was three point two miles from the highway. If she didn't find it by the time the counter hit three point five, she'd give it up and drive back to town.

At the two-mile mark, an abandoned truck, rusted and scavenged, reminded her of one of those wistful Depression photos. Add graffiti—Abandon Hope, All Ye Who Enter Here—and it would have been a New Mexican version of Dante's gate to hell.

Nick clenched her teeth at the thought. Reading Dante had been one of her mother's obsessions, though she read only in Nick's presence, never Elliot's.

"Education can be a curse, especially when it comes to catching a man," Elaine said each time she took Dante from its hiding place. "Good cooking and sex, that's what they want. Never let them know you're smarter than they are."

"Then why do you read it to me?" Nick had asked.

"Because I don't want you to have any of my illusions."

Nick shook her head. The squat adobe farmhouse straight ahead was no illusion, and the well-kept truck parked in front said the ranch was inhabited.

The man who came out to meet her looked much like Gus Beckstead. He was old yet somehow ageless, wearing jeans low on his hips, a checkered shirt, a straw cowboy hat, and a sun-wrinkled face that rivaled the eroded landscape.

He waved away her introduction. "I've seen you in town,"

he said. "You're the one causing all the trouble." He snorted. "More power to you, I say. It's about time Mayor Ralph came down off his high horse. My name's Van Harris, by the way. Come on in out of the sun and I'll give you a beer. It must be a hundred and ten out here."

By comparison, the inside of the farmhouse felt almost chilly.

"My daddy built this place back in the thirties," Harris said. "The walls are two feet thick. When I was a boy he used to tell me that you had to have that much wall between you and the Indians. Of course, the Indians were long gone by then and so was my mother."

"Do you know why I'm here, Mr. Harris?"

"I have a good idea."

"I found an old airplane not far from here, as the crow flies anyway. Out on Gus Beckstead's place."

"That's what I heard, but the mayor says otherwise. He told me himself when I was in town earlier. He said the whole thing was nothing but a mirage." Harris smiled wide enough to crinkle his face. "You don't look like the kind of woman to imagine things."

"Were you living here during World War Two?"

He nodded. "As soon as I saw you drive up I said to myself, 'Van, she's looking for witnesses.' But I didn't see a thing, if that's what you're asking." He winked. "You don't have to look so glum, because I heard it all right, the sound of gunfire. It wasn't no thunder neither. I know the difference. It could have been practice strafing, I guess, but then you wouldn't have found any wreckage, would you? I think it must have been late afternoon, getting on toward dark maybe when we heard it, because my father didn't go out to investigate until the next day. He ran into some kind of roadblock and came back emptyhanded. Since it was wartime, that was the end of it."

"What about you? Did you ever go looking on your own?"

"Being a kid, I snooped some, but my father never would say exactly where he hit that roadblock. Besides, I had school and work to do around the ranch here. Of course, looking at this place now, you wouldn't think anyone had ever put a lick of work into it. But it paid for a while, back during that war, when we could sell our range beef. Nowadays, nobody wants anything raised this close to Los Alamos, not that I blame them, considering what the fallout did to this state. It wasn't so bad around here, but upwind, let me tell you. That's a wasteland."

By the time Nick returned to the motel, her father and his student archaeologists were there ahead of her. The hot water had run out and her cold water shower did nothing to revive her spirits. More than ever she was convinced that the B-17 was part of a military cover-up. Probably Ken Drysdale was right. Real-life logic didn't apply to the military. Maybe they'd been so paranoid about the possibility of invasion that they really did shoot the *Scorpion* down by mistake. If so, they sure as hell wouldn't have admitted it during wartime.

She said as much to her father, once she'd pried him away from his students at the Zuni Café. Their conversation was made difficult by the overexcited discussions following the discovery of another cannibalized bone and what appeared to be an old well.

"On top of everything else," she said, "the mayor's telling people I've been imagining things."

Elliot held up a finger before beckoning to Mom Bennett, who came over to their table, wiping her hands on her apron and smiling. "When's that nice Mr. Guthrie coming back for seconds?"

"Tomorrow, we hope," Elliot said. "He had to drive into Santa Fe. In the meantime, we're looking for a copy of yesterday's *Albuquerque Journal*. It has proof of my daughter's airplane."

"You and everybody else." Mom shrugged. "Good riddance, I say. All you read in the papers is bad news anyway. I'll be back with your dinner in a minute."

Nick rolled her eyes, longing for a green salad instead of Mom's home cooking.

"I know that look of yours," Elliot said. "Your mother used to get the same one whenever she was about to explode. Take a deep breath and relax. All we've got to do is call the paper and order a copy. Better yet, you can call Mark Douglas and ask him to read his article to you."

"You're right, and now's as good a time as any."

She left the table and headed for the old-fashioned phone booth at the back of the café. Information gave her the direct number to the *Journal*'s news desk.

"Mark Douglas, please."

"He's gone for the day."

"I'm calling about his airplane article in yesterday's paper," she said. "Could someone read it to me?"

"I'm the only one on the desk, ma'am, so I can't tie up the line. But I'll give Mark a message, if you'd like."

Nick left her name and asked for a callback as soon as possible.

By the time she got back to the table, her dinner plate was waiting, with no sign of a salad.

"The best I could do was leave a message," she told her father.

She was toying with her food ten minutes later when the pay phone rang.

"That was fast," Elliot said.

Nick held her breath until Mom verified that the call was for her.

She hurried to the phone. "Mark?"

"Nick, it's Ben Gilbert. I called your motel. They gave me this number."

She looked back at her father, shook her head, and closed the phone booth door. Gilbert, though only in his early forties, was her department chairman at Berkeley. The last time they'd spoken had been on one of those colleague dates where they both went Dutch. Instead of rousing her passion, he'd spent the evening complaining about getting stuck with paperwork while envying her Anasazi hunt.

"It's bad news," he said. "I need you at a special meeting of the tenure committee."

"What the hell are you talking about?"

"I'm only following orders, Nick. This comes directly from the chancellor's office. He asked me to contact you personally."

She felt stunned. As far as she knew, the tenure committee wasn't expected to meet until late in the fall semester. Even then her tenure was only a formality, or so Gilbert had promised. She'd taken him at his word. After all, in the small world of archaeology, he too had studied under Clark Guthrie at one time, and later with Elliot, who had helped Gilbert latch on to his job at Berkeley.

"It's out of my hands, Nick," Gilbert added.

"I don't believe this is happening."

"There's more. The meeting's tomorrow afternoon in Sproul Hall. One P.M.."

"I'm in the middle of New Mexico. You know that. I don't know if I can get there by then."

"My instructions are clear, Nick. If you don't appear, you miss your chance for the year. I'm sorry."

"That's unheard of. What the hell's going on?"

"That I couldn't say," he replied, and hung up.

She checked her watch against the Zuni's wall clock,

7:15 P.M. She'd have to drive to Albuquerque tonight and hope to catch a flight to the coast, though she doubted if any would be leaving until morning. A morning flight would be cutting it close. Panic tempted her to start calling the airlines now, but suddenly she was hungry.

She was halfway to the table before she saw the stricken look on her father's face. Standing beside him, head bowed, was Jay Ferrin from the motel.

"What's wrong?" Nick said as soon as she reached her father.

"Nobody ever calls my motel this time of the year," Ferrin said. "Then suddenly we get two emergencies in one night."

Shaking his head, Elliot took Nick by the arm and led her out of the café and into the middle of Main Street. There he stopped to stare up at the stars. "Clark died a few minutes ago of a heart attack. I have to leave for Santa Fe immediately to start making arrangements. It's something I promised him years ago when he named me as his executor. I hate to dump my students on you like this, but I don't have any choice."

"I can't do it, Dad. You're going to have to put one of them in charge temporarily. I have to appear before a tenure meeting tomorrow afternoon. If I don't, I lose a whole year."

"What?"

"That was Ben Gilbert on the phone just now with the news."

"That man owes me, for God's sake. I'll call him right back."

Nick shook her head. "Leave it alone, Dad. Something's going on. You know it and so do I." She hugged him.

"Come on, Nick. You're being foolish."

She might have believed him if she hadn't felt him shaking almost as badly as she was.

"You know what I keep thinking?" he said. "That Guthrie would have loved to have been there today when we found the well. It means my site wasn't as dependent on surface water as

141

we once thought. It also explains the location of ES Number Two, which I intend to rename Guthrie Number One. What do you think, Nick? Would he like that?"

She stared at her father. At times, he had a great capacity for denial. He'd practically turned it into an art form when dealing with Nick's mother.

"ES Number Two is twenty miles deeper into the badlands than ES Number One," Elliot went on as if lecturing. "It's a smaller site, maybe even an aberration because of its isolated location. Or so says the conventional wisdom. But a well. That would provide year-round water. If we find a well out there, Guthrie will be remembered for changing that kind of so-called wisdom. And my guess is that the water can't be more than a few feet below the surface of the old river bed. I'm moving the dig out there before the summer's over."

Nick sighed.

There was no road leading to ES No. 2, just twenty miles of badlands that would have to be crossed in a four-wheel-drive. But Nick would have preferred that journey to the one ahead of her.

22

After a frantic drive across the desert, accompanied by one of her father's students who'd volunteered to return the Isuzu to Cibola, Nick was lucky to find a red-eye into San Francisco. She'd taken only one semidressy set of clothes with her into the desert, a lightweight tan cotton poplin suit. In Cibola, the one time she'd worn it she'd felt overdressed and on the verge of sunstroke. Coming off the plane in San Francisco, with the usual fog bank resting on the coastal hills, the poplin was no protection at all against the summer cold.

Shivering, Nick took a taxi to the downtown BART terminal, where she caught a train into Berkeley. Another cab let her off at Sather Gate, near Sproul Hall. By the time she reached the massive rock building, Nick felt even colder. A perfectly normal reaction, she told herself. Her body needed time to adjust to the dramatic change in climate. But alarms kept sounding anyway. Tenure hearings for the Department of Anthropology and Archaeology were usually held in the Kroeber Building. Sproul was strictly administrative.

The clock on the Campanile said she had five minutes to

spare as she climbed Sproul's granite steps. Ben Gilbert must have been waiting just inside, because he pushed through one of the doors to meet her on the threshold.

"You cut it close," he said. "I was starting to think you weren't coming."

"Who's on the tenure committee?"

Gilbert ran a hand through his short, curly hair while avoiding her eyes. "It's not exactly a tenure committee."

She stared at him, wondering why she'd ever thought him attractive. Never marry a good-looking man, her mother had often advised. Maybe, in that one instance, she'd been right.

Now, seeing Gilbert under the present circumstances, Nick realized he was more politician than archaeologist, and that being chairman of the department was more important to him than doing real work in the field.

"I'm listening," she said.

"It's a disciplinary hearing. I'm serving along with Assistant Chancellor Janet Bombard and Professor Pat Campbell from our department."

Two women and one man, Nick thought, so there'd be no question of sexual discrimination. And Campbell of all people. She was one of the most conservative women Nick had ever met in the field of archaeology. She had a reputation for resenting younger women in the field. No doubt she believed that women Nick's age should have as hard a time as she'd had working in a field dominated by men. On top of that, Campbell made no secret of her belief that Nick's area of expertise, historical archaeology and its study of the recent past, was no better than rubbish picking.

"What am I supposed to have done?" Nick asked.

Gilbert shook his head. "That's not for me to say."

"You bastard," she said. "I have rights."

Ducking his head, Gilbert ushered her down a long corridor to a conference room adjoining the assistant chancellor's office. A heavy wooden table dominated the room. Three chairs had been placed at the far end of the table. Two were already taken by Bombard and Campbell. Gilbert quickly seated himself in the third, leaving Nick the one remaining chair, facing her accusers down the long axis of the table. A microphone was already in place facing Nick's chair. The mike was connected to a cassette recorder next to Bombard, who opened a manila folder in front of her, nodded at the colleagues flanking her, and then switched on the recording mechanism.

"For the record," Bombard said, "state your name and position on the university faculty."

Nick complied.

"Is it correct to say that you are on leave for the summer, working at an archaeological site in New Mexico?"

"Yes, though the work's not funded by this university."

"And did you leave that site to conduct another, unsanctioned excavation."

"Yes, with the permission of Dr. Elliot Scott, who heads the Anasazi dig."

"And did you give an interview to a newspaper reporter named"—Bombard consulted her notes—"Mark Douglas of the *Albuquerque Journal*?"

Nick nodded.

"Out loud, please."

"Yes," Nick answered.

"Do you stand by what you told him?"

"What I said to him is one thing," Nick said, "but I have no idea what he wrote."

"Are you saying that you haven't seen his article?"

"That's correct."

"Again, for the record, you contend that you participated

in the excavation of a World War Two aircraft?"

Nick didn't like the word contend but answered anyway. "A B-17 bomber, yes."

"And that bodies were on board?"

"Yes."

Bombard leaned forward. "Where is the airplane now?"

"Someone's taken it."

"I see." Nodding, Bombard sat back in her chair.

Professor Campbell's eyes rolled; her expression condemned Nick.

"The B-17 story is a hoax," Gilbert said.

Nick opened her mouth to call him a liar, but caution held her back. Clamping her teeth together, she forced herself to take a deep breath. "I'm not the only witness to see that airplane, and I'm not the only one to go inside it either."

"The newspaper has retracted the story," Gilbert said. "They admit, in print, that they were taken in by what they call, quote, 'A total and utter hoax,' unquote."

"The plane was there."

"Let me read you an excerpt from the article." Gilbert looked to Bombard, who nodded her approval. " 'Archaeologist Nicolette Scott looks and dresses like a character from the wild West, a modern-day Annie Oakley, who's as expert with a rifle as she is with an archaeologist's spade.' That sounds anything but professional."

My God, Nick thought, couldn't they see that Douglas meant that description as a compliment, even though it was somewhat flamboyant.

"Do you make it a habit of using a rifle on your expeditions?" Bombard asked.

"The rifle's for protection."

"From what?"

"I shot a rattlesnake near the airplane. No big deal. Now, could I see the entire article, please?"

Bombard ignored the request. "Did you understand the situation, Ms. Scott? You are charged with perpetrating an archaeological hoax and thereby bringing disgrace upon this university." She took a copy of the *National Geographic* from her folder and opened it to Nick's picture. "If it's fame you're after, it might be a good idea if you tried some other profession."

"The newspaper has a photograph of my find, for heaven's sake." Nick thrust her hands into her lap so they wouldn't see how badly she was shaking, not with cold this time, but with rage.

"Photographs can be doctored," Gilbert said. "On top of everything else, one of the wire services picked up the story from the *Journal* before it could be retracted. By now, who knows how many newspapers have carried it. My department will be a laughingstock all over the county."

Cool it, Nick told herself. *Breathe deeply. Count to ten. Don't say a word until you think it through. You can always fight them in court.*

"Your action," Gilbert continued, "could cast doubt on everyone else's work."

To hell with caution, Nick thought. Somebody was out to destroy her, somebody who'd gotten to Gilbert, probably the military. After all, they fed enough weapons-research money into the university's radiation laboratory to blow up the world, not to mention keeping a lot of professors employed.

"If I'm on trial here," Nick said, speaking softly enough to mask her anger, "I have the right to defend myself. The fact is, it might be best if I had an attorney present."

Gilbert started to reply but Bombard silenced him with a look.

"As yet you have no tenure at this university," the assistant chancellor said. "We can terminate you for cause."

"And if I get Mark Douglas on the phone and he confirms what I've said? What then?"

"I've already spoken to his editor. The retraction stands. Your airplane doesn't exist."

"Bullshit," Nick blurted, then gritted her teeth.

Bombard stood up. "This hearing is at an end. As of now, you are suspended pending further action. You will be escorted to your office to collect your personal belongings and then shown off the campus."

"A moment more, please," Gilbert said.

Reluctantly, Bombard sat down again.

"I've known Nick Scott for more than a year now," Gilbert said. "Her work has been competent in the past, as evidenced by a recent article in the *National Geographic*. Her father is a recognized expert on the Anasazi Indian culture."

"We understand that," Campbell said, speaking for the first time. "If we didn't, we wouldn't be here at all, would we? I should point out, however, that Indians are one thing, airplanes quite another when it comes to archaeology. It seems to me none of this would have happened if Ms. Scott here had stuck to a more legitimate field of study such as the Anasazi."

"Exactly my point," Gilbert said. "Between the Anasazi and her other pursuits she's overworked and no doubt suffering from exhaustion. Look at the temperatures where she's been working in New Mexico. Over a hundred degrees every day for the last two weeks. That's enough to fry anybody's brain."

"My brain's fine," Nick said.

Gilbert shook his head. "People having nervous breakdowns seldom know they're in trouble. Besides, I think we owe it to her father's reputation to give Ms. Scott the benefit of the doubt."

"No, you don't," Nick said. "My work stands on its own. My father has nothing to do with it."

Bombard said, "Your unreasonable attitude makes me think

that Professor Gilbert may be correct. Perhaps rest and professional care will bring you to your senses."

She looked at Campbell, whose eyes seemed to say she wanted Nick's blood but whose nod went along with Bombard's comment.

"Very well," Bombard said. "For the moment, you will be placed on medical leave. You will be expected to seek psychiatric help. When that is complete, your case will be reviewed."

Every fiber of Nick's body screamed for instant revenge. She wanted to tell them to go to hell. Only that would be suicide. If a university of Berkeley's reputation terminated her for a hoax, whether guilty or not, she would carry the stigma forever. She had only one chance, then, to prove the existence of the *Scorpion*.

Holding herself as stiffly as a robot, Nick rose from her chair and left the room. To have done anything else, even so much as a nod, would have undone her resolve.

Ben Gilbert caught up with her on the steps outside Sproul Hall.

"I did the best I could for you," he said, latching on to her arm.

Nick twisted free and raised her hand, palm out toward him, a warning not to touch her again. "Either you're a fool or a liar. Who got to you? Who's using you?"

"Keep your voice down."

"Archaeology is my life, you know that. I would never do anything to jeopardize that. That B-17 was there in the desert and you know it."

"I wasn't there, Nick, so how can I know that?"

"You know I wouldn't fake a find."

He retreated a step. "Nick, I have my own future to worry about."

"What the hell does that mean?"

"I'm only the messenger," Gilbert said.

"Are you saying there's more?"

"I've been told to tell you to forget about that damned airplane."

"Who told you that, Bombard? Or is there someone else I have to worry about?"

"Take my advice," Gilbert said. "Lay low for a while."

"And if I don't?"

"There are times when even a famous father can't protect you."

"I earned my own reputation," she said.

"Then don't throw it away."

23

Once free of Ben Gilbert, Nick hurried across the campus. At North Gate, she checked to see if anyone was following before heading up Euclid Avenue to Hilgard. Originally, that area of Berkeley had been strictly residential. But as the university grew, the larger homes had been converted to rooming houses and apartments. Nick's apartment, like many of those on Hilgard Avenue, had been built in the late 1930s, a two-story wood-shingled Victorian with bay windows, gables, and a large front porch, now glassed in to provide an extra downstairs bedroom.

Ken Drysdale was waiting for her on the tiny stoop at the top of the outside stairway that led to her apartment. At her approach he rearranged the duffle bag he'd been sitting on, so she could open the door. More than ever he reminded Nick of her father. When he hugged her, he even smelled the same, a comforting mixture of sweat and verbena aftershave.

"I thought you were hiding out in Hawaii." she said.

"It's safer here," he answered into her ear before breaking contact. "Nicer, too. Besides, in Honolulu the sniffers were all over me." His tone of voice made her glance down at the street, which was wall-to-wall with parked cars as always. Nothing was out of place that she could see. In Berkeley, people had been known to stick with a prime parking place for months, only starting their cars often enough to keep the batteries charged. Drive away for a few minutes and you might end up parking miles away.

At the moment, Nick's ten-year-old Ford was only two houses down, and had been there ever since she'd left for the dig in New Mexico. Chances were, its battery was dead by now.

"Let's get inside," Drysdale said, "before we have sniffers raising their legs on us."

An hour ago Nick might have accused him of exaggerating. But her session with the disciplinary committee and Ben Gilbert had only compounded her growing fear.

"We've got more than sniffers to worry about," she told Drysdale.

With a hand steadier than she'd expected it to be, Nick let them inside, then bolted the door. Shivering, she turned on the wall heater. Most times, she welcomed Berkeley's fog-drenched summer chill. Today, she pulled on a heavy sweater and still couldn't get warm.

"You look exhausted," Ken said.

"Have you looked in the mirror?"

He ran a hand over his whiskered chin. "I'll tell you what, Nick. I'll make us some coffee while you put me out of my misery and tell me what's happening that I don't know about."

In the kitchen waiting for the water to boil, Nick brought him up to date. She started with Guthrie's heart attack and her father's denial of the present by retreating into the past among his beloved Anasazi. Then she moved on to her nighttime dash across the desert and a red-eye flight that got her to Berkeley in time to have her career threatened by lies.

Drysdale looked stunned. "Can they do that without proof?"

"In academe, tenure is the magic word. If you have it, you've got a job for life. Without it, you're little more than day labor. The newspaper retracted. They called my find a hoax. If I didn't have the navigator's diary and the names of the crew, I'd be out of luck."

"What's to keep them from calling that a hoax, too?"

"Nothing at all," she admitted.

Shaking his head, Drysdale poured coffee into two mugs and handed her one. "What about that newspaper reporter? What does he have to say for himself?

"That's what I'm about to find out."

Nick abandoned her coffee to use the kitchen phone, angling the receiver away from her ear so Ken could listen in.

When she asked for Douglas, the *Journal*'s operator connected her with the city editor.

"This is Dr. Nicolette Scott. I'd like to speak with Mark Douglas, please."

"I'm sorry. I guess you haven't heard. There's been an accident. Mark Douglas is dead. They tell me he was smoking in bed and must have fallen asleep with a lighted cigarette. His apartment was gutted completely."

Nick caught her breath, then shook her head violently at Ken. "Mark told me he wouldn't start smoking again even if they paid him," she said into the phone.

"I told the same thing to the firemen. Do you know what they said? Ex-smokers are the worst kind. They backslide and don't want their friends to know about it, to know they lack willpower to stick to their promises. So they sneak smokes and suck on breath spray. Pretty soon they're back where they started, two packs a day, and on the high road to lung cancer."

"I don't believe it," Nick said.

"I didn't want to, but there's something else, too. They found a whiskey bottle beside his bed. If he was drinking, that would explain falling asleep with a lighted cigarette."

"Was he a good reporter?"

"Damn good."

"Did you trust him?"

"Yes, but I can't reprint the B-17 story, if that's what you're getting at."

"I don't believe he died smoking in bed," Nick said. "And I don't think you do either."

"I'm a journalist. I print what I know for a fact, not what I think or personally believe."

"Well, think about this. If it's a lie about Mark smoking in bed, then somebody's covering up his death."

"The firemen could have made a mistake, but the coroner agrees with them."

"My B-17 wasn't a mistake," Nick said. "I was inside it and so was Mark Douglas. There were bodies in that plane. American flyers who deserve a decent burial at least."

"It's in the hands of lawyers, Ms. Scott, and out of mine," the man said, and hung up.

"Too many people are dead," she said to the dial tone.

Ken pried the phone from her and replaced it in its cradle.

Feeling cold again, Nick reached for her coffee mug but it no longer had the heat to warm her.

"There were eleven bodies on a plane that carried a crew of ten," she said. "We dig it up, and suddenly Beckstead, Clark Guthrie, and Mark Douglas are dead."

"It could be coincidence."

"And your sniffers?"

"Maybe I imagined them."

"Sure, and I'm not about to be blackballed either." Nick closed her eyes and saw Mark Douglas leaning on his cane next to the *Scorpion*. She blinked wetly. "I say we fly to Albuquerque and confront that editor."

"What good would that do? He wasn't out there in the desert with you."

"It would make me feel better, at least."

"Think about it, Nick. They're ready for us in Albuquerque, so I say we go at this another way. We could deliver that love letter you found. If we get enough women asking about their missing husbands, all hell could break loose."

"Are you telling me that you found the navigator's widow?"

Drysdale gave her a pleased smile. "Mrs. Ross McKinnon, Glendale, Arizona. A friend of mine at the National Archives owed me. I'm afraid that's all we're going to get, though, unless we fly to Washington and go through the records ourselves." He made a face at the idea. "In D.C. the sniffers run in packs."

She abandoned the tepid coffee to throw her arms around him. "Maybe one name's all we need."

He kissed her. His lips felt warm against hers. She was tempted to surrender, to kiss back and take him to bed. To hide under the covers from whatever was out there. When his lips parted, she broke contact to say, "I promised my father I'd call him as soon as I got the chance."

"I'll give you some privacy," Ken said, and left the kitchen wearily.

Nick dialed her father's office at the university in Albuquerque, where he'd promised to leave a number. Two calls later, she caught up with him at a mortuary in Santa Fe, where he was making arrangements for Clark Guthrie's funeral.

"Clark would have a fit if he knew what this was costing," Elliot said as soon as he heard her voice. "I'm not buying a sarcophagus, I told them, I'm arranging for a cremation. I don't know if I told you, but Clark wanted his ashes scattered among the Anasazi."

"Elliot, listen to me. Mark Douglas is dead, his story has been retracted, and I've been suspended for perpetrating an archaeological hoax."

"What hoax?"

"They say the *Scorpion* doesn't exist, that I made the whole thing up as a publicity stunt."

"Calm down, Nick. We know it existed. It's just a matter of time before everything sorts itself out. My suggestion is for you to get back to the dig and let it all blow over. If we prove my well water theory, your fame is assured. You can come work for me at the university. I'll get you instant tenure. Now, how soon can you get back? I don't like leaving my students on their own."

His question hit her like a slap in the face. The Anasazi were more important to him than anything else. How many times had her mother said exactly that, that the only sure way to get Elliot's attention was to turn yourself into an Anasazi? And each time Elaine had said it, Nick had denied it, defending her father.

She closed her eyes and for a moment felt like joining Elaine in her black well of despair. Then she smiled at the irony of the situation. Wells of one kind or another had obsessed both her parents.

"Mark Douglas is dead," she said. "He can't vouch for me."

"What did you say?"

As calmly as possible, she explained the circumstances of Douglas's death.

"It could have been an accident," Elliot said when she finished.

"I don't think so, and neither does Ken Drysdale. He's flown in from Hawaii to help me."

"And what do you want me to do?"

Did her father sound hurt, or was she imagining things? Whatever the case, she wanted him safe.

"Go back to your dig, Dad. I'll feel better when you're surrounded by students."

"And how are you going to keep safe?"

She smiled. Maybe she was running the Anasazi a close race.

"The first thing I'm going to do is track down that B-17's crew."

"If I don't hear from you soon, I'll come looking."

Nick smiled. That was exactly what she hoped he'd say.

"I'll be leaving for Phoenix," she said, "as soon as I can get a plane."

24

The official temperature at the Phoenix airport was a hundred and six, though Nick figured that had to be a Chamber of Commerce ploy. Judging by the sizzling sidewalk outside the Southwest Airlines terminal, a hundred and fifteen was more like it.

By the time she and Ken found their rental car, the soles of her feet felt scorched despite walking the last hundred yards in the shade of the parking garage. Next time, she reminded herself, stick to thick soled Nikes, not low-heeled pumps, no matter how businesslike they looked. Her choice of a tailored cotton blouse and loose skirt, a hastily purchased Macy's special, was lightweight enough for a California summer. But in Phoenix, she felt decidedly overdressed.

She kicked off her shoes the moment she got into the car. Ken started the engine, set the air-conditioning to maximum cold, and then began adjusting the driver's seat and mirrors as if he were preparing to pilot a plane.

He drove while Nick navigated, getting them lost only once before picking up Highway 17 north to the suburb city of Glendale. There, on Grovers Avenue, they found the McKinnon house, one of those small side-by-side tract homes with aluminum siding masquerading as wood. The walk from the air-conditioned car to the cement-slab front porch seemed to suck the air right out of Nick's lungs. In New Mexico, at least, there wasn't all this concrete and asphalt to radiate the heat.

"Christ," Ken said, "and to think I complain about the humidity in Hawaii."

The door behind the screen opened before Nick had time to knock. The woman standing in the doorway, squinting against the noon sun, reminded Nick of her own mother: diet thin, hair perfectly coiffed, fighting old age tooth and nail.

"Mrs. Lael McKinnon?" Nick asked.

The woman nodded, unlatched the screen, and opened it far enough for Nick to catch hold. When Nick hesitated, the woman beckoned anxiously. "Come in, dear. We don't want to cool the whole outdoors, do we?"

When Ken closed the door behind them, Nick stood blindly for a moment, waiting for her eyes to adjust. The house was cold enough to raise gooseflesh along her arms.

"Thank you for calling ahead," Mrs. McKinnon said. "That way I could have my son with me. He doesn't like me inviting strangers into the house unless he's here."

Nick nodded at the man.

"Please, sit down," her son said, motioning toward the sofa.

As soon as she and Ken complied, Mrs. McKinnon's son helped his mother into an occasional chair and took another for himself.

"Now," he said, "my mother tells me that you called about an old World War Two airplane. Is that correct?"

Nick had been thinking over her answer to just such a question all the way from the airport. Considering the circumstances, particularly the fact that the plane had disappeared, she'd decided to be very cautious. She also wanted to see the widow for herself, before springing a long-lost, and possibly painful, love letter. With that in mind, Nick had brought along a copy of her *National Geographic* story to help smooth the way and gain Mrs. McKinnon's confidence.

She handed the magazine to McKinnon, who left his chair to share the article with his mother.

"As you see," Nick began, "I'm an archaeologist who specializes in the near past. Airplanes are one of my passions, in particular B-17s like your husband flew in."

"My husband was stationed in the Pacific," Mrs. McKinnon responded.

Her son tapped one of the photographs in the *National Geographic*. "This is New Guinea, mother. That's the Pacific."

"I'm not senile yet," she snapped back. "Have you found my husband's plane, is that why you're here?"

"We found a B-17, all right, but any kind of formal identification has yet to be made."

"In New Guinea?"

Nick dodged the question by asking, "I take it from your name, Mrs. McKinnon, that you've never remarried."

In that instant, with her eyes fully readjusted to the dim light, Nick realized that the question needn't have been asked. The mantelpiece, the top of an upright piano, and the end tables at either arm of the sofa were covered with framed photographs of a handsome man in uniform. Some of the snapshots showed him in flying gear. He was smiling in all of them, a fair-haired young man, blue eyed probably, and college age if Nick was any judge.

His son, she realized, had dark hair and brown eyes and looked much younger than she expected. Forty, she guessed before her train of thought was interrupted by Mrs. McKinnon saying, "I never stopped loving Ross."

She nodded to her son, who abandoned the magazine to remove a picture frame from the wall above the mantel. He handed the frame to Nick. It contained a telegram from the War Department, informing Mrs. McKinnon that her husband was missing in action in the Pacific and presumed dead. Side by side with the telegram was a citation, the Distinguished Flying Cross, awarded to Ross McKinnon posthumously. The telegram was dated 1945, the last year of the war.

Doing arithmetic in her head, Nick figured Mrs. McKinnon had to be seventy at least, and her son a surprising fifty.

More troubling than his apparent agelessness was the War Department's lie about where Ross McKinnon died. Unless, somehow, the B-17 in the desert outside Cibola wasn't McKinnon's plane at all, but only contained his diary. Fat chance.

"To answer your question," Mrs. McKinnon went on, "a man like my husband comes along once in a lifetime. I didn't realize that at first, a young woman on her own. I thought I needed a second husband to take care of me and my son, but after a while I gave up looking. My husband is closer to me now than ever. Maybe it's because I'm getting older and will soon be with him."

As if by rote, her son handed his mother one of the photographs from the mantel. Her eyes looked vacant as she stared down at it, her fingers tracing the image.

Nick shuddered. Her own mother had that same lost look in the year before she died. Finally, Elaine had refused to leave the house except to have her hair done, a weekly pilgrimage prepared for with the exactness of an overseas voyage.

"Where did you find the B-17?" McKinnon asked.

Nick was still thinking over possible answers when Ken came to her rescue. "A long way from New Guinea, that's for sure."

"That's no answer."

"Someone from the army contacted me not long after my husband's plane went missing," Mrs. McKinnon interrupted.

"That was when they gave me his Flying Cross and told me what a hero he'd been. I'm sure he bombed Tokyo or something important like that, though the army couldn't say then, because the war was still on."

"Did any of the other members of his crew survive?"

She shook her head. "They all went down together in the *Lady Laurie*."

"Was that the name of your husband's plane?" Ken asked.

"There's a picture somewhere."

Her son plucked the photograph from among those adorning the top of the piano. The plane in the photo had one of those lush wartime pinups with *Lady Laurie* written in script below it.

"My husband was the navigator, you know. He would have named the plane after me if he could have, but the pilot had first say in such matters. His wife was named Laurie. A nice woman. We've kept in touch over the years, though the poor dear's had a stroke now."

"Is she able to talk?" Nick asked.

"I suppose you could try. Her name's Laurie Dexter now. She lives in Monterey, California." Mrs. McKinnon's face pinched with disapproval. "She remarried, you know."

"The plane I found wasn't named the *Lady Laurie*," Nick said.

Tears welled at the corners of Mrs. McKinnon's eyes.

McKinnon said, "They changed it, didn't they, Mother?"

"That's right. Laurie wrote to me about that. She'd gotten a last letter from her husband saying they might have to rename their ship for a special mission."

"What kind of mission?" Ken said.

The woman slowly shook her head. "The censors would never have let anything like that through during the war. But there must have been one, because they won the medal, didn't they? Every single member of the crew."

"Besides Laurie Dexter, have you kept in touch with any of the other wives?" Nick asked.

"I'm afraid not. The fact is, I don't think most of those boys were married. Most of the enlisted men were right out of high school, you know."

McKinnon moved behind his mother's chair and rested his hands protectively on her fragile shoulders. "Why is all this important now? And why are you here if you're not sure about the plane?"

Nick stared at his hands, then at his face. At first, she'd guessed his age at forty, but now she revised the figure down to thirty-five, tops. Which meant he couldn't be the dead navigator's son.

"Excuse me," she said, making it clear she was addressing him, "your name is McKinnon, isn't it?"

"Ross McKinnon, Junior."

"His father would have been so proud of him." Mrs. McKinnon said.

"You never knew him?" Nick probed.

McKinnon shook his head.

Nick took a deep breath. One thing was certain. Eccentric or not, Mrs. McKinnon still loved her dead husband. In that light, Nick didn't have the heart to keep the letter from her.

"The B-17 I found had a scorpion painted on its nose," Nick said. "I can't be sure of much else at this point, but I did find some personal effects. They'd been buried for fifty years and are in very fragile condition, so I couldn't bring the original, but I wrote out a copy. It's a letter to you, Mrs. McKinnon."

Nick handed the woman an envelope containing a transcription of the letter. Mrs. McKinnon handled the paper as if it were the real thing. As she read to herself, tears slid down her powdered cheeks.

Reading over his mother's shoulder, McKinnon asked, "Is that all you found?"

"That and names of the other crew members on board your father's plane. There's a chance, of course, that the letter was being brought home by another crew. In that case, the *Scorpion* would have nothing to do with your father."

"Is that what you believe?"

Rather than speculate, Nick shrugged.

"We're in your debt," Mrs. McKinnon said, rising from her chair to take Nick by the hand. "Thank you, my dear. You've brought my husband closer to me than ever. Now, you'll have to excuse an old lady." She waved away her son's offer of help and left the room.

"May we have the real letter one day?" McKinnon asked.

"If it's up to me, you can."

He nodded. "I'd better see about my mother."

"We were leaving anyway."

"One more thing," Drysdale said. "Would you know your father's army serial number?"

Thank you, Ken, Nick thought, realizing she should have asked the same question.

"It's written on his citation, I believe. Yes, here it is."

Nick wrote it down and thanked him again.

Outside, she and Ken stood on the curb, in the sparse shade of a listless willow, with the car's engine running, waiting for the air-conditioning to make driving bearable.

"Why would the War Department lie?" Nick asked.

"It was wartime. Morale had to be kept up."

"I might agree with you if the *Scorpion* hadn't been stolen out from under me."

"I didn't say I believed it," Ken said. "I merely offered it as a possible explanation."

"And why pretend the crew died in the Pacific? Or hand out medals, for that matter?"

"Like the letter said, it was some kind of secret mission."

"Are you playing devil's advocate?"

"I'm old-fashioned. I like things to make sense."

"What doesn't make sense is that someone's still trying to cover it up fifty years later. And why would P-38s shoot down one of our own planes over New Mexico? Even with that diary entry, I wouldn't have believed it if I hadn't seen the bullet holes for myself. That plane was shot to pieces, Ken, and I want to know why."

"Okay. You're the airplane buff, so answer me this. What's the range of a World War Two fighter, a P-38?"

"Maybe a thousand miles. I'd have to look it up to be sure."

"You're talking combat conditions, Nick. My guess is that the P-38s which hit your B-17 wouldn't have come all that far. Which means all we have to do now is find out what fighter bases were in striking range of where you found the *Scorpion.*"

"You're right. I'm still so mad I'm not thinking straight. Maybe we'll have better luck coming at the truth that way."

"Leave it to me," Ken said. "Us old sergeants have friends everywhere. One of my closest is stationed at the Historical Research Center at Maxwell Air Force Base in Alabama. It's a nasty place in the summer, but for you . . ." He grinned sheepishly.

"I'd hug you if it weren't so damn hot."

"The car ought to be cool enough by now to take you up on that."

They were about to drive away when Ross McKinnon hurried down the walk and knocked on the car window on Nick's side.

"There are some things I'd like to explain to you," he said the moment she lowered the glass. "I'm due back at work right now, but maybe we'd could talk over dinner."

Nick glanced at Ken who shrugged.

"I saw a Hilton near the airport, Mr. McKinnon. Why don't we meet at seven?" Nick replied.

25

With the Hilton Hotel in sight, Drysdale suddenly veered their rental car to the curb and stopped, his eyes riveted on the rearview mirror.

"You can catch a sniffer that way sometimes," he said. "Pull over when they aren't expecting it."

"And did you?" Nick asked.

Drysdale released his seat belt so he could look over his shoulder. "Not so you'd notice. If they were watching the McKinnon house, they could be ahead of us." He shook his head. "I can feel the bastard watching us. I can sense him."

Nick looked for herself but saw nothing.

"Let's face it," Drysdale went on. "You're at risk, Nick, until we get everything out in the open."

"Not if I'm imagining things. Not if Mark Douglas went back to smoking cigarettes."

"Your prospector could have been an accident, that much I can buy. But your B-17 didn't get up and fly away, and those were sniffers at my heels in Hawaii, not door-to-door salesmen. On top of which, it takes some heavy-duty bullshit to get a newspaper to retract a story, even if it is a lie, let alone the truth. So I say we keep moving. At least, I'll keep moving while you stay over to talk to the *junior* McKinnon, who's not quite what he appears to be."

"You noticed that too, didn't you?"

"If you mean his age, you're damned right. The two of them are probably nut cases. So we'd better turn over some more rocks."

"I believed her."

Drysdale shrugged. "Maybe I do, too, but I'd like to find someone else to tell us what happened, someone with all their marbles on board if possible. Which means we have to come up with more names. That's why I'm hopping the next plane to Alabama."

"I should be going with you."

"Don't get ruffled, but this takes a man-to-man approach. Besides, I'm retired military, will full PX privileges. It's easy for me to snoop around the base. You'd stand out, which is what I want you to do while I'm gone. Stay out in the open in public places."

"Stop worrying about me," Nick said. "If someone wanted to come after me, there were plenty of chances out there in the desert."

Drysdale sighed. "I covered your back in New Guinea."

Nick laughed. "You and your headhunters. We never met one, remember?"

"That doesn't mean they weren't there, just like the sniffer."

Nick kissed him on the cheek. "All right. You win. But call me from Alabama, and let me know your schedule."

He leaned over and kissed her back. "I'm already jealous of McKinnon."

"He's probably married."

Drysdale shook his head. "In that case, that mother of his

would have had another wall full of pictures, the wedding, the daughter-in-law, the works."

"McKinnon's too old to be single."

"And too young to be who he's supposed to be," Drysdale reminded her.

Ross McKinnon had a table waiting by the time Nick entered the dining room at seven o'clock. She'd changed into another of her Macy's specials, a wraparound red-and-black poplin dress that would have been too heavy without the Hilton's efficient air-conditioning.

For a moment he didn't appear to recognize her, though she could scarcely blame him. She hadn't looked at all herself in the bathroom mirror upstairs. On some women a new dress and makeup, something Nick seldom used, created a sophisticated look. On her, Macy's and Revlon were a lost cause. All she'd managed to achieve was a sense of looking as if she'd borrowed someone else's clothes.

As McKinnon rose to greet her, she realized that she felt nervous enough to be on a blind date. For that matter, the last time she'd been out with a man, other than at the Zuni Café, was her Dutch treat outing with Ben Gilbert. No wonder she was anxious.

Don't expect to catch a man if you spend your life digging in old graves, her mother used to harp. Strangely enough, Elaine had been right. Nick always felt more at home among the dead, the long dead.

She seated herself before realizing that he'd been about to pull the chair out for her.

"Sorry," he said. "When I go out to dinner, it's usually with my mother. At Lael's age, she expects to be catered to. Liberation is something the Allies did in Europe and the Philippines, not the status of women."

"I appreciate courtesy, too, when my brain's working."

168

He smiled. "You don't look like the archaeologists on television."

"You should see me on a dig. Levis', an old T-shirt, and a baseball cap."

A waitress as efficient as the air-conditioning arrived to take their orders: Caesar salads, quiche with artichokes and sun-dried tomatoes, and the house merlot.

Holding up his glass, McKinnon said, "Here's to dinner with a beautiful archaeologist who, I have a feeling, isn't telling me the whole truth."

"Women never do, you know. It's part of the mystery."

"Would you care to make an exception in my case?"

Sipping her wine, Nick thought that over. Finally she said, "I seem to remember you were the one who had some explaining to do. That's why you asked me to dinner. The truth is in your court."

He laughed. "In the funny papers, why is it that Lucy always pulls the football out from under Charlie Brown?"

"That's another mystery we women keep to ourselves."

He stared at her intently, his head tilted to one side. Then he grinned. "I have a feeling that you'd get along well with my mother. You're both very cryptic at times." His grin faded. "That letter you brought her, she's already memorized it. It's the final justification for her obsession. To her, Ross McKinnon didn't die in the war. He came back to her twelve years later. He made love to her and she became pregnant. As far as she's concerned the child is his, Ross McKinnon, Jr., me. As to who the man really was, I'll never know. I doubt if Lael does anymore. So you see, the only father I've ever known is the one in her memory. The one you brought back to life today.

"The reason I'm telling you this," he went on, his eyes avoiding hers now, "is that I don't want you to be misled by what my mother told you. She doesn't live in the present. To her, truth is somewhere in the past. Her reality is September

1944, the last time she saw *my* father. She made love to him then, and I was born nine months later, not twelve years."

Pausing, he took a deep swallow of wine.

"What about the telegram and medal?" Nick said. "Are they real or imaginary?"

"As far as I know, they're the real thing. I don't think faking them would ever have occurred to her. There have been times, I grant you, when I wanted to find out. But what good would it do if I discovered that it was all a pretense?"

"Except for the twelve missing years, is there something else I ought to know?"

He shook his head. "I'm never quite sure about my mother's world. It's been that way since I was a little boy. She's told me stories of my father's missions during the war, right down to details she couldn't possibly know. My guess is that a lot of her memories come from old war movies, greatly embellished, of course."

"I'm sorry. I might not have delivered the letter if I'd understood the situation."

"Don't be. You made my mother happier than I've seen her in years. There are times when I envy her fantasy."

He blushed, something Nick found naively charming in a man his age.

"Are you married?" she asked, bringing even more color to his face.

"I brought a couple of women home to meet my mother once. One she scared off, the other became Lael's instant disciple. I couldn't marry someone like that. Reality may not be what it's cracked up to be, but it beats 1944. Looking at you is proof of that."

Nick smiled at the compliment while thinking what it would have been like bringing men home to meet her mother. Unlike McKinnon, Nick had never taken such a risk. Elaine's moods had shifted so violently from one day to the next, from the black hole of depression to the sun-searing, manic heights of Icarus.

"What kind of work do you do?" she asked.

"Nothing as interesting as looking for lost airplanes."

"Airplanes aren't exactly my full-time job. Mostly I go on digs with my father, excavating Anasazi Indian ruins in New Mexico. Which reminds me, have you ever heard your mother mention New Mexico in connection with your father . . . her husband?"

"It's all right to call him my father. I do. Hell, he is as far as I'm concerned. And no, New Mexico never came up in our conversations."

"What about his secret mission?"

"I know he was stationed in the Pacific. I've seen the letters for myself. He wrote to my mother from Guadalcanal and Midway Island. As for anything secret or even as interesting as bombing Tokyo, I think that's just wishful thinking on Lael's part. The way I understand it, by 1945 B-29s were doing most of the bombing over Japan, not B-17s. And yes, she's fantasized about his secret missions, though mostly they belong in a John Wayne movie, if you ask me."

"Is there anything else you can tell me?"

He shook his head.

Nick said, "You never did tell me what you do for a living."

"I think it's your turn to come up with explanations," he answered, "but I'll go first if you like. I usually keep quiet about my work because it puts a lot of people off. I'm a district director for the IRS."

Nick laughed. "Archaeologists don't make enough money to cheat on their taxes."

"Then why don't you tell me what you and your friend, Mr. Drysdale, are really doing?"

Nick took a deep breath. "I found a B-17 in New Mexico, with a scorpion painted on its nose and your father's diary hidden on board. The crewmen's bodies were there, too, though I wasn't able to identify them."

His mouth dropped open.

"Before I could excavate properly and arrange for identification and burial, lawyers showed up, and claimed the plane. The next thing I knew, trucks showed up and hauled it away."

"Do you think my father's body was on board?"

"I don't know. We didn't find any dog tags."

"Are you're saying those bodies were there fifty years, since the day my father wrote that letter?"

"I think so, but I don't have any proof."

"That pisses me off, my father—or any flyer—being left in the desert to rot. God, whatever happens, I don't want any of this getting back to my mother. If her fantasy ever shatters, there wouldn't be anything left of her."

"That's a promise," Nick said.

He leaned across the table, staring into her eyes. "What are you going to do about that plane?"

"Your father's diary contained the names of all the crewmen. With luck I can trace them, though what good that's going to do me, I don't know. Still, it's a start. My friend Drysdale is working on that angle right now, trying to come up with names and addresses."

McKinnon leaned back and chewed on his lower lip. After a moment, he grinned lopsidedly. "The IRS keeps track of everybody. If you need help locating those crewmen, let me know and I'll bend a few rules if need be."

"I wouldn't want you getting into trouble."

"I want my father buried." He handed her a business card. "I want the right thing done."

"So do I," Nick said, reaching across the table to shake hands.

26

At first Nick thought the alarm clock had gone off. She blinked, had trouble focusing her eyes for a moment, then zeroed in on the clock radio's glowing red numerals: 6:30 A.M. She'd programmed the alarm for 7:00.

Something whirred. She switched on the bedside lamp and saw paper feeding from the Hilton's in-room fax machine. Most likely, it was some kind of promotional material advertising breakfast. In which case, she'd call the desk and raise hell for disturbing her sleep.

Once out of bed, the air-conditioning made her wish for a flannel nightgown. Goose bumps were climbing her spine as she read the printout. Ken Drysdale was on the other end, faxing her from Alabama where, she calculated, it was an hour later, the beginning of the military's working day.

I have narrowed the field, Drysdale wrote, to the 36th Fighter Training Squadron based near Las Cruces, New Mexico. The only other P-38 base in the region would have been at the extreme limit of their service range. In any case, the 36th has to be the right choice, judging by the hell that's starting to break loose here because of my questions.

What did he mean by that? she wondered. Gooseflesh spread from her spine to every nook and cranny.

This fax is being transmitted without authorization. So there goes my retirement. In any case, I have the names of pilots in advanced training at the 36th as of January 1945. Joseph Abbot, Timothy Carlson, John Clay, Henry Eames, George Fuller, Richard Gilchrist, Gilbert Holcomb, Lawrence Knowles, William Nash, Jessie Peterson, Joseph Twombly, and Ira Weissman. I don't have present-day addresses for them yet, but

The rest of the page was blank.

Dammit. She pulled off the bedspread and wrapped it around her. Why had the fax broken off? Surely nothing could happen to him on an air force base.

Nick scribbled a note on hotel stationary—*Ken, get out of there*—punched in the origination number at the top of Drysdale's fax, and transmitted her reply. After that, she sat huddled on the edge of the bed, watching the fax machine and counting off the minutes on the clock. When five minutes had crept by, she grabbed the phone. She had trouble getting an outside line momentarily, and then called long distance information to get a number for Maxwell Air Force Base. After that, it took three transfers to reach the public information office.

"This is Corporal Miles."

"I'm trying to locate Master Sergeant Lewin," Nick said. "He's stationed there."

"Are you a relative?"

"Actually, a friend of mine, Ken Drysdale, was meeting Sergeant Lewin on your base. I'd like to speak to either one of them."

"Sergeant Lewin is on emergency leave."

"As of when?"

"I'm not authorized to give out that information."

"Mr. Drysdale faxed me from your base just a few moments ago."

"What's his rank?"

"He's retired."

"You must be mistaken. Only authorized, active-duty personnel may use military facilities."

"Mr. Drysdale is a retired master sergeant," Nick said. "I can assure you that he's on that base."

"I'll transfer you to the visitors' center," the corporal replied.

A moment later, a deep male voice said, "This is Lieutenant Murray."

Forcing herself to sound calm, Nick identified herself and explained her quest a second time.

"I'll have to check the visitor's list."

"I'll hold on."

"It will take some time."

"I have no intention of hanging up," she told him.

"Yes, ma'am."

Five minutes later, still waiting, Nick carried the phone into the bathroom and began brushing her teeth. She had a mouth full of foam when Lieutenant Murray came on the line again. "Ms. Scott?"

"Yes?" she managed.

"I have no record of a Mr. Drysdale signing onto the base. Are you sure you have the right name?"

Nick swallowed her toothpaste. "He was there visiting a Sergeant Lewin."

"He's on leave."

"So I've been told. Just tell me when he left and where I can reach him."

"I'm sorry, ma'am. I can't help you on that."

At the sound of the dial tone, Nick clenched her teeth in frustration. Her stomach rumbled, objecting to the toothpaste. For a moment, she thought she was going to be sick.

Shakily, she read the label on the toothpaste tube, fearing to find a Do Not Swallow warning. But there was no such disclaimer.

"Relax," she told herself. "You're panicking."

She drank a glass of water to dilute the contents of her stomach, made certain the in-room hair dryer worked, then stood under the shower a long time, thinking over the situation. The worst Ken had done was break some damned military regulation by using the fax. Surely they wouldn't arrest him for something like that. Besides, Ken would have sense enough to pay the line charges if it came to a confrontation.

What then? Maybe they'd thrown him off the base and didn't want to admit the fact to an outsider. That sounded like the military, all right. But why would they bother lying about it? Why would they say he'd never been there?

Cover-up was part of the military mentality, Ken had told her often enough. Still, it didn't make sense. Most likely, it was some mistake, some paperwork mix-up. Probably he was on his way to the airport. By this evening, they'd be at her apartment in Berkeley laughing about her panic.

She sighed. That made sense. Even the military would realize the futility of locking the barn door after their secrets had escaped.

So why did the goose bumps come back the moment she stepped out of the shower? Because they always did, she reminded herself. Even so, she retrieved the fax from the bedroom and kept it with her while she dried her hair. Her feeling of vulnerability continued until she was fully dressed and sipping what passed for in-room coffee, strong enough to set her teeth on edge and fuel her anger.

If the military or anyone else thought she was going to back off, they had a big surprise coming. She'd raise hell, starting right now. She retrieved Ross McKinnon's business card from her purse and called him at the local IRS office.

"Are you home already?" He sounded delighted to hear from her.

"I haven't left the Hilton yet."

"There's still hope for me, then. How about lunch?"

"I know a great place in Berkeley."

He laughed.

"Is your offer of help still open?" she said.

"Absolutely."

"Ken Drysdale sent me a fax with the names of twelve World War Two pilots."

"The IRS frowns on doing personal business over the phone, which means I'm going to have to see you again to get those names."

"My plane leaves in two hours."

"Tell me which airline and I'll meet you at the airport."

"Southwest."

"Thirty minutes?"

"I haven't had breakfast yet."

"I'll eat one with you, then."

The airport restaurant looked as if it had been cloned from McDonald's, but the croissants were up-market and crispy. Nick, wearing her number-one Macy's special, blouse and skirt, now badly wrinkled despite labeled promises of iron-free care, added marmalade to her croissant while McKinnon read the fax.

As soon as he finished, he asked, "Any idea why it ended so abruptly?"

"If I had to guess, I'd say someone walked in on him and switched off the machine."

"We should make copies of this."

"I already did that at the hotel. You can keep that one. I have another in my purse. I also mailed one to myself."

McKinnon toyed with his croissant. "Why would you take that kind of precaution?"

To avoid answering immediately, Nick bit into her pastry and took her time chewing. What would he think if she told him everything? Would he think her crazy?

She swallowed convulsively. Going down, the croissant felt as though it had sharp edges.

"Do you think your friend's in trouble?" McKinnon asked.

"I hope not."

"Even if somebody walked in on him," McKinnon went on, "that's no big deal. You don't hang a person for unauthorized use of equipment."

"You don't kill someone for writing the truth, either. But the reporter who wrote about my B-17 is dead. So is the man who found it in the first place." Nick shuddered.

McKinnon leaned across the table to take hold of her hand. Concern showed in his face.

"You know something, Ms. Scott. I think you're the kind of woman a man like me could take home to his mother."

The breath went out of her.

"Now stop stalling," he said, "and tell me what the hell's going on."

Nick hesitated. She prided herself on being self-sufficient. She'd had to be. Her mother hadn't been capable of cooking dinner, or choosing what clothes to wear, let alone looking after anyone. Nick had been the woman of the house as far back as she could remember.

McKinnon squeezed her hand. "You have my promise. I'll run these names through the computer as soon as I get back to the office. One way or another, I'll track them down for you." He grinned. "Who knows? We might even come up with some back taxes owed."

Suddenly, the words started tumbling out, her initial discovery of the B-17, followed by Beckstead's death, the arrival of his so-called next of kin, Guthrie's heart attack, and the death of Mark Douglas and his story in the *Albuquerque Journal*.

For a long time after she stopped talking, McKinnon just stared at her. Every once in a while he'd take a bite of croissant and chew thoughtfully, his eyes never leaving her, his free hand holding onto to hers. She regretted her frankness, but the need to tell someone, anyone, had completely overwhelmed her. She'd just have to hope she could trust him.

Finally, she could stand it no longer. "Say something, dammit."

"Jesus, Nick. I don't want to believe any of it, but I do."

"Thank God for that at least."

"How do you feel about displays of affection in public?"

"What?"

Without answering, or letting go of her hand, he rose from his chair and kissed her. His touch was electric, though it didn't rival that first contact with the *Scorpion*'s wingtip. Some romantic she was, Nick thought, and put more effort into the kiss. The wattage was increasing when she remembered where she was and pulled away from him. He licked his lips and sat down again.

What the hell was she thinking? She hardly knew the man. From noon yesterday until now was not enough time to fall in love. It had to be adrenaline, that's all, triggered by Ken's fax, by her fears, and by feeling so damned alone. McKinnon was an available shoulder to lean, nothing more. He was good-looking, though, no doubt about that.

"I don't want you to go," he said.

"Ken expects me to be in Berkeley. If he's all right, that's where he'll come, to my apartment."

"If what you've been telling me turns out to be true, if people have been killed deliberately, then maybe you shouldn't go there."

She thought that over for a moment, fingering the chain that held the dog tag around her neck. "There's some research I have to do. But I'll be careful."

"When I track down those names of yours, it will be from confidential sources. That's not the kind of information I want to leave on your answering machine."

"So say something cryptic. No names or anything. I'll recognize your voice and call you back."

She stood up. "It's time for my plane."

"Be careful," he said.

"You, too."

"Don't worry about me," McKinnon said. "Everybody's afraid of the IRS."

27

Drysdale wondered why the MPs had kept him so long without bothering to question him. For that matter, nobody had said a word after locking him up. That was three hours ago and him sweating blood the whole time. And for nothing, it turned out, because here he was being escorted to his car, MPs on either side of him, practicing that ice-cold straight ahead stare of theirs. Well, by God, two could play that game. He set his teeth and glared.

He just hoped that Nick had gotten his fax. To make sure, he'd phone her the moment he reached the airport.

One of the MPs handed over the car keys and stepped back, hand on his holster, as if to increase his field of fire.

"Intimidation doesn't work on civilians," Drysdale said, then opened the door and slid into the driver's seat.

The moment he closed the door, both MPs pointed him on his way without so much as a word. Even the guard on the gate stayed mute as he raised the traffic barrier and waved Drysdale through without the usual inspection.

Drysdale stepped on it the moment he cleared federal land. At the first side road, he decided to head away from Montgomery, intending to circle around the state capital until he could be certain he wasn't being followed.

In that part of Alabama, the farm houses he passed looked as bleak as those old Depression photographs in *Life* magazine. The countryside in between was heavily wooded, not with big trees but that spindly second growth that comes after clear-cutting. Here and there, cows grazed in small clearings.

He slowed, enjoying the quiet beauty. Lowering the window, he took a deep breath of country air. For the first time since the MPs had walked in on him in midfax, he began to relax. He had the road to himself. In fact, he hadn't passed another car since turning off the highway.

Maybe he'd been worried for nothing. Maybe the MPs grabbing him had been pure chance. Sure, technically he'd been using military property for personal use, but so what. Everybody did it, or so his buddy, George Lewin, had said when he turned a blind eye. So what set off the MPs? The only thing Drysdale could think of was his records check. But hell, that didn't make sense. Old Air Corps records weren't usually classified. And even if they were, any reporter armed with the Freedom of Information Act could get access if determined enough. Besides, old P-38s were nothing but relics, antiques practically, nothing to get stirred up about. The B-17 was ancient history, too, for that matter. Even if they'd lost track of it by mistake and felt guilty about the bodies turning up after so many years, there was no reason to get excited.

So why had the MPs come down on him? Acting on orders, of course. But whose? Just like the lawyers showing up in the desert and stealing Nick's find. Nothing made sense, but it was happening just the same.

Drysdale checked the rearview mirror. Nothing.

You're getting paranoid, he told himself. *Tell that to Mark Douglas.*

Son of a bitch! A windshield glinted up ahead. He double-checked the rearview again. Sniffers liked nothing better than to sandwich you, one vehicle in front, another trailing. But the road behind him remained clear.

He squinted against the afternoon sun. A quarter of a mile ahead, a red pickup truck was parked on a dirt side road. Just sitting there.

Drysdale picked up speed, until he was doing seventy-five as he passed the pickup. In the rearview, dust rose as the truck turned onto the road and followed him.

Drysdale began to sweat. Part of him figured the truck being there was just coincidence, the rest of him felt foolish for turning onto a side road in the first place.

Come on. Don't panic. Chances were that truck belonged to some Alabama cracker. Hell, sniffers stuck to discreet sedans, not flame red pickups riding high on oversize tires.

Still, he regretted his decision not to head directly into Montgomery. On the other hand, that pickup didn't have a chance in hell of catching his rental, a V-8 Thunderbird. All he needed now was a good straightaway, instead of all these damn backwoods curves. One straight mile. He'd settle for that. After that, the pickup would be history. As it was, seventy-five miles an hour was pushing it on such a narrow two-lane road.

Another glance in the rearview told him the pickup was pushing it, too, because there it was, holding its own, two curves back.

A warning sign, a double switchback, forced him to slow down. *There's no use killing yourself,* he thought. *If you do, you won't be of any use to Nick.*

He smiled at the thought of her reading his fax and knowing that he'd come through for her as promised. As soon as he got to her apartment, he'd say, Show a little appreciation. Maybe a hug or a kiss. He licked his dry lips. Appreciation was as good a place as any to start. Who was to say where it might lead?

He checked the mirror again and was reassured to see that the pickup had dropped back a bit.

All right, Nick, I'm on my way. And appreciation won't do it. I'm going to ask you to marry me. I'm going to keep on asking until you either say yes to me or someone else.

Drysdale nodded to himself and backed off the accelerator enough to get better control of the car. After all, it was broad daylight, and chances were that pickup belonged to some kid who liked nothing better than playing tag with tourists.

He was congratulating himself on coming to his senses when he rounded a blind curve and saw another pickup jack-knifed across the road directly ahead, blocking both lanes. Instinctively, he realized there wasn't enough room to brake. Drysdale swung the wheel hard over, heading for a break in the trees.

The drainage ditch, invisible beneath a heavy growth of weeds, was like hitting a brick wall. His air bag inflated as the Thunderbird flipped end over end. The car came to rest upside down.

Stunned, Drysdale managed to switch off the ignition. Then, bracing one hand against the partially crushed car roof, he used his other hand to release the seat belt and began squirming through the open window.

He was congratulating himself on being alive when he saw the man get out of the red pickup carrying a gun.

Ellsworth Kemp drove away from the burning Thunderbird with an entire Milky Way crammed into his mouth. The face grinning back from the rearview mirror reminded him of a baseball player who'd wadded his cheek with tobacco. Kemp resisted the temptation to complete the image and spit. With a Milky Way wad, spitting cost calories and he needed the energy. Dealing with Drysdale had been hard work.

Kemp hated it when they were stubborn, when they fought back. It was so damned futile. They always gave in at the end. He told them that up front. But there were always a few, men like Drysdale, who felt they had something to prove. In his case, Kemp figured it had to do with the lady archaeologist.

Well, fuck it, that was love for you. It was weakness, particularly for a man in his profession.

Driving one-handed, Kemp used the other hand to unwrap a second Milky Way. He sucked on it. He'd read somewhere that shrinks claimed that cigars were nothing but phallic symbols.

He laughed out loud. What would the bastards have to say about him and his Milky Ways?

He shoved the candy bar all the way in, looked at himself in the rearview mirror, and produced a chocolate grin. His teeth dripped caramel, making him look like some kind of kinky vampire.

He chewed noisily before swallowing his Milky Way. After that, he got down to business on the cellular phone, dialing the number he'd been given, aware that it was a scrambled line but following orders to be careful just the same.

"Record your message after the tone," he was told.

"As of now," Kemp reported, "the woman has no backup. She's out on a limb all by herself, with nowhere to go and no more options as far as I can tell. Even so, it might be best to chop the limb off altogether."

Someone picked up at the other end, surprising Kemp.

"Do you recognize my voice?"

"Yes, sir," Kemp said.

"There's been too much publicity already. What happened

today might cause more. It's best if we wait and see before taking further action."

Kemp said nothing, wondering if he'd be blamed for any bad publicity that might result from Drysdale's death. He shrugged. He knew his own limitations. The thought of publicity, or its consequences, had never crossed his mind while on the job. Thinking wasn't what he got paid for.

"I want no tree limbs removed at the present time. Is that clear?"

"Yes, sir."

"You can do a little preliminary spadework, though, if you get my meaning."

"Absolutely," Kemp said, smiling at the euphemism. Keep an eye on the client while digging a nice deep hole, just in case it might be needed later. Six feet long and six feet deep, Kemp's speciality.

"I want you back in Berkeley immediately."

"Yes, sir."

"With luck, there won't be any more side trips."

"Yes, sir," Kemp said, though side trips like today's were what made life worthwhile.

28

The moment Nick entered her apartment she sighed with relief. The light on her answering machine was blinking repeatedly. It had to be Ken, checking in.

She dropped her bag, kicked off her shoes, and made a beeline for the playback button. After three hang-ups, she recognized Ross McKinnon's voice instantly.

"Your records have been checked," he said from the tape. "At least one discrepancy has been found. As a result you're now being audited by the Internal Revenue Service. An agent will contact you."

"Thank you," Nick breathed. Ross had come up with something, at least one name if she were interpreting the message correctly.

Following another hang-up, there was a message from her father. "Call me back or I'll send in the cavalry."

Knowing he'd be at the dig, she phoned the Seven Cities Motel and left a message of her own. "Hold off on the horses a while longer. John Wayne is already helping me."

Two of them, she thought, Drysdale and McKinnon.

Fingering the Japanese dog tag at her throat, she dialed McKinnon's number but was told that he was out of the office and not expected back for the day. When she asked where he might be contacted, IRS paranoia set in. She was quizzed as to name, address, and phone number only to be told that Mr. McKinnon was still unavailable.

After escaping the IRS receptionist, Nick thought about calling Ross's mother, but abandoned the idea in favor of a shower and a change of clothes.

Ten minutes later, with her hair still wet, Nick walked to the campus, hoping to catch Marcia Sheppard in her office at the Asian Studies Department in Dwinelle Hall. Marcia, like Nick, didn't have tenure and had been stuck teaching summer classes. They were both members of the affirmative action committee, another grunt-work assignment for the untenured.

Nick was in luck. Marcia was holding student office hours for her class on twentieth-century Japan, though no one had shown up so far. Her office was one of those windowless cubicles in the bowels of the building. Gray metal shelves filled to overflowing with books and stacks of papers covered every inch of available wall space. The matching desk and chairs, one behind the desk, the other in front of it, were relatively free of clutter.

As usual, Marcia's meticulous wardrobe—a collarless herringbone jacket in old rose over twill oatmeal trousers that coordinated perfectly with a pink silk blouse—made Nick feel like a bag lady in her jeans and sweatshirt.

"If you're here on committee business," Marcia said, "I gave that up the moment my tenure came through. I couldn't get out of summer school, though."

"Congratulations," Nick said.

Marcia nodded. "I heard about your run-in with the disciplinary committee. From the rumors going around, it sounds like you got a raw deal to me."

Nick closed the door, sat in the student chair, straight-backed and uncomfortable, meant to discourage lingering, and removed the dog tag from around her neck. "I'd like you to take a look at this for me."

Marcia cleared a space on her desk, retrieved a magnifying glass from a drawer, and carefully examined both sides of the metal disk. Only then did she say, "Where did you get this?"

"On one of my airplane digs," Nick said, manipulating the truth. "I found it among the bodies."

"This is a very rare piece. Not many dog tags or medals survived the war. You see, after we dropped the bomb and Japan surrendered, their soldiers were terrified of our troops. They thought we'd do the same things to them that they'd done to those they conquered. As a result, most Japanese soldiers destroyed the evidence of their military service before the occupation forces landed."

Marcia held the disk between her fingers, turning it under the magnifying lens. "This one in particular is a collector's item. It belonged to an admiral, one Hitoshi Manabe. I'd take good care of it, if I were you." She handed it back. "It ought to wrapped in cotton and sealed in plastic."

"I'll put it in a safe deposit box as soon as I can. In the meantime"—Nick fitted the dog tag into place again, out of sight under her sweatshirt—"is anything known about this Admiral Manabe?"

Marcia plucked a reference book from a shelf directly behind her, checked it briefly, then retrieved another volume, this one in Japanese, which she studied for several minutes. Finally she said, "The name sounds familiar, but I can't place it."

Marcia went back to her books, pulling another volume from her collection. "Here's a reference. He was a member of the Japanese General Staff during the war. He died in 1945. It doesn't say how."

Marcia ran a hand through her blond hair, somehow without mussing it. Nick sighed. Her own hair, glimpsed in the bathroom mirror before leaving the apartment, had looked as though a cow had been licking it.

"I found the dog tag in a B-17, one of ours," Nick said.

Marcia raised an eyebrow.

"In New Mexico. The tag was hidden inside a diary whose last entry was dated January, 1945, eight months before the war ended in the Pacific."

"It's probably a war souvenir."

"I don't think so."

"Why?"

"That B-17 got me hauled before the committee."

Marcia arched an eyebrow. "And you think the dog tag has something to do with it, too?"

"I was hoping you could tell me."

"The military isn't my specialty. Have you ever heard of Akihiro Yoshida?"

Nick shook her head.

"His book on the Japanese war machine is considered a landmark work. I'd like him to take a look at your dog tag."

"Lead me to him," Nick said.

"It's not that easy. He's retired from the faculty and a bit of a recluse. I don't know if he's even in town for the summer. Would you trust me enough to leave the tag with me? I'll show it to him as soon as I can."

Nick hesitated. If she involved Marcia, sooner or later word was bound to get back to the disciplinary committee. But Marcia had tenure now, so she'd be safe enough. Besides, Nick suddenly realized that she didn't want her job back anyway, not on the committee's terms anyway.

Nick handed her the dog tag. "You might as well know the rest of it. The B-17 I'm talking about didn't crash in New Mexico. It was shot down, probably by our own air force."

"Yoshida will love that." Marcia slipped the tag over her head. "I'll call you as soon as I've spoken with him, or I'll leave a message on your machine. Now show me where you found it on the map."

Marcia reorganized her desktop to accommodate a large atlas. As soon as she turned to the page featuring New Mexico, Nick fingered the spot.

"That's pretty damned close to Los Alamos. Considering the importance of that place in 1945, it's always possible the Japanese could have captured one of our planes and were using it on a suicide mission. In that case, it would have been hushed up."

"Fifty years have passed. Besides, a B-17 couldn't fly nonstop all the way from Japan, or from any of the islands they held in 1945."

"Maybe they took off from an aircraft carrier." Marcia rubbed her hands together as if warming to the subject. "Like Jimmy Doolittle's planes."

"A B-17's too big."

"In wartime, strange things happen. People innovate. Think about it. If the Japanese had bombed Los Alamos, history might have been changed."

Memory brought back Ross McKinnon's hurried diary entry. *Our own planes are shooting us down.*

"There are times when history should be changed," Nick said.

Dismissing the comment with a wave of her hand, Marcia scooted around her desk and opened the door. "Let me call Bill Varney over at the Lawrence Lab and see what he has to say.

He was one of the wunderkinder at Los Alamos back in 1945. He's also my ex-father-in-law."

Ellsworth Kemp eyed Dwinelle Hall with anxiety, hoping the morning rooftop fog wouldn't settle any lower. The concrete building was huge, a monstrosity, not at all like the ivy-covered colleges you saw on TV. It had to cover a square city block at least, maybe more. And God alone knew how many exits it had.

To make matters worse, once every hour students swarmed in and out to the accompaniment of bells from the clock tower, another monstrosity as far as he was concerned. So chances were he'd seen the last of the Scott woman. For all he knew, she'd escaped him in that last crush of students. And if she'd come out another entrance, it was good-bye until he picked her up again at her apartment. Or until her car moved, activating the tracking device.

He munched on a Milky Way and shifted positions, moving from one concrete bench to another. Five minutes more, and he'd give it up.

He triggered the timer on his wristwatch. When he looked up an instant later, he grinned. Damn, he was good. And everybody else so damned stupid. People were like sheep, creatures of habit. They go in one door and come out the same way. More like lemmings than sheep, he amended. Two lemmings, because Scott had picked up a friend, a blonde. Perfect. Blondes stood out, allowing him to fall well back as the pair began walking.

Kemp smiled. He'd have to be blind to lose a blonde like that.

Their route took them past that damned clock tower, called the Campanile according to his map, then east across the campus all the way to Gayley Road. There, on a wide street, he fell back another fifty yards.

When Gayley ran into Hearst Avenue, the two women

turned north. After a block or so, Hearst branched right and became Cyclotron Road.

He snorted. Goddamn eggheads and their word games. Where else would Cyclotron Road lead but to the Lawrence Berkeley Laboratory.

Kemp whistled as he walked, pretending to shoot the red squirrels from the trees along the way.

29

It was Nick's first time at the Lawrence Lab. Because of the nuclear research done there, she'd been expecting armed patrols backed up by snarling guard dogs. What she had to settle for was a visitor's badge and Marcia as an escort because Professor Varney's secretary was on her break.

"Exactly what does Varney do?" Nick whispered as they approached the man's office.

"He doesn't like to talk about it," Marcia answered. "And I'm sure as hell not going to ask."

"Weapons?"

Marcia put a finger to her lips and knocked on the man's door.

Expecting a demented Dr. Strangelove, Nick could only blink in surprise at the man who ushered them into his office. He was short, round, and jovial, and reminded her of a cross between Burl Ives and Santa Claus. His office was large by university standards, with two windows, and enough clutter to house generations of insect life. Most of the piles of paperwork had brightly colored Post-it notes attached with Day-Glo instructions: Do Not Dust Or Remove. Two chairs, recently cleared of debris if the stacks on the floor next to them were anything to go by, faced his jumbled desk. The only wall not covered with bookshelves was a collage of framed photographs.

A perverse part of Nick's brain couldn't help thinking that buried somewhere in all that mess was a forgotten formula to blow up the world.

"I could make us tea." Varney reached into one pile of litter and came up with a box of assorted herb teas. "There are cookies around somewhere." The only cups in sight were filled with pencils, marker pens, and paper clips.

"Thank you, no," Nick said. "I've already had too much coffee as it is."

Marcia took her eyes off the cups long enough to decline his offer.

"Well, then," he said, nodding at Marcia, "on the phone, you said you had a mystery concerning my days at Los Alamos."

"Nick's the one with the mystery."

Varney smiled and the resemblance to Santa Clause became stronger. Had Nick been twenty years younger, she'd have climbed on his lap and given him her wish list. Instead, she recounted her discovery of the *Scorpion*, its condition, its eventual removal from the site, and the deaths surrounding it. All the while she spoke quietly, with only her fingers trembling at the exertion of holding her emotions in check. She concluded by pointing out that her discovery in the desert had gotten her suspended from the university.

When she finished speaking, Varney didn't answer immediately, but leaned back in his chair, laced his hands behind his neck, and closed his eyes. After a while his head began nodding as if agreeing with some unspoken questions. When it changed direction, becoming negative, he said, "I don't think there could have been an attempted attack on Los Alamos, by your B-17 or anything else, without rumors getting out. Besides, we were the best-kept secret of the war."

His eyes opened to a squint. "I doubt if the Japanese had so much as a clue about us. As for your identity disk, my guess would be that it's nothing but a war souvenir."

"I thought the same thing," Marcia said.

"There were eleven bodies on the plane," Nick said. "A B-17 carries a crew of ten."

Varney unlaced his hands and leaned forward. "There's another possibility, though I hope it's not true. That plane could have been part of some radiation experiment."

"It was full of bullet holes," Nick said.

"An atomic detonation stirs up a lot of debris. Rocks, even pebbles, are as good as shrapnel when hurled against a target with enough force."

"And the P-38s?"

Varney shrugged. "There are such things as coincidences."

"You don't cover up coincidences." Nick was losing patience, both with Varney and herself. What had she expected from a physicist? She would have been better off consulting an aeronautical engineer.

"I can see that you believe what you're saying," Varney said. "Maybe I do, too, because I've spent half my life dealing with the military. They'd stamp everything top secret if they could get away with it. That way they wouldn't have to answer to anyone. Which is damn near true when it comes to Los Alamos. If your airplane was connected to that place, you might as well forget about it. They'll stonewall you to doomsday."

He was probably right, Nick knew that, but she couldn't let go. "Did you ever hear rumors about something unusual, any kind of sabotage?"

Varney's laugh was pure Santa Claus. "Our biggest dangers were backbiting and infighting. One faction, I remember, me among them, was worried about burning off the earth's atmosphere the moment we tested that first bomb. Another group, big guns we called them because they were so damned loud and explosive, had only one fear, that the war might end before they got the chance to test their new toy."

He smiled grimly. "I can still see it as if it were yesterday, Army CIC agents swarming everywhere like flies on cow pies. Christ, they were all over Oppenheimer, thinking he might be a Communist spy, and all the time Klaus Fuchs was spoonfeeding the Russians everything there was to know. What a joke, but that's the army for you."

"Those must have been exciting times," Marcia ventured.

"Most of the time, I felt like an imposter. Here I was, a kid really, in the same room with the likes of Teller, Enrico Fermi, and Leland Hatch. Those men are legends. Me . . ." He shrugged. "After the war, I settled for the peace and quiet of teaching. Sometimes, though, I wonder what it would have been like if I'd taken some of the offers I had when the shooting stopped."

He snorted. "I'd be rich, that's for sure. Leland Hatch himself offered me a job. He wasn't head of CMI then, but was running some kind of start-up company in Chicago before he joined the Los Alamos project."

"Why didn't you take him up on the offer?"

"When the Germans surrendered he was brokenhearted. He thought the Japanese would collapse immediately and that his beloved bomb would never get a proper testing—on human targets."

Varney shook his head. "Come to think of it, if the Japanese had been flying that B-17 of yours, Leland Hatch should have been their target. He and his group of followers. Like I said, he asked me to join his gang once. They called themselves the wasps or some damned thing, because they had what Hatch called radioactive stingers."

Hair prickled on the back of Nick's neck. Someone like

that might have seen nothing wrong with using soldiers as guinea pigs. Maybe the crew of her B-17 had been exposed to radioactivity, perhaps during the Trinity test even, and then shot down to hide the evidence.

Varney swiveled his chair, spilling papers from his desktop, so he could point at the photos on the wall. "That's my memory wall. Hatch and his wasps are in one of those pictures."

"I'd like to see it," Nick said.

With a grunt, he eased himself out of the chair and walked along the wall, peering at the dozens of photographs. Finally he nodded, took one from its hook, and wiped the frame on his trouser leg before handing it to Nick.

Pictured were three men, one an army officer in uniform, his rank not distinguishable in the photo. All looked young, no more than their late twenties or early thirties.

"Hatch is the one in the middle. He always insisted on that."

"How old was he?" Nick asked.

Varney shrugged. "They say he got his Ph.D. at twenty. Back then, he looked like a teenager, but he had to be twenty-four or five at least."

"And the others?" she said.

"The one in uniform was a general, Tom Gault, I think. Hatch loved having military men around him. I always thought he would have worn a uniform if he could have gotten away with it, Wehrmacht gray or American khaki, it wouldn't have mattered as long as the rank was high enough."

Varney thumped himself on the forehead. "Now I remember. They called themselves scorpions, not wasps."

Nick dropped the photograph, breaking the glass. "The plane I found in the desert," she said, "it had a scorpion painted on its nose."

"Son of a bitch."

"Did they ever use B-17s at Los Alamos, maybe to drop dummy bombs or something like that?"

Varney shook his head. "That kind of thing was done up in Wendover, Utah. At least as far as I know. I was a junior man back then, you've got to understand. Look at the pictures." He waved at the wall. "You don't see me standing with Oppenheimer or General Groves, do you? Not like Hatch. Sure, he was younger than me, but he had the drive." Varney hunched his shoulders. "Obsession would be closer to the mark. And he was a member of the inner circle. That's where the real power lay. If a B-17, your B-17, went down anywhere near their precious security zone, those men would have known about it."

He went from photograph to photograph, tapping a fingernail against a face here and there. "Not many of us are still around now. Those that are left, like me, have signed too damned many oaths to tell the truth anymore."

"The picture I dropped," Nick said, "would you have a copy of it?"

"It's one of a kind, I'm afraid."

"Could I make a copy?"

"Why not? We've got a pretty good Xerox. Old Hatch may be a little grainy but still recognizable. Just what do you have in mind for him?"

"I'd like to ask him about his scorpions."

"Good luck to you."

"That sounds like a eulogy," Marcia said.

Varney stared at Nick for a long time. Finally he shook his head sadly. "My advice to you, young woman, is to forget you ever found an airplane or heard the name Leland Hatch. He's one of those men with eyes that burn right through you. He's a believer. To him, ground zero was Mecca. He worshiped there. He worshiped power, and there was nothing more powerful than the bomb. I cried when we dropped it. Leland Hatch danced a jig."

30

Leland Hatch ground his teeth as he listened to Kemp's report. When the report ended, Hatch took a deep breath to calm himself. Finally he said, "How long was she with Varney?"

"A little more than an hour."

"I didn't think she'd get that far." With a shake of his head, Hatch condemned his own stupidity. He should never have put the Scott woman in a box. Thanks to him, her job was gone, her career threatened, and her friends were dying. He'd given her no way out. Thinking about it now, he realized he should have tried bribing her the moment she found that B-17.

"What now?" Kemp said.

"Back off."

"Are you sure?"

"I know where she's going next."

Hatch tossed the phone aside and strode to the tinted floor-to-ceiling windows that looked down on New York's Fifth Avenue. It wasn't true that people looked like ants from this high up, he thought. Ants were more organized, they had a purpose, a common goal.

Technically speaking, of course, he could push a button, activate a phone line, and order any one of them squashed. It was also true, technically speaking, that to do so would involve him in a criminal conspiracy.

He smiled at the thought. He was already a conspirator, he and Ellsworth Kemp.

But the time was coming when Kemp would have too much accumulated knowledge. Then he'd have to be silenced. Such an act would require participation in still another conspiracy, unless Hatch himself performed the act.

At his age, though, that might not be so easy. That left his son, Lee, who still had a clear conscience as far as the *Scorpion* was concerned.

Hatch sighed. It would have to be Lee. Only blood was safe. Blood was immortality.

Still, he hated the thought of destroying Lee's illusions. Yet the only other option was to let Nick Scott run her course. And that could be dangerous, even if Hatch did know her every move in advance. Good intelligence went only so far. After that you had to be on the killing ground personally.

Hatch returned to his desk and played back the latest intelligence reports detailing the Scott woman's activities. Part of him couldn't help admiring her. She was far more resourceful than he'd ever expected. Not for a moment had he considered the possibility that she'd get as close to him as she had by talking to Bill Varney. Of course, the man knew nothing. How could he? He was a second-rate scientist with no foresight. Proof of that was the fact he hadn't joined CMI when he had the chance.

Hatch closed his eyes and, like a chess master, calculated the woman's possible moves. Whatever she did, he'd be right with her every step of the way via his highly paid intelligence system.

There was also the possibility that he was worrying for nothing. Maybe her friend's death in Alabama would bring her to her senses and make her back off.

Nodding, he picked up the direct line to his son, bypassing both their secretaries.

"We need to meet," Hatch said without preamble. "How's your schedule?"

"I'm free."

"We'll meet at home, then, just the two of us. Tell no one about it."

"Is there a problem?" Lee asked.

"In the meantime," Hatch continued, ignoring his son's question, "I want you to contact my pilot directly. Tell him to have the plane standing by on a permanent basis from now on, twenty-four hours a day."

Hatch paused, testing his son's reaction. Dealing with company planes, even Hatch's personal jet, was usually a matter for a secretary. To ask an executive of Lee's rank could be construed as menial.

"Anything else?" Lee said.

Hatch sighed with relief. His son knew when to obey orders. "Tell the pilot his mission will be highly confidential. I expect him and his copilot to stay on board until they hear from us."

"Consider it done."

"We might need security for what I have in mind."

"Kemp's men?"

Hatch smiled. His son was catching on.

"How many will be needed?"

"He has six, doesn't he?" Hatch asked, probing his son's knowledge of the company.

"We lost one last month, don't you remember?"

Hatch snorted. "You can't expect a mercenary to stay sharp unless the training's realistic."

"I'll have the five of them on standby at the airport."

"I'm proud of you," Hatch said and hung up before sentimentality got the better of him.

Then he rang for his secretary. The moment she entered he said, "I want you to arrange for a security sweep here and at my home."

"There's one due next week," she pointed out.

"I want a full inspection, every room, every phone, within the hour."

Nodding, she retreated, closing the door behind her.

Obedience was a wonderful thing, Hatch thought, especially in women. Affirmative action and equal rights were as dangerous to this country as drugs. Nick Scott was proof of that. If she got any closer to the truth, he'd have to pull the plug on everybody. He made a list on the legal pad in front of him. Her father, his students at the dig, the IRS man, they'd all have to go, along with anyone else she'd contacted.

"I hope you're satisfied, Ms. Scott," he said. "You are about to cause a massacre."

Hatch drew a line across the bottom of the legal pad on his desk. "That's your line in the sand, Ms. Scott. Cross it and I'm going to have to kill you."

Nick crossed the threshold of her apartment just as the phone began to ring. Thank God, she thought. She tossed her purse onto the sofa and dashed into the bedroom. It had to be Ken.

She snatched up the phone and collapsed onto the bed in one motion.

"Ms. Scott?" a man asked.

"Yes."

"This is Captain Evans, Alabama State Police."

She sat up. "Yes."

"Do you know a man named Ken Drysdale?"

"Yes."

"It's bad news, I'm afraid. Mr. Drysdale was involved in an automobile accident shortly after leaving Maxwell Air Force Base. He's dead and your name was listed as next of kin in his wallet."

The breath caught in her throat.

"According to our preliminary investigation," he continued, "Mr. Drysdale stopped at a bar for drinks once he was off the base. An hour later his car ran off the road and caught fire."

"He wouldn't drink and drive," she managed to say.

"No other cars were involved. His was the only vehicle on a country back road. He simply lost control."

Nick swung her legs over the side of the bed and stood up, locking her knees to keep from crumpling to the floor.

"Are you sure it's Ken Drysdale?"

"Like I said, we salvaged his wallet, and the rental car was in his name."

"Has there been a blood-alcohol test?"

"Not yet."

"What about an autopsy?"

"I'm sorry, Miss Scott. That's all I'm authorized to say at the moment." He sounded as if he were reading from a prepared statement. "We'll contact you concerning funeral arrangements once our investigation is complete."

The dial tone started Nick shaking. Only a teeth-clenching act of will kept her from hurling the phone through the bedroom window.

"Oh, Ken."

She sagged onto the bed, still holding the droning phone, and wanted to cry. But anger wouldn't let her. Ken was dead and it was her fault. She'd taken advantage of his love.

"Forgive me."

For what? she asked herself just as he would have. For giving up, because that had been her intention after speaking with Professor Varney. His warning had been clear enough. Anything to do with Los Alamos was off-limits. And it was foolish to think a man like Leland Hatch would be involved, let alone care one way or another about a relic B-17 in the desert. What possible reason could he have after more than half a century?

None at all was the logical answer. But if not Hatch, someone cared enough to kill Ken Drysdale. That much was certain.

Nick no longer had any choice. If she gave up, Ken's life would have been thrown away for nothing.

She needed to call her father, to seek solace as she had as a child when the burden of dealing with her mother had become too great.

She was about to dial when the phone rang in her hands. Distantly, she heard a voice saying, "Hello, Nick. Are you there?"

"Ross?" she asked tentatively.

"Yes, it's me. When I didn't hear back from you, I started worrying."

"Ken Drysdale is dead," she blurted. "They're claiming it was an auto accident but I don't believe it. I think he was killed because he was helping me. The same thing could happen to you."

McKinnon didn't answer immediately. The longer the silence continued, the more certain Nick was that she'd done the right thing. It was better to warn him now and avoid having someone else hurt because of her.

"Like I told you before," McKinnon said finally, "I'm not my father's son but I intend to avenge him just the same. For my mother's sake if nothing else, I'd like to see him properly buried."

"Chances are we'll never find him, or any of them."

"Then we'll put his memory to rest."

"I don't want you on my conscience," Nick said.

"You don't have any choice. I have the address of one of those P-38 pilots. And I've already taken a leave of absence."

"Where are you calling from?"

"The airport in Phoenix. I just now made a reservation for Boise, Idaho, where the pilot lives. I made a reservation for you, too, at the airport in San Francisco. Your plane leaves at six tomorrow morning."

"I'll make it."

"And I'll be waiting for you in Boise."

31

Ross McKinnon met her at the airport gate with a kiss that took her breath away. She held on, feeling a sense of instant comfort along with a rising excitement nearly equal to discovering a B-17.

"Whew," she said when she finally came up for air. "That's what I call an IRS audit."

He stepped back to get a better look at her. "I like the look, lots of leg."

She blushed. Despite the early morning rush to get to the airport in San Francisco, she'd chosen her clothes carefully. It was her one Saks outfit, a long-sleeve black velvet turtleneck sweater over a plaid kilt, slit up the side the way no Scotsman had ever intended. Her brown leather scuffed briefcase, the one she used for her classes, clashed.

He took her by the hand and led her away from the boarding area and into the main terminal. "I'm sorry about your friend, Ken. Are you sure it wasn't an accident?"

She nodded, looking around, heeding Ken's warning about

watching her back. No one except McKinnon seemed to be paying attention to her.

"There's still time for you to back out," she told McKinnon.

"I'm already in too deep." He smiled. "Love is a crime when it leads to misuse of an IRS computer."

Nick stared at him. Could he love her after so short a time? For her part, she was attracted to him certainly, but she'd been attracted to her department head before she got to know him better.

"The timing is bad, I know, but I wanted to let you know how I felt."

She squeezed his hand briefly, then got down to business. "Tell me about the pilot."

"That list your friend faxed to you contained twelve names. I could find only one of them in our computer, Joseph Twombly. By cross-checking, I confirmed that he went through advanced fighter training at Las Cruces, New Mexico, in 1945." McKinnon pursed his lips.

"What's the problem?" she asked.

"Very few people escape our computers. So odds are some of the other names should have shown up, too."

"Does this man Twombly know we're coming?"

"I called to make certain he was home, that's all. I didn't give my name or say what we wanted."

Nick took a deep breath. "Let's go before I chicken out."

"If I'm reading the map correctly, he lives less than a mile away. We can walk."

Nick remembered driving through Boise as a child. Then it had seemed like a small town, dominated by pine and cottonwood trees along the banks of the Boise River. Since then the population had nearly tripled. Now what trees she could see had a gentrified look, but the air smelled fresh enough, with only a hint of jet fuel from the nearby airport.

By the time she and McKinnon reached the Twombly house thunderheads were gathering along the horizon to the north. The house, like its neighbors, was a red brick square with two aluminum-framed windows flanking a front door. An aluminum awning overhung a concrete porch just large enough for Nick and McKinnon to stand side by side. A gray-haired man with a deeply wrinkled face opened the door.

"You must be the ones who called," he said. "What are you selling?"

"Joseph Twombly?" Nick asked.

"That's me."

"We want to talk to you about the war."

"Sure you do. But what the hell. I'm willing to talk to anybody these days, especially a good-looking woman like you. And who's to say? I might even buy something if you two are entertaining enough."

"Here's my card," Nick said.

Waving aside the offer, Twombly opened the screen door and ushered them into a small living room crammed with furniture. He pointed them to a sofa and took a facing recliner, whose upholstery was worn shiny. Behind the recliner stood a Formica-topped table with matching chrome-and-Naugahyde chairs. The top of the table was covered with potted plants, violets mostly, and a few begonias. Somehow Nick had been expecting to see flying memorabilia.

She smiled at the man. To have flown in World War II, Twombly had to be seventy at least, more likely seventy-five, but his eyes were twinkling as he admired Nick's legs. In contrast to the life in his eyes, his face had a pallor of illness.

"I understand you flew P-38s during the war," she said.

"Now, how the hell would you know that?"

"I'm an archaeologist, Mr. Twombly. Old airplanes fascinate me."

"Maybe so, but that doesn't answer my question, does it?"

He chuckled. "It's too bad my son isn't here. He'd get a kick out of this. Usually when I tell old war stories, I drive him and his wife away. Now here you are, making a special trip to see me. All the way from. . . ?"

"Berkeley."

He winked. "Seeing a woman like you makes me wonder if I haven't been a widower too long. And don't judge a man by his age, either. I still fly, young lady, and own my own plane, a Beechcraft. That's why I live here in the old neighborhood, close enough to the airport to walk, when I'm up to it anyway. My son keeps saying a man my age should give up flying. It pisses him off every time I pass my physical and get my pilot's license renewed. He works for the FAA, you understand, so I have to mind my Ps and Qs. I . . ."

He paused to wait out the sound of a jet passing overhead. "That's a 727."

"You have a good ear," McKinnon said, speaking for the first time since entering the house.

Twombly tapped a fingernail against the face of his wristwatch. "It takes off every day heading for Seattle at this time."

Nick, who'd been sitting on the edge of the sofa, sighed with relief. Twombly's comment about judging someone by their age was on target. She'd been expecting a stereotype, someone fragile, maybe even senile.

She leaned back, exposing more thigh and drawing his attention immediately. While rearranging her kilt more modestly, she said, "Tell me about your training at Las Cruces."

The twinkle went out of his eyes. "To tell you the truth, all that stuff about me bending ears with old war stories is nothing but bunk. The past is gone, I say, and talking about it won't change anything."

"Like I told you," Nick said, "I'm an archaeologist. Four days ago I was digging for Indian relics near the town of Cibola, New Mexico. Do you know what I found? A B-17."

210

Twombly's eyes narrowed. "That's a four-engine bomber. I flew fighters."

"There were bodies on board," Nick said. "I didn't have time to identify the remains properly, but I'd say they'd been there since the war."

"So?"

"I found something else, too. A diary belonging to the navigator."

"Was it in Japanese?" Twombly asked.

"He was an American, Ross McKinnon." She nodded at McKinnon. "This is his son."

Twombly shuddered.

"My mother was told he died in the Pacific," McKinnon said. "What do you say?"

"Did the B-17 have a name?"

"There was a scorpion painted on its nose," Nick said.

"Christ! They swore us to secrecy. We were ordered never to speak of the *Scorpion* no matter what."

"Who ordered you?"

He shook his head.

"Fifty years have passed," McKinnon said.

Breathing heavily, Twombly levered the recliner back a notch, then settled back and closed his eyes. If anything, his pallor looked worse. Sweat beaded his brow, confirming Nick's earlier thought that he wasn't a well man.

"Are you all right?" she asked.

His nod was halfhearted.

Without being asked, she fetched a glass of water from the kitchen. He drank a few sips, then pressed the cool glass against his temple. But only the sound of an airplane passing overhead seemed to revive him.

"I may be the only one left who knows what happened," he said after a while. "The fact is, I shouldn't be here at all. I should be long dead."

McKinnon started to say something, but Nick signaled for silence. She sensed that Twombly needed to talk. It was merely a matter of letting him go at his own speed with a little prompting.

"Fifty years is a long time to keep a secret," she probed gently.

"You're right. Besides, it's too late to court-martial me now. And those boys should be buried, no matter who they were."

He paused for breath. "We were at Las Cruces and then, when the war had only a few months to go, they shipped my squadron to the Pacific. But when we got there, we sure as hell made up for lost time. Every nasty mission that came along, we drew it. At least, it seemed that way at the time. Thinking back on it now, I believe we did draw the short end of the stick, because every damn one of us got shot down, me included. All the others died. But me? Me the Japs caught. If the atomic bomb hadn't ended the war, I would have died, too. Hellsakes, I was half blind from starvation by the time they liberated us. One survivor out of twelve, that's me."

He blinked at Nick, but she had the feeling that he was seeing only the past. She was about to prompt him about the *Scorpion* when he continued.

"Before we were sent off to the Pacific, a general showed up at our base in Las Cruces. None of us had ever seen a general before. This one had three stars and had just flown in from Washington. And what does he do? He shakes hands with all of us. Then he briefs us, not our CO, but he personally. We were to intercept a B-17 over the desert, he says, and gives us the exact coordinates. When we asked why, he said the plane had been captured by the Japs and was on a suicide mission. It would have been shot down long before it reached New Mexico, only the big brass had decided it was best if that happened over as desolate an area as possible."

Twombly stared down at his lap where his hands were

tightly clasped. "You found it, so you know what kind of country that is. After training there, even the Pacific looked good. Anyway, that day over the desert it was like shooting fish in a barrel. They couldn't even shoot back. The reason, we were told, was that the Japs had stripped the plane of all its machine-guns so it could carry more explosives. Now you tell me there were Americans on board. So why did the general lie to us?"

"Someone's still lying," Nick answered. "Right after I found the *Scorpion*, someone stole it away."

"The military?"

She shrugged. "I don't know, but it had to be someone with clout, that's for sure."

He rubbed his forehead without raising his eyes. "God, I think I've known something was wrong all along. I never said anything to the others in the flight. What was the sense? It was over and done with. But on one of my passes, I got close enough to see their faces in the cockpit. I thought they looked like Americans, but I figured I was imagining things. Hell, we'd been told they captured American uniforms along with the plane. Now you tell me I was right all along. That we killed our own and they couldn't even fight back."

Tears streamed from his eyes when he raised his head to look at McKinnon. "Your father, too. My God, I'm sorry."

"You were following orders," McKinnon said.

Twombly shook his head. "You know what makes it worse? They gave us medals for shooting down that plane. A formal ceremony, with all of us lined up on the runway in front of our planes. Then the next day, we were ordered to the Pacific. Out there, we *deserved* medals. If what you tell me is true, and I believe it is, I can't help thinking they were trying to get rid of us. That's why we got all the shit details. Hell, we weren't much better off than kamikazes. I guess we were an embarrassment to the bastards, because they'd made a mistake about that B-17 being captured."

213

"And if it wasn't a mistake?" Nick said.

"It had to be. Why else would they order one of our own planes shot down?"

"That's what I'm trying to find out."

"Bastards, that's what they are. An old man like me ought to be able to die with a clear conscience."

Nick leaned forward and spoke softly. "Did you know what was going on at Los Alamos back in 1945?"

"We knew that part of the state was a no-fly zone, but we didn't know why. We figured something secret was going on, but nobody suspected the bomb."

His hands unclasped to grab his knees. "I'd like to have my P-38 with me right now. I'd strafe a few of the bastards, that's for sure."

"I know how you feel," McKinnon said. "But we don't know who to shoot."

"Maybe I should start writing letters to the newspapers or some damned thing."

"I don't think that's a good idea," Nick said. "One newspaper has already retracted its story about my discovery of the *Scorpion.*"

"You mean I'm supposed to just sit here and do nothing after what you've told me?"

She hesitated to say more, but if she didn't, he might blunder around and get himself killed. "I'll make you a promise, Mr. Twombly."

"Joe."

"All right, Joe. Here's the deal. When we get to the bottom of this, I'll pass the information on to you."

"No offense," he said, "but people, especially young ones like yourself, get busy with their own lives and forget about old geezers like me. So give me your phone number and I'll keep in touch. That way, I'll know who to strafe if I can find myself a P-38."

Nick glanced at McKinnon, who shrugged.

"I'm not going to be home for a while," she said, "so I'll give you my father's number at the University of New Mexico. He's not there at the moment, but your call will be forwarded automatically. All you have to do is leave a message and I'll get it."

"Fair enough."

"One more thing. Do you remember the general's name who gave your squadron the orders?"

"You'd think I would, wouldn't you? Hellsakes, maybe they never told us, I don't know. In those days, when you saw someone with three stars, you came to attention, saluted, and stared straight ahead."

"I'd like to show you a photograph. Actually, it's a copy of a photograph and pretty damned grainy at that." She dug into her suitcase for the photocopy she'd obtained from Professor Varney, the one taken at Los Alamos showing Leland Hatch arm in arm with a general.

"That's him, all right," Twombly said without hesitation. "I remember the other guy, too, the one standing next to the general." Twombly pointed at Leland Hatch. "That's the civilian the general brought with him."

"You didn't say anything before about a civilian," McKinnon said.

"I didn't remember him until I saw the photograph."

"Do you know his name?" McKinnon asked.

"Nobody ever said, I don't think."

"Did the civilian say anything?" Nick said.

Twombly shook his head. "Whatever he had to say, he whispered it in the general's ear."

32

By the time Nick and McKinnon were ready to leave the Twombly house, the distant thunderheads she had seen earlier were directly overhead. The temperature had plummeted, from somewhere in the eighties down far enough to raise a shiver along her arms. Of course, Twombly's photographic identification of Leland Hatch had aided and abetted her cold chill.

Twombly, who'd followed Nick and McKinnon outside, took one look at the thunderheads and insisted on calling them a cab. While they waited, he said, "Usually I walk to the airport, but today . . ." With a shake of his head, he stared up at the threatening sky.

"It's a bad day to fly that small plane of yours," McKinnon said.

"Mostly I just watch these days. Takeoffs and landings, and maybe kibitz with some of the other old-timers. I still fly, though, when the mood hits me. Sometimes, when I close my eyes, I'm young again and flying a P-38."

He grinned. "And you know what? My hands still squeeze

the gun handles, and my thumb still reaches for the cannon button. Four fifty-calibers and a twenty-millimeter. That's one hell of a lot of firepower. A B-17 could take a lot, though, not like the kills I had in the Pacific before they shot me down. Still, it was a miracle that B-17 didn't explode in midair."

When the cab arrived, Nick said, "We can give you a lift to the airport, if you'd like."

Nodding, Twombly climbed into the front of the taxi just as the first rain began falling. "It's best to leave the backseat for the paying clients," he told the driver.

At the airport, Twombly followed them into the waiting area, sitting with them while they waited to board the next flight to the Bay Area.

"You've brought back a lot of memories," he said, "and not all of them bad. We were a tight-knit group, the twelve of us in my squadron. We were young enough to think we were immortal, even though the odds were that all of us wouldn't be coming back. I figured, like everybody else, that it wouldn't happen to me. But one survivor out of twelve is worse than bad luck."

"I'm sorry to have caused you pain," Nick said. "But I had to know what happened out there in the desert."

"The three best friends I ever had in my life were in that squadron. Henry Eames, Dick Gilchrist, and Gil Holcomb. If they were here right now, they'd be raising hell, knowing we were lied to, that we shot down our own men. They'd want me to do something. Dick and Gil burned, you know. That's the way fighter pilots go usually."

Nick touched his hand. "They'd want you to stay alive," she said. "And keep their memories alive, too."

Twombly shook his head. "Somebody's got to pay."

"That's why we came to see you," McKinnon said. "Working for the IRS makes me an expert on collecting what's owed."

When the boarding call came, Twombly took Nick's hand.

217

"I don't blame you for the truth. Hellsakes, I'm glad you came. You've given me something to look forward to. Justice for those boys on that B-17. Otherwise, it was nothing but murder."

Once the 727 broke through the thunderheads into clear air, Nick used the cellular phone in the seat back ahead of her to call her answering machine. The thought crossed her mind that her phone might be bugged, but in that case it was already too late. There was one message, from Marcia Sheppard. "I just got back from showing the dog tag to Professor Yoshida. He's very excited about it and wants to see you. He'll be in my office at nine tomorrow morning. If you can't make it, let me know."

Nick passed the message on to McKinnon, then consulted her address book before phoning the Zuni Café in Cibola, where it was dinnertime.

"It's a good thing you're not here," Elliot said as soon as he came on the line. "Mom Bennett's fixed turkey and dressing again."

Maybe she was tired; maybe talking to Joe Twombly had been too stressful. Whatever the case, just the mention of turkey and dressing made her queasy.

"Are you all right?" McKinnon asked over the engine noise.

She nodded in midswallow, wondering how long bad memories last. A lifetime. Twombly was proof of that.

"Where are you?" Elliot asked.

"Somewhere over Idaho, on our way back to San Francisco."

"Who's with you?"

"His name's Ross McKinnon. His father was on the *Scorpion*."

"Jesus."

"You'll like him," Nick said, deciding now was not the time to explain that McKinnon wasn't actually related to the father he was named after. In a way she envied McKinnon his cloudy lineage. In her case, she knew what genes she carried along with the worry that one day she too would fall prey to a dark depression.

"Why Idaho?" Elliot asked.

Briefly, Nick summarized her interview with Joe Twombly.

"That's hard to believe," Elliot said when she finished. "He actually told you they'd been ordered to shoot down the *Scorpion*?"

"Yes."

"And he identified this man Hatch?"

"That's right and there's more. Ken Drysdale is dead." Haltingly, she filled in the details as reported by the Alabama State Police.

When she finished her father said, "For your own safety, Nick, I think you ought to be back here with me. Bring this man, McKinnon, with you if you'd like."

"I can't drop this, not yet."

"I'm coming after you, daughter. Somebody's got to keep an eye on you."

She relayed the comment to McKinnon, who said, "I've already volunteered for that job."

"Did you hear that?" she asked her father.

"How old is this man?"

"Younger than you'd think."

"Please," Elliot said. "I need you here."

"I have an appointment tomorrow morning."

"Let me speak to this McKinnon."

Nick handed over the phone, watching as McKinnon listened, nodding occasionally. Finally he said, "I think you're right, Mr. Scott. We'd all be safer there."

Nick grabbed McKinnon's arm. "We don't want to get ourselves trapped in the middle of that desert without any witnesses around."

McKinnon leaned against Nick so she could listen in. "Did you hear what your daughter said?"

"Yes," Elliot answered.

"She has a point, but I think I've got the solution. I work for the IRS, Mr. Scott. In case you haven't noticed, we're paranoid about security. Our offices have bullet-proof glass and unlisted addresses in some cases. We also have an internal security system for those times when we have to go into the field looking for tax evaders. Once we get to Cibola, I'll call in my location. After that, if I don't check in every twelve hours, my people will send in the FBI to rescue us."

"Excellent," Elliot said. "When can I expect you here?"

McKinnon gave Nick a questioning look.

"Late tomorrow," she said into the phone.

"If you're not here by dark, I'll be coming after you," Elliot said.

"Would you really abandon the Anasazi for me?" Nick teased.

Her father chuckled. "I found another kiva and want you as a witness and an independent check on my work."

"Cannibalized bones?"

"That and water. Both ritual, both controlled by their shaman, would be my guess, though I don't intend to do any guessing in writing quite yet."

"Where's the new kiva?" Nick asked, picturing the cave in her mind. A second kiva there would have had to be aboveground and should have turned up long before now.

"Nearly a quarter of a mile from the cave, over the old riverbed if my calculations are correct. That's why I think water may have played a greater role in ritual life than we originally thought."

"I'll be there."

"Now let me speak to your friend alone," Elliot said. "Man to man."

A few moments later, McKinnon hung up the cellular phone and grinned at Nick. "Your father's very protective."

"What did he say?"

McKinnon wiggled an eyebrow. "He mentioned something about shotguns."

She aimed a gentle elbow at his ribs.

He leaned across the seat to kiss her on the forehead. Loosening her seat belt, she adjusted his aim until their lips touched. A definite improvement, she thought. A little more electricity and he'd be right up there with B-17s and proof that the Anasazis had one another for dinner.

33

Marcia was waiting outside her office at nine the next morning. As usual, she looked ready for a fashion show in her black-and-gold striped trouser suit and V-neck red vest.

"Professor Yoshida is waiting inside," she said. "Your dog tag is on the desk."

"Aren't you joining us?" Nick asked.

Marcia shook her head. "With a man like Akihiro Yoshida, you wait to be invited. I wasn't."

"I'm going in," McKinnon said.

Marcia shrugged. "I have a class anyway. I'll be back in an hour."

Nick knocked and entered the office, with McKinnon right behind her. Professor Yoshida rose from behind Marcia's desk to greet them. In his dark suit, white shirt, and conservative tie he looked more like a politician than a teacher. His head was shaved, making his age difficult to read, but he had to be in his sixties at least. Nodding, he came around the desk to shake hands formally, then waited for Nick to be seated before returning to his chair.

"Ms. Sheppard told me about your discovery," Yoshida said. "If you don't mind, Ms. Scott, I'd like to hear it for myself."

Carefully, aware that he was a professor emeritus, she detailed her discovery of the *Scorpion*. As she spoke, he stared at the dog tag on the desktop.

When she finished, he said, "Describe the scorpion that was painted on the nose."

"It was bright yellow with red eyes. Its tail and stinger were raised as if poised to strike."

He nodded. "Yes, that's how the story goes."

"I don't understand."

"As you know, my area of expertise is the Japanese military during World War Two. I was born in this country but was interned along with my parents. The war was a turning point in my life, and I've been studying it and its effects ever since. Your Manabe"—he tapped the dog tag—"was a member of the Japanese General Staff who disappeared mysteriously late in the war. Some say he was killed in an air raid and his body never found. Others say he's still alive. The point is, a lot of people, myself included, thought he was more myth than man."

Nick and McKinnon exchanged bewildered looks.

"I know what this must sound like," Yoshida went on, holding up a hand to forestall argument. "But hear me out. A story arose in Japan after the war. You might call it a fairy tale or an urban myth. Most people give it no more credence than those stories you hear about automobiles that would run on water if they weren't suppressed by the oil companies. Or the match that lights forever. In Japan, this particular myth is called the Manabe Mission. Had it succeeded, or so the story goes, the atomic bomb wouldn't have been dropped and hundreds of thousands of lives would have been saved."

Yoshida shook his head. "Seeing this identity disk and knowing where you found it makes me think the story is true."

Hair rose on the back of Nick's neck.

"Scorpion was Manabe's code name. It was a deliberate misnomer. It was meant to sound aggressive, to deceive the war lovers on the General Staff, but it actually referred to a peace mission. Hitoshi Manabe was its envoy. Secretly, he was sent by the emperor to meet with the president in Washington. He was to have been flown there on a B-17. But, as the story goes, the plane was shot down and the result was Hiroshima and Nagasaki."

"A B-17 has a crew of ten," Nick said. "But there were eleven bodies on the *Scorpion.*"

He nodded. "There's more to the story. The president had promised safe conduct, at least that's the way I've heard it told."

"We talked to one of the pilots who shot it down. They were told the plane had been captured by the Japanese and was on a suicide mission."

Yoshida closed his fist around the dog tag. "It's true, then. The war lovers intervened. There's no other explanation."

"Does the myth mention any other names?" Nick asked.

"Some versions mention meetings in Switzerland with diplomats and generals alike, but those figures are always vague and shadowy."

"Does the name Leland Hatch mean anything to you?" Nick said.

"He was at Los Alamos, I know that much. And he's very rich and very powerful."

"His name has come up in connection with the *Scorpion.*"

Yoshida stood up. "I'm an old man. I have little to lose. If I were your age, I would forget I ever heard the name Manabe. Or Leland Hatch for that matter."

34

Hatch gave no thanks for the report, but merely hung up the telephone. Good intelligence cost money; thanks weren't necessary, except to himself for having the foresight to provide backup.

But from now on, that wouldn't be good enough. Impersonal phone calls, technology, and satellite uplinks could only do so much. From now on, he didn't want to hear that the *Scorpion*, and everyone involved, was dead and buried. He wanted to see it done with his own eyes. That way, nothing could ever come back to haunt him again.

He called his son, who arrived less than a minute later.

"Kemp is waiting for me in Albuquerque," Hatch told him without preamble. "I'll be leaving for the airport as soon as you and I reach an agreement here. And one thing's certain. We're going to have to get our hands dirty."

Lee stared.

"Sit down," Hatch told him. "There's something I have to tell you. I never meant to, but now I have no choice. It goes all the way back to the Manhattan Project and Los Alamos, early in 1945. By then, the Japanese were in no position to attack us or anyone else. For all intents and purposes they'd lost the war. The only question was how and when they'd surrender. If it came to us invading the Japanese mainland, the military was predicting one million American causalities. So the bomb was a godsend."

Hatch paced as he spoke. "Then came the peace feelers, and suddenly an envoy was on his way to Washington to see the president. We were flying him in in one of our B-17s, a plane called the *Scorpion*. That's when a group of us decided the bomb had to be tested in combat. We arranged to have that plane shot down over this country, in New Mexico to be precise. Later, we told the president that the airplane had been part of a plot to assassinate him and had been shot down in the Pacific."

Hatch paused, waiting for his son's reaction. After a moment, Lee said, "I hope I would have done the same thing. But that's ancient history, surely?"

"The *Scorpion*'s come back to haunt us. An archaeologist named Nick Scott dug it up in the desert near a town called Cibola. Ever since then she's been raising hell." Hatch tapped himself on the chest. "It's my fault, really, because I didn't stop her soon enough."

Hatch precisely summarized the steps he'd taken so far, mostly through his intermediary, Ellsworth Kemp.

"I thought getting rid of the old prospector and reporter would be enough," Hatch concluded. "I miscalculated."

"So now we have to eliminate them all. That's what you're thinking, isn't it?"

"I wanted to keep your conscience clear."

"My conscience hasn't been clear since you fired my predecessor and gave me his job."

"I'm sorry."

"Hell, don't be." Lee grinned. "I wanted that job. Besides,

I've never forgotten what you told me. 'A conscience is for fools.' I was five years old when you said that."

Tears filled Hatch's eyes. "You remembered that?"

"I've taken all your advice."

"I'm proud of you."

"I don't think you would have promoted me if I hadn't listened. Now, why don't you let me fly to Albuquerque and take care of things for you?"

"You sound like me. It does a father's heart good. But I think I have to be there this time. I know every last detail, going all the way back to Los Alamos."

"We'll go together, then."

"I want you in reserve, if you don't mind, son. As soon as I land in New Mexico, I'll send the plane back with orders to stand by at the airport. If something unexpected comes up, though I can't think what, considering the backups I already have in place, I'll use the satellite uplink to call in the cavalry, *you*. If that happens, bring Kemp's security team with you."

"That's a lot of witness we'll have to worry about."

"Like I said, I've planned ahead. The Scott woman, her father, and a man named McKinnon will be handed to Kemp on a platter. When they're dead, I'll take care of Kemp if I can catch him with his back turned. If Kemp survives, you and the security team will take care of him. In that case, I want you bringing up the rear carrying an Uzi. A few more bodies won't matter as long as no one's left to point a finger at us."

"What about the B-17?"

"By now it's nothing but scrap metal."

"And the bodies inside?" Lee asked.

"Cremated."

Hatch stood up to embrace his son.

"Be careful in that desert," Lee said. "I saw on the news that they're having a heat wave in New Mexico."

35

The late afternoon temperature at the Albuquerque airport was a hundred and seven when Nick and McKinnon arrived. An hour later nearing Cibola, it was a hundred and fourteen degrees, well beyond the capacity of the rental car's air-conditioning.

Nick fiddled with the car's radio until she found her favorite station in Gallup. The heat wave was expected to continue three more days, with record-setting temperatures predicted for the badlands.

"Coyote Rock," the announcer said, "has already recorded one hundred and sixteen degrees. And tomorrow is supposed to be higher yet."

McKinnon grunted. "It feels like hell has opened up."

The truth, Nick knew from her study of the great drought that afflicted the Anasazi, was a high-pressure area with anti-cyclonic circulation. The result was intense surface heating and clear skies. But hell was more apt. God knew what it would be like out at the dig site. A hundred and twenty in the sun probably, maybe ten degrees less inside the cave. The thought made her thirsty. In temperatures like that, survival would be a matter of drinking water constantly. She hoped her father was keeping up his intake of liquids.

"Let's stop at the Zuni Café first," she said, "and order milk shakes. Doubles."

"How far is it now?" McKinnon asked.

"Ten minutes."

"Make it fifteen. I think I'd better slow down before this car explodes."

It was dinnertime when they parked in front of the Zuni Café. At the sight of her father's Isuzu Troopers parked safely out front, Nick let out a sigh of relief. Weather like this could be as dangerous as any assassin.

When she stepped out of the car and onto the road, the asphalt squished underfoot. By the time she reached the sidewalk, the soles of her feet felt seared.

Inside the café, the Coca-Cola thermometer read ninety-eight degrees. The wall-mounted air-conditioning unit sounded as if it were rattling to death.

Mom Bennett was sitting at the counter fanning herself with an old magazine. At the sight of Nick, she smiled, and said, "It's pot roast tonight, dear. I hope you don't mind helping yourself. It's the last I'll be cooking till this heat wave blows over."

"Nick!" her father shouted from a large table at the back of the café, where he was hemmed in by his students. "Come and sit down and we'll serve you."

Just the sight of him calmed her. It had been the same when she was a child. Burying herself in his arms and hugging him for all she was worth warded off the sense of chaos that pervaded the house when Nick was alone with her mother.

Two of Elliot's students vacated their chairs at Nick's approach. Another time she might have insisted they stay put, but for the moment she had only energy enough to introduce

229

McKinnon before collapsing onto a chair next to her father. McKinnon sat on the other side of Elliot.

"Something cold to drink," Nick pleaded. "Milk shakes if you can."

The students, looking skeptical, left the table to consult with Mom Bennett.

"We're celebrating," Elliot said, raising an eyebrow to indicate he wanted to keep his students ignorant of the *Scorpion* and its ramifications. "That kiva I told you we found—what's left of it anyway—was definitely built over the old riverbed. There were shards everywhere, the remains of ancient water jars. My guess is that it represented more than a symbolic entrance into the underworld. It was a well, symbolic or otherwise, from which sprang life-giving water. Probably the priests were in charge of it."

Nick smiled. Dead civilizations were much less stressful than dealing with the living.

"The drought is well documented," Elliot went on. "No rain from 1276 to 1299. If our new kiva dates from then, it's possible that some kind of religious schism occurred. After all, the priests were responsible for keeping track of the seasons to make certain the crops were planted on time. So when it stopped raining who else would get the blame? Chances were, they threw the priests out after a while and anointed new ones. In such a scenario, water might have become an object of worship."

Around the table, his students nodded.

"If Clark Guthrie were here, you wouldn't sound so certain," Nick said. "Don't try to prove your theories, he'd say. Let the facts speak for themselves."

"She's right," Elliot said for the benefit of his students. "It's too early to make assumptions. But next year, Nick, we dig at Site Two."

She groaned. To get from Site No. 1 to No. 2, twenty miles

of desert had to be crossed without benefit of road. Site No. 2 was smack in the middle of true badlands, where the plant life was so stunted it cast shade fit only for lizards. And next year meant next summer, working in hundred-degree-plus heat at an Anasazi site that offered shade only inside the cliff dwellings themselves.

Milk shakes arrived, thick and tasty enough to guarantee that Mom Bennett herself had a hand in making them.

"Do you remember the kiva at Site Two?" Elliot asked. Without taking her mouth from the straw, Nick nodded. Their initial work out there, a partial excavation, had taken place three years ago, when Nick was still a graduate student working on her doctorate. At that time, the kiva had seemed unique because of its location at the bottom of a shallow gully near the base of the cliff dwellings themselves.

"I've been checking my maps. It's built directly over the riverbed, I'm sure of it. And if you'll remember, that kiva is unusually deep."

Nick didn't answer until she reached the bottom of her glass. "By the time that kiva was built, the river had been dried up for centuries."

"Exactly. I think it's a well as much as it is a kiva. Certainly a place for rain ceremonies, or don't you agree?"

"It sounds logical."

Elliot nodded. "Think back. There's a large stone in the center of the floor. My guess is, if you pull it up you'll be looking into a well. It explains survival at such a remote and barren location."

"How deep would it have to be?" Nick asked.

"I'm no geologist, but I'd say the water couldn't have been too hard to get at. Otherwise, they wouldn't have settled there in the first place. On the other hand, that stretch of desert would certainly have kept their enemies at bay. So what do you say, Nick? Shall we go looking for water out there?"

Before she could answer, McKinnon laid a hand on her arm. "I think we have more important things to talk about."

Elliot stared at Nick for a moment, then nodded. "I know that look." He turned to his students. "In this heat, we'd better get an early start in the morning."

They got the point, said their good-byes quickly, and left the café in a group.

For the next thirty minutes, between mouthfuls of Mom's pot roast, Nick and McKinnon took turns bringing Elliot up to date on their investigation. At first, Elliot listened calmly, nodding occasionally, making no comment. But when Nick recounted Akihiro Yoshida's story of the Manabe Mission, Elliot shook his head hard enough to rattle cartilage.

"Since we know the B-17 was there," Elliot said finally, "I think it's safe to assume that someone wants us to disappear the same way the plane did."

"You believe Yoshida, then?" McKinnon asked. "That peace was sabotaged so we could use the bomb?"

Elliot nodded. "People have been saying pretty much the same thing for years, that there was no need to drop the bomb, that the Japanese were already defeated. Some think we dropped it as a warning to the Russians. Others say Hiroshima and Nagasaki were nothing but testing grounds."

"Christ," McKinnon said. "I think I'd better call in and set up an alert."

"Are there any strangers in town?" Nick asked.

Elliot shook his head.

"How much water do you have at the site?"

"Normally I'd say a week's worth, but in this heat, maybe half that."

"Tomorrow we load the Troopers with food and all the water we can carry and stock up the cave."

"We can't hide out there forever," Elliot said.

"Like I told you on the phone," McKinnon said. "Once an IRS alert is in effect, I have to check in every twelve hours. If I don't, help will be on its way. I can also call in a rescue team by punching a special code into my cellular phone."

"Wouldn't it be safer if we turned ourselves in to the IRS?"

McKinnon shook his head. "Only as a last resort. Otherwise, I have to explain why I broke the rules for Nick."

"Don't we all," Elliot said. "Still, your plan sounds as good as any. So make your call. And who knows? Maybe I can get some work out of you two while we're at the site. In the meantime, I think I better go back to the motel and get my students out of here."

Elliot paid for dinner, including his students', then gave Mom Bennett a hug.

As soon as she broke free, she winked at Nick. "I know how you feel about turkey and dressing, dear. So as long as you're here, you won't see it on the menu. I promise."

Nick added a hug of her own before leading the way outside onto Main Street. Even with the sun about to set, the temperature hadn't diminished. Heat waves rising from the surrounding desert gave the illusion that Cibola was an island encircled by molten lava.

"What's the problem with turkey and dressing?" McKinnon asked as they waded toward the Seven Cities Motel.

"Thanksgiving," Nick said cryptically.

"Food poisoning," her father added. "My wife wasn't the best of cooks. Come to think of it, none of the women in my life are gourmet chefs."

Nick glared. "If it wasn't so damned hot, I'd kick you."

Elliot ducked his head.

One of these days, Nick thought, she'd tell him the truth, that Elaine had disappeared into one of her black fugues that Thanksgiving week, talking only when Elliot came home in the evening. The rest of the day, she'd curled into a ball behind the sofa, leaving nine-year-old Nick to cope with the turkey and dressing.

At the motel, Elliot, with Nick at his side, called a meeting of his students. He told them he'd been forced to call an early end to the dig, assuring them that they'd receive full credit for an entire semester's work. His announcement brought smiles to their faces. And who could blame them? Nick thought. This kind of weather was an invitation to heat stroke.

Elliot broke out some six-packs of beer, further adding to the air of celebration, while everyone pitched in to load the students' personal gear into one of the Troopers and Nick's rental car, which was to be dropped off at the airport in Albuquerque.

Nick and McKinnon drove the second Trooper, the one she thought of as her own, to the general store, where Mayor Ralph, eyes shining with avarice, was waiting. They'd called him at home in advance. The size of their order brought him running.

Except for the front seat, every inch of the Trooper was crammed with bottled water, canned goods, and three individual backpacks filled with high-energy rations. Portable stoves, pots, pans, plastic dishes, and sleeping bags were already at the dig site.

The .30-.30 Nick kept hidden under the front seat didn't seem like enough fire power, so she purchased two hunting rifles, .30-.06s, plus ammunition, maxing out her credit card.

As soon as they got back to the motel, they loaded both weapons, then got busy carrying the mattress from Nick's room into her father's. That way, the three of them could stick together during the night, with one awake and one on guard at all times without alarming the students in the other rooms.

By then it was nearly midnight. The outside temperature, somewhere in the nineties if Nick was any judge, had the window-mounted air conditioner complaining.

"We can't hear anybody coming with that racket," McKinnon said. He'd volunteered to take the first watch.

"He's right," Elliot said.

Nick sighed and switched off the air conditioner.

"As soon as we kill the light, I'll open the door and watch the street." He pulled a chair into position. "Say when."

"It's going to be a long night," Nick said.

The moment McKinnon doused the light the phone rang.

Something clattered as Elliot fumbled for the phone in the dark. Finally he said, "Who's this? Joe Twombly?"

"That's the P-38 pilot I told you about," Nick said.

After a moment, Nick found her father's outstretched hand.

"This is Nick Scott," she said into the phone.

"I called to thank you," Twombly said. "I always figured I didn't have anything else to look forward to, but you changed that."

"I don't understand."

"I told you about my son, didn't I? I'm sure I did. Flying's in his blood, too. That's why he works for the FAA. Well, I've been onto him, checking into flight plans, if you understand my meaning?"

Perhaps it was the darkness of the motel room, but her brain didn't seem to be functioning properly. "I'm afraid I don't understand," she said.

"They couldn't kill me in the war no matter how hard they tried. But now the cigarettes have caught up with me and my lungs. That's no way for a fighter pilot to go."

"I'm sorry," she said.

"Don't be. Just tell that friend of yours, that McKinnon fellow, that he's a lucky man."

"I just may do that."

"You're my kind of woman, all right. I knew that the moment I laid eyes on you. I'd give your friend some competi-

235

tion if my last flight wasn't coming up. Now let's talk about that man Hatch. I've been racking my brains about him ever since we talked. No matter what, I'd say he has to be made to pay for what he's done."

"What flight are you talking about?"

"The trouble is, the rich think they can get away with murder," Twombly went on, ignoring her question. "Ever since we talked I haven't been able to get the *Scorpion* out of my mind. I keep seeing it over and over again. Only for once I'm not dreaming. It's broad daylight and I can't get those men out of my mind. They were flyers like me, and they died because of that man, Hatch."

"I think you should be careful," Nick said. "You're now the only witness left."

Twombly laughed. "Be careful at my age, with my lungs? Shit, it's that bastard Hatch who should be careful. I looked him up, you know, at the library. He lives like a king. He has his own jet plane, for God's sake, not a small one, but one of those big commercial jobs. Imagine that, not having to wait in line like the rest of us, or get stuffed into your seat like a sardine. No, indeed. Our Mr. Hatch has an entire airplane to himself. Probably he has his own bedroom on board, and who knows what else." Twombly clicked his tongue. "I say someone ought to shoot down that plane of his, with him on board."

"Neither of us has a P-38," Nick reminded him.

He laughed. "Don't be so sure. Besides, there's always a kamikaze attack."

"Where are you?" Nick groped for the light, then thought better of it.

"Back where I started from, you might say."

In the background, she heard someone shout, "You're set, Twombly."

"You haven't answered my question. Where are you?"

"Where else would a pilot be, Ms. Scott, but the airport?

That's my mechanic calling. When the time comes, a man like me wants to be in the air."

"The way to get at Hatch is to make everything public," she said.

"You tried that and it didn't work. Now I've got to call my son again and make final arrangements. In the meantime, you take care of yourself and that young man of yours. I'll see you in the funny papers, or maybe on the radio."

"Mr. Twombly, I—"

A dial tone sounded in her ear.

"What was that all about?" McKinnon asked.

"I don't know," she said. Probably it had been nothing more than an old man's fantasy. But Joe Twombly hadn't struck her as a man given to boasting.

Nick lay back, laced her hands behind her head, and stared into the darkness until it was her turn to stand watch.

36

They left Cibola at sunrise. Nick drove the Isuzu Trooper, while her father and McKinnon shared a single bucket seat between them. The two loaded .30-.06s were propped against the passenger door, safeties on and muzzles down against the floor mat.

Normally, the desert would have been cool this early, chilly even. But today, Nick guessed the temperature had to be well into the nineties already, hot enough to make her long to switch on the air conditioner. But the Trooper was too heavily loaded to risk overheating.

Shaking her head, she turned on the radio in time to hear a cheerful announcer in Gallup say, "We've got a real humdinger ahead of us, folks. It's going to be another record day. One hundred and twenty degrees in some areas. The authorities are urging everyone to take special precautions."

The announcer lowered his voice in an attempt to sound grave. "Everyone, particularly children and the elderly, should stay inside unless absolutely necessary. Keep cool and drink

238

plenty of liquids. Highway travelers should carry emergency water with them at all times."

His voice perked up again. "We'll be back with more news in an hour."

"If you ask me," Elliot said over a commercial, "we're in luck. Who the hell would be dumb enough to come after us in this kind of weather? Besides, they can't be absolutely certain where we are. The fact is, maybe we should change plans and head out to Site Two."

"Sure, and test your new theory while we're at it." Nick shook her head. "It's going to be hot enough at ES One without risking a trip across those badlands."

"There's water under that kiva," Elliot said. "I know it."

"We've got all our supplies at Site One. And once we're inside that cave, there's only one way to get at us. That's head-on. That's why the Anasazi built there."

"Is there a back way in?" McKinnon asked.

"Not really," Nick said. "Just a fissure in the rock that the Indians used as a chimney. I tried climbing it once and damn near got stuck."

Nick checked the rearview as she'd been doing every few minutes since leaving the motel. The road behind them was empty.

"One hundred degrees at seven A.M. in downtown Gallup," the announcer said. "Breakfast is cooking on the sidewalks. So's our music."

Up ahead, she spotted the marker they'd erected at the turnoff to ES No. 1.

"Hold on," she said for McKinnon's benefit. "Here's where we leave the good road behind."

Slowing the Trooper dramatically to keep dust to a minimum, Nick swung off the asphalt highway and stopped on the dirt track. By prearrangement, her father and McKinnon jumped out quickly and uprooted their site marker, a six-foot post topped by a red plastic ribbon. Once they'd stuffed the marker into the back of the already overloaded Trooper, Nick crept ahead in first gear for the next mile or so, until they were far enough from the highway to keep their dust from showing. They still had nineteen miles of dirt road ahead of them, though the rising heat waves kept them from seeing more than a half mile at a time.

"My God," McKinnon murmured. "I thought the country around Phoenix was desolate, but this is downright hostile. What kind of Indians would live in a godforsaken place like this?"

Out of the corner of her eye, Nick saw her father rub his hands together, the way he did when explaining finer points to his students. "First, you have to understand that the climate has changed since the Anasazi flourished a thousand years ago."

For the next hour, Elliot outlined his vision of Anasazi life, beginning well before the birth of Christ with nomadic hunter-gatherers and culminating in the great cliff-dwelling cities two thousand years later.

Finally, Elliot said, "The arrival of the Spanish explorers in 1540 changed everything. For all intents and purposes, the Anasazi culture came to an end."

McKinnon shook his head. "Christ, those Indians must have been a tough lot. I'm surprised they didn't wipe out the Spanish."

"Gunpowder is a great pacifier."

"Thank God," Nick said, startling her father until he saw her pointing to the canyon entrance up ahead, where the road passed through a narrow gorge not much wider than the Trooper. "We're here."

"My Anasazi knew what they were doing. A perfect defensive position. The only way in or out is through this pass, except to the east. Otherwise you have to climb over a mile of rock."

"What's to the east?" McKinnon said.

"Badlands all the way to Site Two. And once you start that way, there's no turning back. You're hemmed in by flash-flood gullies a hundred feet deep."

"This whole damn place is a bottleneck," McKinnon said. "Sure, you can defend it, but you can also get yourself trapped in here."

"Exactly. That's why I'm certain my Anasazi knew where the water was and how to get it."

Once through the narrow pass, the road led directly to the mouth of the cave, which at the moment looked as if it were grinning at them from the base of a mountain of red rock. Nick parked within a few feet of the mouth before killing the engine.

"As soon as we unload," she said, "I'll stash the car at the back of the canyon."

McKinnon stepped out of the Trooper, took one look around, and said, "This place makes me believe in spontaneous combustion."

"It's going to get a lot hotter," Elliot told him, "so we'd better start lugging the gear inside."

By the time they had everything stowed at the back of the cave, they'd consumed half a gallon of water each, though it seemed to leak from their pores as fast as they could swallow it.

"I'm going to move the Trooper while I still have the energy," Nick said.

"Maybe I should go with you," McKinnon said.

She shook her head. "We're used to this place. You aren't. The shade in here isn't going to last, so you'd better take advantage of it."

He followed her to the front of the cave just the same, where he took her in his arms and kissed her. This time, she thought, the electric tingle was right up there with a B-17.

"If your father weren't here," he murmured into her.

"You'd what?" she said teasingly.

He smiled.

"That suggestion could lead to sunstroke."

"What a way to go."

When he tried for another kiss, she pushed him way, but not too hard. "Save your energy until we get out of this."

"My mother waited too long," he said.

She was still thinking that over when Elliot tapped her on the shoulder from behind. "Underground kivas were as good as having air-conditioning." He grinned to let her know that he'd overheard their conversation. "Unfortunately, the floor of this cave is solid rock. Here, everything had to be built aboveground. Of course you two could always take an upstairs apartment if you want privacy." He nodded at the aluminum ladder leaning against the side of the three-story cliff dwelling. "Pull it up after you, if you want. I don't mind. It's the one place where there's always shade, too."

Feigning outrage, Nick stepped out of the cave and into the burning sunlight. A cliff dwelling wasn't her idea of a honeymoon suite. Besides, it was to be their second line of defense, and would have to be stocked with water and emergency rations as soon as she got back.

"Take one of the rifles with you," McKinnon called after her.

Nick hesitated. Her own .30-.30 was stashed under the front seat of the Trooper as always, but if she ran into trouble on the way there she'd need firepower. She backtracked and hefted one of the .30-.06s. It felt heavy and awkward compared to her lever-action .30-.30. Still, an oh-six would knock down a buffalo, whereas a .30-.30 was more of a varmint gun.

As always, she double-checked the safety before carrying the rifle with her to the Trooper. Before getting in, she checked the road. McKinnon was right about that. The narrow entrance to the canyon was as much a trap as a defensive position. Here, the Anasazi could have fought off the Spaniards. Only by the time they had arrived, the site had long been abandoned. The fact that it had been was a good argument against her father's water theory. Why leave, if there was water to be had?

She shook her head. Absolute answers were seldom to be had in archaeology.

Gingerly, she opened the door on the driver's side. The metal was hot to the touch.

Taking a deep breath, she climbed inside, checked under the seat to make certain the .30-.30 was where it should be, then started the engine and pulled away from the cave mouth. A hundred yards away, behind an outcropping of rock, she backed the Trooper against the cliff.

Since the Trooper's white paint made it highly visible, she scooped red dirt onto the hood and grill. It wasn't exactly camouflage, but it might fool somebody from a distance. For a moment, she considering cutting brush and doing a better job of concealment. But the heat was too intense. Already, her sweat was starting to dry up, a sign she needed more water, and soon.

She was halfway to the cave when she remembered the .30-.30. But surely two .30-.06s would be enough firepower for whatever might come up. She nodded and kept going. How would a man like Hatch find them out here in the middle of nowhere anyway?

"Are you sure they're at the site?" Hatch asked Kemp the moment he boarded the CMI jet in Albuquerque.

"Absolutely."

"You've been in touch?"

Kemp nodded. "I verified their position not twenty minutes ago."

Hatch turned to the pilot, who was waiting for instructions. "I want you to return to New York immediately, refuel at the airport, and stand by for instructions from my son. Is that clear?"

"Yes, sir."

Hatch dismissed the pilot with a nod, then stared at Kemp. "Are we going to need backup?"

"I don't know why you bothered coming, sir. I can do this myself, like always."

"I want to see this taken care of." Hatch smiled. "Just hearing about it wouldn't be good enough."

Kemp shrugged. "As I said, I've verified everything. We have them trapped. Shooting fish in a barrel would be risky by comparison. Even if it wasn't, we could seal them up and wait them out if we had to."

"Starvation takes time. I'm too busy a man to wait that long. Now, how long's it going to take to get us there?"

"I have a helicopter waiting. I've already flown the route myself."

"I hope they didn't see you."

"I was very careful."

"What about the satellite uplink gear?" Hatch asked.

"Everything's loaded onto the chopper."

Hatch nodded. "You never did give me a time frame."

"I thought it best to fly as far as the highway, then drive the rest of the way."

"In this heat? Let's hear your argument."

"Just before you reach the site, the road—it's nothing but a dirt washboard, by the way—passes through a narrow rock canyon. To be on the safe side, we use our Land Rover to block the road at that point. That way, they can't drive out and nobody can drive in."

"And the Land Rover?"

"Already camouflaged and waiting for us in the desert," Kemp said.

"And if we fly all the way in?"

"The terrain is rough. The closest we can land safely is about a half mile away."

"Christ," Hatch said. "I'd forgotten how damned hot it was in this part of the country. But I see your point. How long a drive after we leave the chopper?"

"An hour, no more."

Hatch sighed. "My pilot said it's a hundred and eighteen degrees on the tarmac. It feels worse. I'm going to need a good night's sleep before we tackle this, say tomorrow at sunrise. Now, is there anything else I should know?"

"They bought a couple of deer rifles at the general store, ammunition, and plenty of food and water."

"Did you go into town to find that out?"

"Of course not."

"Should we worry about the rifles?"

"Our only worry is the bodies as far as I can see."

"What have you got in the chopper?"

"A couple of assault rifles, both fully automatic, an Uzi, a rocket launcher, and some explosives."

"You've done your homework. I appreciate that." Hatch nodded at Kemp to lead the way down the ramp. Once they were on the tarmac, Hatch laid out his rules of engagement. "The rocket launcher is a last resort only. A deliberately damaged archaeological site will cause a lot more fuss than missing archaeologists, or even bodies showing up in the desert. The authorities may not like what they find, but what are they going to do about it? They'll have no witnesses. So we'll dump them in a ravine somewhere. With any luck, the scavengers will help us out. If they don't, we're still free and clear."

At least Hatch would be, he amended to himself, since he intended to be the only survivor.

Hatch nodded with approval as Kemp set the helicopter down next to the Land Rover the next morning. Their flight had been smooth and uneventful. Seeing Kemp at work, the consummate professional, Hatch decided he was too old to risk tackling the man himself. After all, shooting a man in the back seemed easy enough in theory, but observing Kemp in person was a revelation. He was an athlete. He transferred the two hundred pounds of uplink equipment to the Land Rover as easily as if he'd been shuffling papers. The heat didn't seem to faze him, while Hatch already felt wilted.

"Let's set up the uplink before we make a move," Hatch said. "I want to speak to my son on a scrambled line."

Kemp assembled the gear quickly, giving the impression that he could have done it blindfolded. More than ever, Hatch knew that he needed backup.

"Lee," he said the moment the satellite connection was made, "where are you?"

"At the airport."

Hatch smiled. His son had foreseen his father's wishes.

"How soon can you get here?"

"A flight plan's already been filed. We can be in the air as soon as we get clearance."

"Hang on for a moment." Hatch released the transmit button and spoke to Kemp. "I took the precaution of alerting your security force before I left New York. We've come too far, and this is too important, to take chances now."

"We'll have too many witnesses," Kemp said.

Hatch blinked. Had Kemp suddenly become a mind reader?

"I've changed my mind. I want to sanitize the area. We'll need manpower to dig that many graves. They'll also be available to back us up in the event of a worst-case scenario."

"It's your money. But it will all be over by the time they get here. Trust me."

"Of course," Hatch said, though he trusted only blood, only his son. He triggered the microphone. "Lee, you ought to be in Albuquerque in four and a half hours. Do you agree?"

"I'll be there."

"Kemp and I will be at the location in about an hour, say ten o'clock. One, your time. Fifteen minutes after that, everything should be taken care of, if nothing goes wrong."

"It won't," Kemp mouthed.

Nodding, Hatch went on. "As soon as the smoke clears, I'll make contact and give you our exact coordinates."

"Be careful, Dad."

"Absolutely," Hatch said, the concern in his son's voice bringing tears to his eyes.

37

A car horn honked in the distance.

Nick, who'd been at the back of the cave with McKinnon and her father cataloging artifacts, dropped the piece of Anasazi history she'd been toying with. It crashed into dust on the rock floor. The sound bounced off the three-story cliff dwelling above, a mocking echo. "What the hell is that?"

McKinnon sprang to his feet, grabbed one of the rifles, and sprinted to the front of the cave. When he came back he was pointing the rifle at Nick and her father.

"That's the signal. They're right on time."

"Who?" Nick said, waving away the rifle only to see it steady on her.

With a flourish, he whipped out a cellular phone one-handed. "The big man himself, in person. Leland Hatch and one of his henchman. Like I said, all I had to do was punch in the code."

"You son of a bitch," Elliot shouted as he lunged at McKinnon.

Sidestepping, McKinnon dropped the phone and buried

the butt of his rifle in Elliot's stomach. With a gasp, Elliot collapsed onto the cave floor, his mouth opening and closing as he fought for air. Nick fell to her knees beside him, holding him tightly. When he'd recovered enough to sit up, she looked up at McKinnon, who'd backed away far enough to have slung the second .30-.06 over his shoulder.

Fear started her trembling. "Why?"

"My mother's getting worse," McKinnon answered. "You talked to her. You must have seen it for yourself. She'll need institutional care for the rest of her life. That costs money, and money doesn't mean anything to a man like Hatch."

"A minute ago you wanted to get me into bed."

"What does that have to do with it?"

"I thought you wanted to see your father buried."

"He's not my father. He left me nothing, not even memories."

Nick's fear gave way to rage. It was like nothing she'd ever experienced. An icy calm settled over her, filling her with a white-hot resolve. Just an opening, she thought, that's all she wanted. A chance no matter how slim, and she'd take it.

He must have sensed the change in her, because he began backing away. "The safety's off, Nick. All I have to do is pull the trigger. I'm not much of a shot, but nobody could miss at this range."

Without taking his eyes off her, he bent down, retrieved the cellular phone, the smallest she'd ever seen. "I'm sorry," Nick," he said. "The fact is you never had a chance."

He punched a single button on the phone, then spoke into it. "I have the weapons." He listened for a moment, nodding at whatever was said in response. "That's fine by me."

Somehow Nick managed to control her voice. "What now?"

"Now I live up to my bargain. I walk to the front of the cave, turn over the guns to them, and I walk away a rich man."

"Leaving us for dead?"

"Maybe if you beg, he'll offer you money, too."

Staring at McKinnon, she wondered how could she have been so wrong about him. Surely treachery showed on a man's face? It had been clear enough on Ben Gilbert's face at the disciplinary hearing. Or had that been embarrassment? Whatever it had been, McKinnon's showed no signs of it. Perhaps she'd been too busy assessing the wattage of his kisses.

"You're like my mother," McKinnon said. "You don't use your head when it comes to sex. Neither of you live in the real world."

Gritting her teeth, Nick helped her father to his feet and began nudging him toward the extension ladder.

"Start climbing, Elliot," she said. "I don't think he has the guts to shoot us."

McKinnon shrugged. "I wouldn't want to be trapped up there in this kind of weather."

"You're on my turf now, you bastard."

"Good-bye, Nick." Keeping his rifle aimed at her, McKinnon backed toward the mouth of the cave.

"Move," Nick urged her father.

He scrambled up the ladder, with her literally at his heels. Once on the top story, they pulled the ladder up after them and repositioned themselves beneath the fissure in the rock wall. Cases of water had already been stacked on the roof, the only permanently shady spot in the cave.

When she looked for McKinnon, she realized that he'd stopped short of the cave mouth to watch their climb. Seen against the light in silhouette, his posture suggested that he was enjoying their plight. In that instant, she knew what had to be done.

"We'll climb out the fissure," she said.

"Look at me," Elliot said. "I'll never fit."

"If we can get to the Trooper we'll be all right."

Elliot shook his head. "There's something I have to say

while I've got the chance. I always knew about your mother, you know. I knew she wasn't capable of doing the cooking and the cleaning, that you got stuck with it. If you remember, I tried to hire help, but your mother drove them away."

She touched his arm. "I've always known you knew."

"About the Anasazi," Elliot said, "they're my way of coping with reality."

"You might as well come down," McKinnon shouted from the cave mouth. "They've left their car in the pass just like I told them. Even if you had the rifles, you'd still be bottled up in here."

He raised his hand to shade his eyes against the outside glare. For a split second, Nick thought her eyes were playing tricks as McKinnon was lifted off his feet and hurled backward. Then came the sound, the roar of a long burst from an automatic weapon. Ricocheting bullets sang like hornets inside the cave.

"Jesus," Elliot said.

"Climb. They're not going to leave us alive as witnesses."

"You first, Nick, in case I get stuck."

Halfway up, another burst of gunfire ricocheted into the cave wall next to them, gouging shrapnel from the red rock. A splinter sliced open her cheek. Behind her, Elliot shouted and fell. When she looked down, he was lying on the roof of the cliff dwelling, one leg obviously broken.

Even as she started to climb down, he straightened the leg. "Go!" he shouted at her.

Two silhouettes stood at the mouth of the cave.

Elliot gestured angrily. "They can't get to me without the ladder. I can last for days. Get help."

She opened her mouth to protest but settled for a nod. He was right. Even if what McKinnon had said was true, that the road was blocked, there was still a chance.

"Two days," she said, "I'll be back by then. If I'm not . . ."

"I'll be here," her father said. "Now move."

She pulled herself headfirst into the fissure, then kicked the ladder onto the top of the cliff dwelling. Around her, startled bats fluttered and squeaked. Clenching her teeth, she wormed her way toward the distant daylight.

She'd always admired bats, but from a distance. Without them, the insect population would explode. But up close, amidst their guano, the smell was not to be believed. And whether the cuts was she feeling on her hands and arms came from sharp rocks or razor fangs didn't make much difference. She was going to need a rabies shot, if she survived.

And survival was as much in Elliot's hands as hers. If the grand old man of archaeology was right, they had a chance.

On the other hand, it didn't make any difference. They no longer had a choice. They were both committed. So keep climbing, she told herself. And pray that Elliot knew his Anasazi.

From the cave, she heard more gunfire. Dear God, had they somehow reached her father? No, that didn't seem likely. They'd have to build a ladder, and there wasn't any material for miles. Of course, they could chop handholds in the rock walls given time enough. But she wasn't about to let that happen; she wasn't going to give them the time.

Twice she slipped, ripping skin from her hands and arms. But she kept going, climbing with her eyes shut to protect them from the stinging sweat that reeked of bat urine.

Blistering sunlight told her she'd broken free of the mountain. Blindly, she groped across the scorching rock face. When her eyes finally adjusted, she wasn't more than a quarter of a mile from the Trooper. All that stood between her and the vehicle was a twenty-foot drop onto rocky soil. She would have preferred to search for an easier way down, but there was no time. She stretched the front of her soaking T-shirt far enough to wipe her eyes, then jumped, rolling as she landed.

Instantly, she was up and running, conscious of nothing worse from the fall than raw knees. Ahead of her, the Trooper shimmered in heat waves. Half blinded by sweat, she lost sight of it completely for a moment. But she kept running, praying the emergency water was where it should be. If it wasn't, she'd be dead in a day considering how much she'd sweated away already.

Halfway there, her legs felt as if they were moving in slow motion. Sucking air in lung-searing gasps, she spurred herself forward with the thought of Elliot being stranded and left to die. And all the while, she expected to feel bullets ripping into her back and pitching into oblivion like McKinnon.

Reaching the Trooper was like a miracle. On wobbly legs, she opened the door and climbed into what felt like an oven on high broil. But the water was right where it should be, thank God, half a dozen one-gallon jugs lashed in place by bungee cords.

She grabbed one of the jugs, gulped water until she had to come up for air, then groped under the seat. The .30-.30 was there, too, along with a box of shells. Shakily, she pulled out the rifle and levered a cartridge into the chamber. Then she retrieved the box of cartridges and stuffed half a dozen loose shells into the pocket of her jeans.

Now all she needed was a few seconds leeway. The key was to lure them out of the cave, but not so quickly that she wouldn't be out of range.

Still panting, Nick rolled down her window, then reached across the seats to do the same on the passenger's side in case she needed a clear field of fire.

Releasing the emergency brake, she started the engine and eased the Trooper forward, creeping along the curving rock abutment toward the cave. If they heard the engine and were waiting for her outside the cave, she'd be dead in seconds. If they'd gone inside, she and her father might have a chance.

38

Hatch, following well behind Kemp, stepped over McKinnon's body and entered the cave.

"We have them now," Kemp said. "There's no way out." Using the toe of his boot, he prodded McKinnon's lifeless body. "I hope this poor bastard got paid in advance."

He had, in an offshore account, but Hatch wasn't about to say how much. A sum like that might make Kemp greedy before his usefulness came to an end.

"He should have kept them down here where we could get our hands on them," Hatch said before realizing the mistake had been his, that he'd given the order for Kemp to shoot. He nodded; he was getting too old for things like this. It was time he turned CMI over to his son.

He stared into the cave, but his eyes couldn't cope with the shadows. "Do you see them?"

"Fuck it," Kemp said. "It's like looking into an inkwell. What do you want to do, wait or blast them out?"

"For Christ's sake. I'm not about to dawdle in this kind of heat. Besides, there's an easier way." Hatch smiled. One thing he wasn't too old for was negotiation. In that area, he could still show Lee a thing or two.

"Follow me," he told Kemp, "and watch the master at work. I'll talk them down. Once I do, you finish them."

Mindful of the cave's rocky floor, Hatch slung the Uzi over his shoulder and strode to the base of the cliff dwelling. "Ms. Scott," he shouted, craning his neck, "allow me to introduce myself. My name's Leland Hatch. I have a lucrative offer for you."

A baseball-size rock sailed over the edge of the roof, missing him by inches.

Retreating beyond Kemp's field of fire, Hatch said, "Soften them up."

Stone and mortar exploded in a line along the wall just below the roof as Kemp fired a burst from his assault rifle.

Even as the echoing roar died away, Hatch heard a car engine revving outside the cave. Before he could move, Kemp took off at a dead run. The moment Kemp reached sunlight, he dropped to one knee, raised his weapon, and fired until he ran out of ammunition.

"Goddamn," Kemp muttered when Hatch joined him. "That bitch is getting away."

A quarter of a mile away, red dust billowed behind a white utility wagon that was heading east into the desert.

"I thought there was only one road in and out," Hatch said.

"There's nothing out there but badlands."

"Are you sure?"

"I'll show you on the map," Kemp said.

"How the hell did she get out of the cave?"

"That I don't know."

"Did you see her father?"

Kemp shook his head. "He must be up there, though. Somebody threw that rock."

"To hell with him. He's not going anywhere on foot. Now

get the map and show me where she's going."

As soon as Kemp returned from the Land Rover, he spread the map on the ground inside the cave to be in the shade. "See for yourself, Mr. Hatch. There's nothing in that direction but an old Indian ruin. To get there, you follow a shallow valley, more like a salt flat really. There's a deep ravine on both sides for a hundred miles at least. When the ravines run out, you've got desert for another hundred miles, and no roads anywhere."

Hatch studied the map. It appeared that Kemp's analysis was correct, that the Scott woman had driven herself into a dead end. On the other hand, escaping the cave had shown a great deal of resourcefulness. So he wasn't about to underestimate her again.

His inclination was to go after her first, then come back to finish off her father. He paced far enough to spot a thermometer hanging from a hook on the rock wall.

"Can you believe it! It says it's a hundred and five in here."

"The forecast calls for a hundred and twenty in the badlands. Maybe more where the Scott woman's headed."

"She'll be dead in a day, then," Hatch said.

"She keeps water in the car."

"How much?"

Kemp shrugged. "Not enough to survive indefinitely."

"Get us some water."

While Kemp fetched, Hatch inventoried the supplies stored against the rear wall of the cave. Once satisfied that there was nothing that could be used as a weapon, he sat down to study the cliff dwelling. It was a full three stories high. Even if Elliot Scott climbed down, he'd never make it to the highway in this kind of weather without water.

"Dr. Scott!" Hatch shouted. "Make it easy on yourself. Give us the ladder, and I promise you a painless death."

Another rock sailed over the parapet.

"We're out of range, but suit yourself. We're going to have

ourselves a nice cool drink and then go after your daughter, who's been foolish enough to drive out into the desert."

"You've never met her, have you?" Scott called out.

"Not in person, no."

"She's always been headstrong, and very determined."

"So am I."

Hatch unslung the Uzi, aimed at the stone parapet where he guessed Scott to be hiding, and fired off an entire clip of ammunition.

Kemp came running at the sound.

"Just getting in the mood," Hatch told him. "Now empty every bottle of water in this cave and then we'll go after the woman."

39

Nick stopped a half mile from the cave, waited for the dust to settle, then looked for signs of pursuit in the rearview mirror. No dust. Nothing. She grabbed her binoculars from the glove compartment, stood on what passed for a running board, and focused on the cave. The Land Rover had been moved but wasn't following her.

Maybe she'd miscalculated. Maybe they'd wait for her there instead of risking the desert. If so, she'd have to go back and confront them, though the .30-.30 was no match for their firepower.

She drank more water, then took another look through the binoculars. "Yes," she said, raising a clenched fist.

There they were, the two of them, coming out of the cave, moving toward the Land Rover. She crossed her fingers. "Come on, you bastards. Chase me."

Hearing the words out loud, Nick smiled at her own madness. Here she was, a mouse, daring the cat to come out and play. Only this mouse, she reminded herself, was playing on her own turf.

She snatched the open water bottle and drank again, this time until she sloshed. Overhead, the sun seemed to fill the entire sky, leaving blue to show only around the edges. Everything else was fire.

Rubbing the sweat from her eyes, she went back to the binoculars. By God, the Land Rover was moving, coming her way at last.

She climbed back into the Trooper, but didn't start rolling until the Land Rover was clearly visible in the rearview mirror, maybe a quarter of a mile behind her. From now on, she'd be the perfect bait, tantalizing close, but still beyond rifle range.

She reset the odometer. The cliff dwellings at Site No. 2 were twenty miles due east. The first two or three miles were the easy ones, she remembered, with only an occasional flash-flood gully to make four-wheel drive an absolute must. Ten miles an hour was possible. After that the trip would be hell.

Carefully, she edged the Trooper up to speed, then assessed the Land Rover's response.

Christ, they looked to be doing twice her speed. Clenching her teeth, she focused on the ground ahead. The boulder-size rocks didn't worry her. It was the smaller ones, the ones that the tires might kick right through the gas tank. Still, she didn't have much choice.

Gingerly, she accelerated. At fifteen miles an hour, she expected disaster at any moment.

After what seemed like hours, she glanced at the odometer. She'd come slightly less than three miles. Already the temperature gauge was creeping toward the red line. But what the hell. She'd burn it up if she had to, as long as it got her to the ridge, the only feature on the landscape worth mentioning before the site itself. At the ridge she'd make her move. From there, it was a four-mile trek to her destination.

Her sigh turned into a groan. Breathing was like inhaling fumes from a flamethrower.

Ahead, mirages crawled along the horizon like indolent monsters. She had the feeling that she was about to drop off the edge of the world and fall into hell where she'd be consumed by fire.

She shook her head. *Don't start hallucinating. Drink more water.*

Driving one-handed, she sucked on the mouth of a plastic water jug. Maybe Hatch and his crony wouldn't have the sense to do the same. Maybe they'd start out thirsty when she put them on foot. On the other hand, maybe her memory was playing tricks, maybe she'd remembered Chaco Ridge incorrectly. Maybe . . .

Concentrate, she told herself. There was no room left for doubts. She was committed.

As if urging the Trooper to greater efforts, Nick leaned forward in her seat. Thank God the needle on the temperature gauge had steadied, just short of the red zone. In this kind of weather, she wouldn't have blamed the Trooper for blowing up. She'd never felt heat like this before. It had to be a hundred and twenty. Even with water, how far could she walk in weather like this?

Behind her, the Land Rover was matching her speed.

So far, the only vegetation she'd seen looked dry and brittle, waiting only for the slightest breeze to blow it away. The poor Anasazi, she thought, having to cross such country on foot. How had they carried their water? How much could she carry, along with the .30-.30?

Mile after mile passed. And with each of them, the landscape grew more barren, until at last there was nothing to see except mirages.

Finally, Nick saw an island poke its head above the heat

waves. She shook her head, then blinked repeatedly. Unless she was hallucinating, the sharp sawtooth rocks that marked the beginning of Chaco Ridge were dead ahead. She stepped on the accelerator. She needed more space, more time. A smoke screen of dust rose behind the Trooper.

The Land Rover was totally obscured by the time she braked next to the first outcropping of rock. She killed the engine, released the hood latch, and threw open the door.

With hands steadier than they had any right to be, she removed the distributor cap and shoved it into her jeans next to her key ring. She could hear the approaching Land Rover but didn't waste time looking for it. Instead, she emptied all the water jugs except two. Wrapping a couple of the bungee cords around her waist, she grabbed the last two jugs and the .30-.30, slung the binoculars around her neck, and sprinted for the rocks.

By the time she took cover, Nick was gasping for breath and blinded by sweat. Her hands were shaking so hard she couldn't steady the gunsight.

"She stopped," Hatch said. "We've got her."

Kemp slowed the Land Rover to a halt well short of the Trooper.

"Get closer."

"I don't see her," Kemp said.

"She must be hiding in those rocks. All we have to do is flush her out."

Kemp shook his head. "She fooled us once." He slipped the gearshift into reverse and began backing away. "A sniper could pick us off from those rocks."

"She's an archaeologist, for Christ's sake. Look. Her hood's up. The car's conked out, that's all."

"It's safer if we go on foot."

Hatch glared. His head ached. He was grimy and soaked with sweat, and the tepid water he'd been drinking had left him queasy without quenching his thirst.

"Forget it, Kemp. This heat isn't fit for a lizard. I'm not walking any farther than I have to."

Kemp switched off the engine. At a guess, Hatch figured they were a hundred yards from the rocks.

"You stay here, then, while I go take a look-see," Kemp said.

As he was opening the door, steam exploded from the radiator an instant before the sound of the shot arrived.

"She's shooting at us!" Kemp rolled out of the car and onto the ground.

Hatch tried to do the same, but landed on his shoulder. His arm went numb.

Another bullet slammed into the front of the Land Rover.

"Goddammit," Kemp shouted under the car. "I told you so."

"Shoot back," Hatch ordered.

Peering under the car, Hatch saw Kemp crawl to the back door. Water was gushing from the radiator.

Kemp fired a long burst from the assault rifle.

"Do you see her?" Hatch shouted.

"I think she moved as soon as I started firing."

Hatch thought that over. The ridge of rock petered out about a half mile to the east. So all they had to do was follow until she ran out of cover. Logically, Kemp should take one side, Hatch the other. But Hatch wasn't up to that kind of walk, not in this heat.

"She's on foot," Hatch said. "All you've got to do is run her down."

"The Land Rover's finished. Maybe we can hot-wire her car."

When they reached the Trooper, the keys were missing and so was the distributor cap. Empty plastic water bottles lay on their sides, their contents absorbed by the sand.

Kemp kicked the door panel in frustration. "We're stranded out here."

"She didn't know enough to shoot what's really important." Hatch gestured toward the back of the Land Rover. "Set up the satellite gear. We'll call in our coordinates."

Kemp nodded. "With help on the way, there's no sense going after her. She's got nowhere to go, and if she tries circling back, we outgun her."

Hatch squinted at the sawtooth ridge. As far as he could see, there wouldn't be any shade until the sun was damn near down. He checked their water supply. Six quart-size bottles remained in the case. That should be plenty, since Lee would be arriving before dark, or tomorrow morning at the latest. But what if Kemp was wrong about the badlands? What if the woman had an escape route. In that case Lee would arrive too late.

Hatch clenched his teeth. He'd underestimated the Scott woman once. Twice would be unthinkable.

"You go after her," Hatch said. "My son and I will catch up."

Kemp shook his head. "Like I said, she's not going anywhere. The best thing we can do is find ourselves some shade and wait."

"Where?"

"Under the car."

"Would five million dollars change your mind?" Hatch said. "Shall we say payable into your offshore account the moment the woman's dead?"

"Payable in advance. You can use the satellite to make the transfer right now."

"Why not?" Hatch said, figuring he could retrieve the money later anyway.

"And I'll take half the water," Kemp said.

"Not until you've set up the satellite gear."

40

Nick collapsed onto the rocky soil at the eastern end of Chaco Ridge. Ahead lay another three and a half miles of desert before she reached Site No. 2. So far, she'd walked half a mile without so much as a sip of water, but now she had to drink. Otherwise, she'd keel over and fry like an egg.

She filled her mouth with the warm water and swished it around before swallowing. Instantly, she felt more thirsty than ever. Five swallows, that's all she was going to allow herself. Five swallows every half mile.

At the count of five, she recapped the jug and focused her binoculars back the way she'd come. Both men appeared to have stayed with the Land Rover.

Come on, you bastards. Chase me.

Didn't they know that without transportation they were as good as dead? They had to follow her; they had to think she'd lead them to water.

She fiddled with the focus. Was that movement or a mirage? She nodded. Finally one of them was coming after her. Common sense said it had to be the henchmen, not someone Hatch's age.

Good enough, she thought. If she survived, she relished the idea of returning to confront Leland Hatch face to face.

In the meantime she'd have to pick up her pace. She drank more water. And why not? Either Elliot was right about the kiva being a sacred well or she was dead already.

When the first jug ran out, she fastened the empty container to the bungee cord around her waist. Otherwise, she'd have nothing to refill for the trip back.

Kemp located her tracks at the far end of the ridge. She appeared to be heading due east. Somewhere out there, he knew, was another Indian ruin, though why she'd head for it, he had no idea.

He shaded his eyes, but saw no sign of the woman, only heat waves obscuring the horizon. She was setting a faster pace than he'd thought possible under such conditions. He picked up his own. By God, no woman was going to outwalk him, not with five million dollars waiting to be spent.

A mile later, he finished the first of his three bottles of water and discarded the empty. And still he couldn't see her.

When the next bottle ran out, he stopped and looked back the way he'd come. The ridge had long since disappeared into the heat waves. He had one bottle left for the return trip. If he didn't turn back now, he might not make it without more water.

"Think," he muttered. If he felt like shit, think how she must feel. He promised himself that when he caught up with her, he'd drink her water and make her watch.

By the time Nick reached Site No. 2, she could barely walk. Her knees were raw from stumbling the last half mile. What water she had left sloshed in the bottom of the jug. By to-morrow, she wouldn't have the strength to move if she didn't find more water.

Above her, cliff dwellings clung to the side of a nearly vertical red-rock wall, the only landmark for miles. Up there would be shade, but no water. Instead of bats, there were scorpions. She remembered them from the last dig.

The kiva, as she recalled, was in a gully at the base of the cliff. According to her father, it had been built over the bed of an ancient river that had eroded the cliff out of red sandstone thousands of years ago.

Keeping her eyes on the ground, she walked along the base of the rock wall. She found the gully easily enough, though it didn't look like much of a riverbed to her. There was no sign of a kiva.

Think, for God's sake. She'd been an undergraduate when her father had brought her here. At that time, the kiva had been fully excavated.

She raised the plastic jug to eye level. There couldn't be more than two swallows left. She licked her lips. She was dead, no doubt about it.

She put the jug to her lips and sucked it dry. The water was warm, almost hot, but tasted wonderful. She dropped to her knees and closed her eyes. Her memory played back Elliot giving orders to his students to have the kiva covered with plywood to protect it from the elements.

She opened her eyes. Memory put her very close to the spot. On hands and knees, she felt the ground around her. Less than ten feet away, her probing fingers found the edge of the plywood. She cleared away the drifting sand, then slid the wood to one side. Cool, dank air rose from inside the kiva.

She lay on her stomach to peer inside. A ladder built by Elliot's students was still in place. The thought crossed her mind that it might not hold her weight after so many years, but she had no choice.

She dropped the plastic jugs and rifle into the pit, then brushed out her footprints in the immediate area. That done, she lowered herself feet first into the opening and climbed into the kiva. Once she'd stowed her rifle, she mounted the ladder again and wrestled the plywood back into place. Instantly, the darkness was tomblike and absolute.

She descended carefully, felt her way to one of the ledges where the ancient Anasazi had sat during their ceremonies, and lay down to rest.

Time passed. She heard nothing, no sound above or water below. The thought flashed through her mind that she had climbed into her own grave.

Sitting up, she reached into the pocket of her jeans and fished out the miniflashlight attached to her key ring. After offering a prayer to the God of batteries, she switched it on. The beam was weak, useful only for finding keyholes, but somehow it seemed like a good omen.

She switched it off to conserve power, then thought over her next move. How long could a man survive in this heat? That would depend on his water supply, on how much he could carry. Judging by her own condition, twenty-four hours from now she'd be comatose, even if she did nothing but lie here in the cool darkness. So that would be her deadline. In twenty-four hours, she'd leave the kiva. By then her pursuer would be in no condition to give chase. If she'd miscalculated, she'd die. If not, she'd start back for her father, assuming she'd found water by then.

41

Hatch punched his password into the uplink transmitter while congratulating himself on his foresight for having brought along the equipment. He savored the technology. In his mind, he watched its signal bounce off the CMI satellite and then home in on his private jet.

Almost instantly, his son answered with crystal clarity. "Is everything all right?"

"There's been a slight complication. I'm stranded in the middle of nowhere until you get here."

"We're locked on your signal and your coordinates have already been programmed into our tracking beacons."

Hatch smiled. Foresight, that was the key to success. Having Lee in the air as backup was a master stroke. Probably he was sitting in the copilot's seat, which he'd loved doing since his first flight as a child.

"What about Kemp?" Lee asked.

"It's a hundred and fifteen degrees here, and getting hotter by the feel of it. The girl's on foot, and I sent Kemp after her. With luck, the desert will do our dirty work. All we'll have to do is bury them. What's your ETA? I'm running out of water."

"We're on final approach to Albuquerque now. I've arranged for humvees to be waiting at the airport. We'll be with you by nightfall."

"Don't risk the desert at night. I may be thirsty, but tomorrow morning will be soon enough for you to get here."

Off-mike, Hatch heard the pilot alerting the Albuquerque tower that there was traffic ahead.

"Jesus!" Lee said.

"What's happening?" Hatch asked but got no response.

"Son of a bitch," he could hear the pilot say. "That idiot's coming right at us!"

"Go left."

"He turning in to us!"

"Pull up!" Lee's voice cried out. "Oh, shit—"

There was a burst of static before the transmission ceased. "Lee!" Hatch shouted. "Talk to me."

Even as he spoke, Hatch knew it was useless. His son was dead. History had repeated itself; it had come back to haunt him. All those nightmares had been a warning against this. In his mind's eye, he saw the jet, like the B-17 before it, plummet toward the earth.

Peering up at the cliff dwelling, Kemp tasted blood from his sun-cracked lips. The woman had to be up there; there was no other possible place to hide.

Suicidal, that's what she was to come to a place like this. There was no vegetation, so there sure as hell couldn't be any water.

Wearily, he tracked her footprints, but there seemed to be no definite pattern. One thing was certain, she'd visited the base of the cliff. He followed her trail along the rock wall looking for a way up. At one point he found what might have been handholds, though time and erosion had shallowed them.

Kemp prided himself on being a strong man, in prime condition. But he also knew his own limitations. If he tapped his energy reserves by climbing up after her, he'd be pushing his luck. Longingly, he eyed his one remaining bottle of water.

He shook his head violently. The heat must be getting to him. He wasn't thinking straight. Hatch would be here soon enough with help.

Kemp opened the bottle and drank deeply, then craned his neck. "I'm coming up, bitch. When I get my hands on you, you're dead."

Wait a minute, he thought. She was armed, for Christ's sake, and here he was standing out in the open.

He flattened himself against the rock wall and found himself staring west into the sun. How long before it set? At least two hours, he guessed. The thought panicked him. He had to get under cover before then.

Suddenly, he banged himself on the forehead. If he felt like this, she must be half dead by now. All he'd have to do is climb up and finish her off, dump her body over the side, and then hunker down until reinforcements arrived.

"Bitch," he muttered, and started to climb.

Two stories up, he grabbed an ancient windowsill and pulled himself through the opening. His feet were about to hit the floor when something stung his hand. He screamed with rage. Reflex hurled the scorpion against the wall. Goddamn. The floor was alive with them. He stomped until there was nothing left but goo. Then he cut open the wound and sucked out the poison.

Nick heard his muffled shout but couldn't make out the words. But his tone of voice sent a chill up her spine despite the heat. She fed the rest of her shells into the .30-.30, braced herself against the kiva wall, and waited.

An hour passed, then another. By now the sun would be setting. Soon there wouldn't be enough light for him to find her hiding place.

She sucked on a pebble, but couldn't raise any spit. If she hadn't gotten out of the sun, she'd have been desperate by now. She smiled in spite of herself. Desperation wasn't that far off.

She closed her eyes against the darkness. Her father would be waiting in the dark, too, alone in that cliff dwelling. She had to survive. She had to make it back to him. He was depending on her.

Breathe deeply, she told herself. *Rest. Hoard your strength.*

After a while, exhausted sleep brought Nick's mother back to life. "You can't know what it's like," Elaine said, "to live inside a black well of despair."

A five-year-old Nick grasped her mother's hand. "I'll pull you out."

"Don't ever let go of me. If you do, I'll fall forever. I'll die in blackness."

Nick jerked awake, gasping. Once her breathing slowed, she dropped to her hands and knees and felt her way across the floor of the kiva. When earth gave way to stone, she switched on her flashlight. The stone was about two feet square, showing chisel marks around the edges.

So far, so good.

Using her Swiss pocket knife, Nick dug along one side of the rock. An inch down doubts assailed her. Maybe it wasn't a wellhead, but only bedrock.

In the next instant, she found the bottom of the slab. After that it was only a matter of clearing enough earth to give her a handhold. When that was done, she used the butt of her rifle to lever the stone to one side.

But there was no well shaft beneath it, only smaller stones.

She sank onto her side to rest. Maybe it had been a well once, but now it was dry.

Elaine's words came back. "I'll die in blackness."

Nick shook her head. In the morning, she'd climb out of the kiva and start back. No matter how hopeless the trek, frying in the sun was better than waiting in the dark to die.

In frustration she reached out, grabbed a rock, and threw it against the wall. Was it her imagination, or had it felt damp?

She touched another one. It, too, felt damp. She leaned her ear against the rock and heard a distant trickle. Frantically, she began digging down through the loose stones.

42

By morning, Kemp knew he was in trouble. His hand had throbbed all night. His fingers had swollen to the point where they wouldn't bend far enough to pull a trigger. His water was gone. He couldn't even raise enough spit to swallow. And he was on his own. He knew that, because if help were coming, it should have been there by now.

Groaning, Kemp rose to his feet. Immediately, his knees threatened to buckle. Walking stiff-legged, he shuffled to the opening in the rock wall and peered over the side. The three-story drop was inviting, but there was no guarantee it would kill him. Thank God he had one good hand left to work the rifle when the time came.

Suddenly, the ground outside the dwelling moved. He rubbed his eyes. No, he wasn't seeing things. It was that bitch.

An angry surge of adrenaline revived him. If he was going to die, he wouldn't do it alone. And shooting her wasn't good enough. He'd climb down there and make her beg.

Nick slid back the kiva's plywood cover and blinked against the fiery sunlight. The blistering heat felt refreshing now that she'd drunk her fill.

She took a quick look around, saw nothing, set her rifle on the earthen lip, then retreated down the ladder to fetch the plastic jugs that had taken most of the night to fill. Over the centuries, the ancient underground river had dwindled to a brackish trickle. But to Nick, it had tasted like pure nectar.

Just as her head emerged aboveground a second time, a rock clattered from the cliff above her. Looking up, she saw the man clinging to the ancient stone and mortar wall, a rifle slung over his shoulder. He was watching her, smiling. She tossed the jug aside and lunged for the .30-.30.

Seeing her reach for the rifle, Kemp changed handholds, preparing to jump the remaining two stories. But his swollen hand had no grip to it. His other hand scrabbled, but the centuries-old mortar crumbled under the strain.

Screaming, he fell straight back, landing on his assault rifle. Along with the sound of his spine snapping came the final thought that the woman had lured him out there on purpose to kill him.

43

Nick found Leland Hatch under his disabled Land Rover. His eyes were closed, his lips swollen and cracked, his body bloated. He'd soiled himself where he lay.

"Hatch," she said, "can you hear me?"

His eyes opened to slits wide enough to show his hatred. "You killed my son," he croaked.

"Was that who you sent after me?"

"You shot down his plane."

She shook her head. The man was out of his mind from thirst.

"Water."

"I'm sorry." She'd finished the last of it half a mile back.

She left him where he lay and staggered to the Trooper. If it wouldn't start, she'd be as bad off as Hatch in a few hours.

The Trooper's door was dented, but otherwise it looked exactly as she'd left it, the hood still up. She crossed her fingers before replacing the distributor cap.

Then she slid behind the wheel and turned the key. The engine started immediately.

Maneuvering cautiously, she turned the Trooper around and kept as far as she could from the Land Rover. The thought of pulling Hatch out from under that car and loading him into the backseat made her pause. After a moment, she shook her head. It was a risk she couldn't take. She was weak. What energy she had left had to be saved for her father. His life depended on her.

She put the Trooper into low gear and headed for ES No. 1. After less than a mile, she switched on the radio to keep from thinking about the look on Hatch's face. But country music wasn't her idea of soothing. She was about to change stations when the music gave way to a news bulletin.

"Here is an update on yesterday's midair plane crash," the announcer said. "The death toll now stands at ten, including the pilot of a small private plane that apparently lost control and slammed into a four-engine jet that was about to land at Albuquerque airport.

"According to witnesses, the private plane, identified as a single-engine Beechcraft, had been maneuvering like a fighter just moments before the crash.

"The four-engine jet, owned by the CMI Corporation, exploded on impact with the runway. Among the dead were CMI's executive vice president, Leland Hatch, Jr.

"The pilot of the Beechcraft has been tentatively identified as Joseph Twombly, a highly decorated pilot from World War Two."